Praise for Silvia Violet's *A Carnal Agreement*

4 Hearts "I thought this was a wonderful historical that had some unusual elements that kept me reading until late at night. I liked the heroine most, she was plucky and not afraid to go after what she wanted even if it wasn't politically correct." ~ *Julia, The Romance Studio*

4.5 Ribbons "Silvia Violet's A CARNAL AGREEMENT is one hot regency novel. If you're picking this one up expecting dandies and fainting couches you're in for a real surprise, though you may require the fainting couch during some of the more explicit scenes. Both Cassandra and Mark are open and honest characters. I loved reading about them." ~ *Chrissy Dionne, Romance Junkies*

"A Carnal Agreement was not like any novel I have ever read by Silvia Violet. This story shows her versatility as a writer and I simply thought it very entertaining and an all around good read." ~ *Tali Ricci, Joyfully Reviewed*

A Carnal Agreement

Silvia Violet

A SAMHAIN PUBLISHING, LTD. publication.

Samhain Publishing, Ltd.
2932 Ross Clark Circle, #384
Dothan, AL 36301
www.samhainpublishing.com

A Carnal Agreement
Copyright © 2006 by Silvia Violet
Print ISBN: 1-59998-294-3
Digital ISBN: 1-59998-090-8

Editing by Jessica Bimberg
Cover by Vanessa Hawthorne

First Samhain Publishing, Ltd. electronic publication: August 2006
First Samhain Publishing, Ltd. print publication: November 2006

Dedication

To Meredith, who furthered my love for history and demanded the best from my writing. Thank you for giving me the confidence to write this book.

Prologue

London, June 1818

Cassandra Braxton, Viscountess Reddington, rarely moved in society, but she felt an obligation to lend her sister moral support as Amanda made her debut. Cassandra was no fan of the overly crowded balls filled with pushy mamas eager to see their young daughters married off. But for the sake of her sister, she was willing to endure almost anything.

She had been tempted, however, to acquire a sudden headache and excuse herself from the festivities on this particular evening. Cassandra's aunt and her sister were attending an engagement ball given in honor of Cassandra's former schoolmate, Lady Katryn Wentworth. When Cassandra left Miss Langford's Academy for Young Ladies, she had hoped she would never lay eyes on Katryn again. A more arrogant and spiteful girl she had never known.

Alas she had seen her former schoolmate several times in the last few years, once in a rather compromising position. And now Katryn was to marry the Earl of Southwood, a man known for his quiet, bookish nature, a strange catch for a woman such as she.

The party began as any other. Cassandra circulated dutifully through the ballroom and several small salons, skillfully avoiding Katryn and her betrothed. As she listened to the formal announcement of the betrothal and the ensuing congratulatory speeches, she breathed a sigh of relief. She could soon return home and seek her bed.

Her attention wandered, and she noticed a rather striking man standing in one of the doorways leading to the balcony. He was nearly concealed by a large potted plant, but she saw him well enough to tell he wore no jacket. His cravat was untied, and his waistcoat was wretchedly crumpled. One might suppose he'd been in an altercation or had scaled the side of the house to reach the balcony rather than using the stairs.

Cassandra took a few steps back from the crowd to study this curious man where no one would observe her. He was tall, several inches over six feet and more muscular than most men of the *ton*. He looked as if he used his body for things far more vigorous than driving a curricle through Hyde Park. His bronze hair and the powerful lines of his face made her think of a lion on the prowl. Something about him seemed familiar, though surely she would remember the occasion if they had been formally introduced. He was not a man many women would forget.

As he drained his glass of champagne, he flashed a wicked smile. What *was* he up to?

Cassandra forced herself to stop staring before anyone noticed her inappropriate attention. Katryn's brother was giving the engaged couple his blessings. He blathered on about what an upstanding man Southwood was when the stranger from the balcony began approaching the family as if he intended to give the next speech.

Intrigued, Cassandra worked her way through the throng to stand closer to the unfolding drama.

The man paused in front of Katryn's betrothed. The Earl failed to conceal his disdain. Katryn's brother stopped mid-sentence, and the stranger took the pause as his cue to begin. "I could not resist taking this opportunity to give my congratulations."

Several people gasped and frantic whispers rustled through the crowd. Lady Bowerton looked as if she might faint. Katryn's face grew red, and she stepped between the two men.

"I can see you didn't expect me." The man turned to face the crowd. "But since I'm here, I thought the happy couple would be offended if I failed to offer a toast." He looked down at his empty champagne glass. "Blast! It's empty."

Katryn stepped forward, anger plain on her face. "You have had quite enough. It would be best if you left before embarrassing yourself further."

"Oh no, my dear," the stranger said, daring to reach out and stroke her face. "Learning your true nature has made me more sober than I have ever been."

Suddenly Cassandra knew why the man looked familiar. Several months ago, she had come to London to discover the true measure of her husband's depravity. Katryn had attended one of her husband's orgiastic parties. This man had been her escort.

The man reached around Katryn and relieved Southwood of his champagne. The earl's eyes widened, but he said nothing. Cassandra expected some of the footman to come forward and remove the intruder, but even they appeared too fascinated to move.

The man smiled and raised his glass. "To an old school chum." He looked at Southwood. "Congratulations on securing the hand of the coldest bitch in all of London." The intruder downed his champagne in one swallow.

Chaos erupted in the ballroom. The man walked toward the crowd before any of Katryn's stunned relatives could respond.

His path brought him toward Cassandra. As he moved past her, his arm brushed her bare shoulder. The heat of his body shocked her, and her knees threatened to give.

When she steadied herself, she turned to look for him, but he was gone.

Chapter One

January 1, 1819

Once Mark Foxwood made the decision to leave London, he could not get away fast enough.

The jolting carriage provided little comfort, but it was the best money could buy. While Gillinvray had never officially recognized him, being the duke's bastard had some advantages. His father showered him with money and gifts, and bored society women flocked to men who stood at the edge of their world. Of course, his lack of bloodline played merry hell with his worth in the marriage market.

But he had given up the romantic fantasy of marrying and having a family of his own, and he had damn sure given up the notion of falling in love. Katryn had seen to that.

Since making an ass of himself at her engagement ball, Mark had tried his damnedest to blot her from his mind. But neither the gallons of liquor he drank nor the endless stream of women he bedded helped.

He had spent evenings in the lowest, scariest drinking holes he could find, beating the stuffing out of more than one of London's lowlifes. Still, he thought of Katryn. He dreamed of her soft, lush body, of the light in her eyes when she screamed his name as she came. He had thought her passion genuine. But it had all been a game.

He slammed his fist against the side of the carriage. *Damn her for her treachery!*

The vehicle slowed to a stop, and a footman appeared at the door. "Yes, sir?"

"Why have we stopped?"

The footman averted his gaze. "You knocked, sir."

"That wasn't a knock. Tell the driver I expect to reach Devon by nightfall. And look at me when I speak to you."

The boy looked up. "Yes, sir." He failed to keep the quiver from his voice.

Mark cringed at the fear he had put in the boy's eyes. The lad could not be more than fifteen. Since when had he become such a tyrant?

Katryn, you vicious bitch! See what you've reduced me to.

He sighed and closed his eyes. If he did nothing else in this new year, he would stop wallowing in grief. Months of excess had not rid him of his memories, so he would purge his mind with asceticism. He would winter in the country, continuing a series of improvements on Northamberly, the partially ruined castle given him by his father—or rather his patron as Gillinvray preferred to be called.

He told no one where he was going, and he hoped to God no one had the audacity to come looking for him. He especially didn't want to see any of his mistresses. An overabundance of sex had not served to drag him out of hell. He hoped a few months of celibacy would do the trick.

Part of his mind, the sensible part, told him he would never make it. Going for months without the company of a woman wouldn't be easy, but he was determined. If he wanted to truly live again, he had to rid himself of this curse. If living like a monk would cure him, that was exactly what he would do.

ଔ ଔ ଔ

Devon, three days later

A child? Cassandra's husband knew better than anyone how impossible that was. She had known he would find a way to plague her from beyond the grave.

For three years Cassandra had suffered the humiliation of being Lady Reddington, never thinking she might be freed from her chains so soon. And now, when her inheritance would protect her sisters from a similar fate, she learned no money would be forthcoming.

Mr. Jenkins, her solicitor, had worked for Lord Reddington's family for decades. He understood the cruelty they were capable of. Unfortunately he saw no way to break the will. The clause sealing her fate was completely legal. But she had asked Mr. Jenkins to remain at Reddington Abbey on the wild hope that somehow they would find a solution.

Once she made arrangements for the solicitor to be shown to one of the guest rooms, she donned her riding habit and headed for the stables. But even the sight of her beloved mare, Artemis, did little to improve her mood.

The air was bitterly cold. Martin, the head groom, asked her more than once if she truly wanted to venture out. In the state she was in, she doubted she would even notice the cold. She had to get out of the confines of the house. Riding had been her only taste of freedom in three years.

As she galloped across the fields faster and faster, she could no longer think, she could only feel. Cassandra longed to keep flying free, but she slowed as she and Artemis approached the base of the cliffs obscuring her view of the sea. Artemis could only cover the rocky terrain at a walk, and while Cassandra had allowed herself a brief escape, she needed to face her dilemma head on.

As she pulled her wrap tighter against the cold, the words of Reddington's will echoed in her head. No matter how many times she went over them, she had no idea how to beat Reddington at his final game. Of course, like all his schemes, it was genius. How could she have had a child when he...no, she wouldn't think about that now. Such memories would only lead her deeper into despair.

There had to be a way around his stipulation. She couldn't let Reddington ruin her chance for freedom, not after everything she had suffered at his hands.

When they reached the cliff top, Cassandra brought Artemis to a stop and looked out at the sea. The presence of a rider on the beach arrested her attention. None of the villagers had reason to be out in this frigid wind. No gentlemen from the area had the equestrian skills to negotiate his way down. None of her neighbors were so tall or golden-haired, nor did they move with the grace she observed as the man dismounted in one fluid motion.

When he turned in her direction, she was suddenly back in London at Katryn's engagement ball. The alluring stranger. His daring toast. This was the same man.

In the ensuing whirlwind after he left the ball, she had managed to discover his name, Mark Foxwood. He was rumored to be an unprincipled rake of the first water, the bastard son of the Duke of Gillinvray, and Katryn's former lover.

Now Mr. Foxwood stood on the beach below her. Her heart raced. She had been unable to put him from her mind since that evening. Night after night he had appeared in her dreams.

She wondered what he was he doing in this remote, unfashionable part of Devon. Then she remembered a conversation overheard last week in the milliners. Northamberly, the half-ruined castle on the land next to hers, was to have a resident after years of vacancy. It had been gifted to a young man by its owner. The new landlord planned to inspect it and spend the remainder of the winter here.

The castle's previous owner was the Duke of Gillinvray. The drafty, damp castle was certainly nothing a legitimate son would care to inherit. Gillinvray's giving it to Mr. Foxwood made perfect sense.

As she pondered Mr. Foxwood's presence in the area, inspiration hit like lightening. He might just be the answer to her prayers.

Chapter Two

"You're going to do what?" Cassandra had never seen her husband's valet so flustered, not even when he had told her of Reddington's death.

"I'm going to conceive a child," Cassandra repeated. "The will says I must *have* a child, but surely if I'm carrying one, that will be sufficient."

Mr. Jenkins nodded. "It would, my lady, but—"

"No buts. It's the only solution. No one knows Reddington's dead. We will postpone the announcement of his death as long as we can."

Mr. Jenkins stared at her as though she were some exotic creature in a zoo. "I don't know how long—"

She interrupted him again. "Three months. Give me three months. If I'm not with child by then, I will start looking for a position as a governess or companion. It's unlikely an English family will have me after my association with Reddington, but my French is excellent, and I can always go to America if I must."

"Certainly such action won't be necessary, my lady," Mr. Jenkins replied. "I would be glad to assist you in finding a situation more comfortable for you."

"While I am grateful for your offer, I cannot settle for such unless I make every effort to thwart Reddington first. I have spent my whole life being controlled by others. I want an opportunity to be on my own."

Cassandra turned toward her husband's valet, Loring. He'd been more of a friend to her than anyone in the household, and she hoped he would see the sense of her plan. Loring frowned. "Do you really think we can hide his death so long, my lady?"

"I don't see why not. You said he had little contact with his London friends while in Paris. Besides, it's winter and hardly anyone is in town. If anyone questions his lengthy absence, they will probably conclude he's hiding out from his creditors."

"What about the fact I have returned?" Loring asked. "While I took care not to appear at Reddington House, I might have been seen in London. We cannot hide my presence for long."

"We simply say Reddington finally tired of you trying to curb his excesses and turned you out. When I learned of his actions, I insisted you remain with the family."

"I suppose such an explanation is plausible," Mr. Jenkins said. "But I do have one serious concern."

He paused and his face reddened. Cassandra guessed what he intended to ask, but she didn't want to volunteer more than she had to. "What is it, Mr. Jenkins?"

"Who will you get to...assist you in producing this child?"

"Ah. I saw the perfect candidate when I went riding this morning. Mark Foxwood."

"No!" Mr. Jenkins yelped.

Loring choked on his tea.

Cassandra bit her lip to keep from smiling. "I don't see why not. He's unmarried, and his reputation indicates he'd be more than willing. I believe he's spending the winter at Northamberly Castle."

Loring shook his head vehemently. "I cannot agree to it, Lady Reddington. I could not permit you to so much as dance with a man like Foxwood. He's one of the worst rakes in London."

"He's exactly the sort of man I need for a scheme like this. It's hardly something a gentleman would agree to."

"Nor is it something a lady should do," Mr. Jenkins said. "Give me a few days to research the will. There may be a way to break it that I hadn't thought of." A troubled looked passed over his face, and he shifted uncomfortably in his chair. "I might even be convinced to lose the will if necessary."

"No." Cassandra barely restrained herself from leaping out of her chair. "I will not permit you to further compromise your integrity for me. You are already on shaky ground for helping me hide his death."

"Even if I agreed to this, I would still know the baby wasn't Reddington's."

"You would have known it wasn't his if I'd become pregnant before he died," she said.

Mr. Jenkins coughed uncomfortably.

"You can't prove he's dead. You haven't seen the body. And you won't be able to prove the baby isn't his."

"Technically that is true, but it is a twisted presentation of the facts. It hardly absolves me of blame."

"Perhaps not, but I still refuse to ask more of you." She took a deep breath and looked imploringly at both Loring and Mr. Jenkins. "Compared to things I saw and dealt with as Reddington's wife, conducting an affair with Mark Foxwood will seem positively tame."

Loring shook his head.

Cassandra smiled. "All right, perhaps not, but it will be nowhere near as scandalous as things Reddington did every day. Please, this may be my only hope to free myself. I know women are supposed to be content to marry and come under the protection of their husband, but I can't marry again. I need to be on my own. I think I've earned my freedom after three years in hell."

Mr. Jenkins sighed. "Yes, you have, Lady Reddington. I wish I knew another way to help you, but I don't. I will go along with your plan, but I cannot give you more than three months."

"That is all I ask. Loring?"

"I have spent the last three years trying to protect you. I don't think you understand the kind of man Mark Foxwood is. I wish you would at least consider someone else."

"He is the perfect candidate. His estate neighbors ours. You can still watch over me. I promise to abandon the plan if he frightens me in the least."

Loring sighed. "I won't stand in your way."

"Excellent. Mr. Jenkins, if you uncover anything new once you return to London, send word immediately, and I will abandon my plan."

"I will, my lady."

She looked from one man to the other. "You don't know how much your support means to me. I don't know if I could have weathered this marriage without you. Hopefully in a few more months I will be able to put it all behind me and look forward to the future and to raising the child I have wanted. Loring, I do hope you will stay on here when this is done."

"I will stay as long as you like, my lady."

"If you will excuse me, I must prepare myself to make a call on Mr. Foxwood."

ি ি ি

Mark lounged on a window seat in his study, one long leg stretched out in front of him and the other bent so his booted foot rested on the cushion. The winter afternoon had been still and quiet. The thick snow covering his fields muffled even the cries of the birds. When someone rapped on his front door, the sound made him jump.

He listened carefully to determine who dared annoy him when he'd only been in town a few short days. He thought he heard a woman's voice. For a moment, he tensed. Surely his last mistress hadn't the gall to follow him all the way to Devon. He thought he'd made it painfully clear their association was over.

Andrews, the butler who had remained at Northamberly on order of his father, had been instructed to hire more staff for the house. The woman was probably a local girl who'd come seeking a position as a housemaid. Andrews would handle it.

He leaned his head back and closed his eyes, but two pairs of approaching footsteps followed by a knock on the door interrupted his peace.

"Come in." He'd actually thought about jumping out the window and making a run for it. What was the point of being secluded in the country if he was forced to entertain visitors?

The door opened slowly. Andrews entered, followed by a woman whose clothing and demeanor clearly indicated she was not applying to be his housemaid. Her thick, chocolate-colored hair was piled on her head, but her attempts to restrain it had failed. Tight curls fell across her cheeks and down her neck, bouncing as she walked into the room.

Her smooth, ivory skin was so perfect he almost thought her a statue come to life. Her pale green gown dipped low on her chest, revealing a bosom as full and rich as her hair. When she smiled at him, his body responded involuntarily, forcing him to lower both legs to the floor.

One day. He'd been one damn day without a woman, and his cock was already begging him to seize her and rip off her beguiling dress. He had to get rid of her quickly.

Refusing to return her smile, he picked up his snifter and crossed the room. He turned toward his disobedient butler. "What is the meaning of this? I told you I wasn't at home to anyone, especially any females."

"I'm sorry to disturb you, Mr. Foxwood, but her ladyship said it was an emergency." Neither Andrews' tone nor his expression indicated there was any sincerity behind his apology.

Mark studied the woman again. His gaze raked her from her disarrayed curls to the pointed toe of her calfskin boot barely visible beneath her lacy hem. "Andrews, I don't know this woman. How can any emergency of hers possibly be a concern of mine?"

Mark truly had no idea who she was. Yet, there was something familiar about her. Where had he seen her before?

Andrews declined to answer the question. The coward. He stepped back and closed the door, leaving Mark alone with a woman who was causing the exact response he'd intended to avoid while he was here.

"Since you've already disturbed my peaceful afternoon, you might as well go ahead and tell me who the hell you are and what you want."

The woman didn't flinch. Instead, she spoke in a strong, steady voice. "I'm Viscountess Reddington. I beg your pardon for bothering you, but I need assistance with a rather delicate matter. I was hoping you would be willing to help me."

"I'm not impressed by your title, and I'm not here to aid damsels in distress."

The infuriating woman had the audacity to smile. "No, I didn't think you were, but the kind of help I require happens to fall in your area of expertise."

The only thing he'd like to help this little minx do was remove her clothes and spread her legs for him. Come to think of it, sexual escapades were about the only area of expertise anyone in society thought he had. "I can't imagine what that would be."

"Before I can explain what I need, I have to tell you something that must be kept secret. I am going to trust you are enough of a gentleman to do so."

"Not many people consider me a gentleman, but you are welcome to take the risk."

She paused, took a deep breath and exhaled slowly. He realized that was the first sign of nerves she'd shown. "My husband is dead. He died under suspicious circumstances in France."

"I hope you don't think me an investigator."

She gave him a scathing look and continued. "He could hardly have been a more wretched person, and I must admit I'm glad to be rid of him. However—"

"I suppose under the circumstances I should offer my congratulations rather than my sympathies." Mark couldn't help but smile at her honesty. God, she was refreshing, so different from the simpering misses who pandered to him in London.

She laughed, a pure, clear sound which heightened his arousal. "Thank you. He may be gone, but he is still managing to vex me. It is necessary for me to conceal his death for as long as possible."

She paused for a moment, and Mark found himself more intrigued than he should be by her story. "Go on. You've already proven yourself to be the most interesting woman I've talked to in months."

"Reddington's will specifies that I am to be disinherited unless I have produced a child." She took a deep breath. Mark watched her ample chest rise and fall. "I need to be with child before anyone finds out my husband is dead."

Mark nearly choked on his brandy. "Are you proposing what I think you are?"

"I need a man to get me with child and allow me to pass the baby off as Reddington's."

"And you thought me a likely candidate?"

"I understand you are quite skilled in such matters." Her cheeks turned a delightful shade of pink. "But that's not the only reason I chose you. You live nearby—my estate lies across the lake." She pointed through the window towards the back of his property. "You are unmarried, and you…well, you don't have a title of your own to pass on."

Anger boiled inside him. This woman dared come here and propose to use him like some farmyard stud. Why he let it get to him he did not know. Women had treated him thus since he reached his majority. They saw him as a toy for their amusement. He was Gillinvray's bastard, not a man in his own right. He wasn't allowed the name he deserved. Why should he think even his seed belonged to him?

He hated her for her presumption. And yet, angry as he was, he couldn't help but think what a delight it would be to bed her. She was outspoken, lush, and startlingly direct. He bet she would go up in flames when he touched her. Considering Reddington's reputation, she had likely been trained in all manner of delights.

She might provide him with the most fun he'd had in years. The eager young widows and overused professionals he'd been with in London had done nothing to ease the knot Katryn's betrayal had lodged in his chest. But maybe he didn't need celibacy. Maybe what he needed was something new, a rare delicacy to replenish his appetite for life. Lady Reddington was certainly unique.

He would do it, but it would be on his own terms. "I will entertain your proposal, but first I require some information. How long were you married?"

She looked surprised by his question but answered without hesitation. "Three years."

"If you did not conceive a child in this time, what makes you believe you will be able to now?"

"Ahhh, a good question." She exhaled slowly. "I've never tried."

"You mean you took precautions to prevent children?"

She shook her head. "No. I mean I am still untouched."

This time Mark did choke. The brandy burned his throat and lungs. He coughed loudly, bending at the waist and gasping for air. It took him several long minutes to get himself under control. When he did, he lifted his head and studied her.

She was smiling, obviously enjoying his discomfort. She looked like a cat who had licked up a large bowl of cream. No man could be married to this woman for three whole years without taking her to bed. The idea was ludicrous.

"Surely you jest. I can't believe your husband, a man who certainly needed an heir, would not visit your bed."

"Oh, he visited, and he wanted an heir, but it did not work."

"What do you mean it did not work?"

"He didn't work. His…manhood refused to cooperate."

Mark bit his lip to keep from laughing at both Lord Reddington's predicament and the obvious difficulty she had finding a polite way to say such a thing. "I'm sorry to be offensive, but I've seen Reddington with other women, women whom he hired for their skills in the bedroom."

She scowled. "It's not me if that's what you think. I am not so odious he found himself unable to bed me."

"No, my lady." He studied her intently, staring boldly at her breasts until, finally, she blushed. "It is nearly impossible to imagine a man finding you unattractive."

"From what I came to understand, he only managed to make himself useful if the woman he was with…if she…abused him."

"What?" Mark couldn't believe what he was hearing. How had Reddington managed to hide this from the *ton*?

Her cheeks turned a deep pink. "Please do not ask me to explain more. I cannot. All I know is what he wanted was not something he chose to ask his wife to do. He tried to perform his duties with me and cursed me up and down for not being able to inspire him."

Mark didn't mean to laugh. Her husband had surely trapped her in a living hell. If Reddington weren't already dead, he would go after the man himself. Yet, the image of Reddington bent over while a woman whipped his ass was too much.

"I am glad you find my situation humorous. At least it brings amusement to someone." Lady Reddington's tone was severe.

"I am sorry. It is simply difficult to believe he was even more perverted than I thought." When Mark closed his eyes in an attempt to compose himself, he heard a snicker. He looked up and realized Cassandra was laughing too.

"It shouldn't be funny," she said as the color in her cheeks intensified. "But when you have to live with it, laughing can be the only way to bear it. Combine his perversion with his drinking and gambling and perhaps you can understand why I don't mourn him."

Mark sobered. "Yes, I believe I do. Why did you accept the marriage?"

She sighed. "Reddington's father knew exactly what his son was. He despaired of ever finding him a wife, but when he found out my father was up to his ears in debt, he offered to pay off some of his bills in exchange for one of his daughters. If I had refused, my sisters would not have enough money for a London season or a chance to marry someone more amenable. I agreed to be the sacrificial lamb."

"I'm sorry." Mark didn't know what else to say. That a father could let such a thing happen to his daughter made him ill.

"I chose it, and I suffered. But now I'm going to be free if I can get around the stipulation in the will. Here's my proposal. I will be your mistress for the next three months. If I become pregnant, I will announce my husband's death and pretend the child is his. If not, I will announce his death anyway and begin looking for a position as a governess or companion. Either way, you will be free to go your own way."

Mark shouldn't say yes. He didn't need this complication in his life. Worse, something told him walking away from this woman wasn't going to be as easy as he would like. Once he had his hands on such a fascinating bedmate, he wouldn't want to give her up. But aside from the pleasure she would bring him, he truly wanted to help her get back at both Reddington and her father.

Finally, exhaling the breath he'd been holding, he said, "I agree, but I have a few conditions of my own."

She looked wary, but she nodded for him to continue.

"If you wish to be with child in three months, then we need to make frequent efforts to render you pregnant. Therefore, you will live here for the duration of our liaison."

She started to protest, but he held up his hand and kept talking. "I want you easily accessible. More importantly, you will be ready to serve me whenever I want, day or night."

Her cheeks were flaming red. "I refuse to be treated like a servant."

"That you may. But if you wish me to be your personal stud, the only compensation I will accept is the free use of your body."

The color drained from her face, and for the first time since she'd entered his study, she looked truly rattled. Excellent. If he got to her with his words, how much more might he affect her with his touch?

"I will pay your price," she said after a few moments of consideration. "I will go home now to collect my things and return in a few hours. I trust you understand no one else is to know of our arrangement."

"I'd planned to spend the next few months in solitude. I expect no visitors. Should I have unexpected guests, I will allow you to return home until they leave."

"Good, it is settled."

Mark studied her intently. An unfamiliar and unpleasant sensation squeezed at his chest. He could only assume it was pangs of remorse for agreeing to divest this woman of her innocence. "I will give you one more chance to reconsider. I am not a gentleman. You cannot expect me to behave as one when I bed you."

She gave him a tight smile. "If I expected such, I would never have come here."

"Very well."

He started to follow her to the door, but she turned and said. "I can show myself out."

He gripped her arm. "I wish to seal our bargain."

Cassandra stepped back, intending to tell him there was no need, but her protest died when he pulled her hard against him.

His lips hovered inches from hers. She could scarcely breathe.

"Does the lovely viscountess have a name? I refuse to use titles in bed."

"Cassandra. My name is Cassandra." It came out as a choked whisper.

"Excellent, you may address me as Mark."

She nodded.

"Cassandra, darling, you have any idea how much danger you are in?"

"What do you mean?" She never got an answer. Instead, he brought his mouth down on hers.

There was nothing gentle about the way he kissed her. He was branding her as his property rather than sealing their bargain. Yet her body responded in ways she'd never dreamed of. Heat flooded her, and an aching tightness coalesced at the juncture of her thighs. She couldn't breathe. She thought her lungs would burst, but she didn't want him to stop.

When his tongue pressed against her lips, forcing them open, she moaned. Her response mortified her, but she couldn't help it. He stroked the inside of her mouth with his tongue, and her knees buckled. She would have crumpled to the floor if he hadn't wrapped his arms around her back, bringing her whole body in contact with his.

His hips pressed into hers, and the hard ridge of his arousal made her shiver. At least he wasn't going to have any problem fulfilling the bargain. He rubbed himself against her, and of their own volition, her hips moved to meet his. She leaned into him, craving more contact, but he broke off the kiss and pushed her away.

She stumbled before she could stand up straight. When she looked at him, his chest was heaving and he'd braced himself on his desk. She was grateful he also struggled for air. If he'd been unaffected, she might have died from embarrassment.

"That definitely had promise," he said, when his breathing had returned to normal. "I think I might rather enjoy our little arrangement."

Cassandra's heart raced. She had to get out of there. "Go. Gather your things. Don't bother with too many clothes. I don't think you'll be wearing them often."

The urge to slap him was so strong she nearly succumbed. How dare he talk to her like she was a whore he'd sampled and chosen to buy? Without a word, she turned and walked out, unable to resist slamming the door behind her.

What had she gotten herself into? Mr. Foxwood—Mark—was still as startlingly handsome as he'd been at Katryn's ball. He was also domineering, insufferable, and far too pleased with himself. She needed to be the one controlling this arrangement. She had contracted his services after all. Instead, he'd made her feel like she was begging him for attention and willing to pay with her body.

Damn him for kissing her when she wasn't prepared. How much worse would it be when things went further? She couldn't afford to lose command of the situation. At least now she was aware of her vulnerability. Next time she would be better prepared.

She remembered his thick shaft pressing against her. Was it truly as enormous as she imagined? Would it even fit inside her? She must have been crazy to agree to let him bed her whenever he chose?

She was desperate. That was the problem. Desperate to gain the means to prevent herself from being at a man's mercy again. If she had to endure three months of Foxwood's arrogance, so be it. There wasn't much she wouldn't do to gain her freedom.

Chapter Three

Cassandra was nearly ready to leave. Her belongings had been packed and sent ahead to Northamberly Castle. Loring implored her to travel the short distance in the closed carriage, as would be proper for a lady. She assured him there was no need to pretend her arrangement was other than it was. She was not a respectable lady paying a call.

She intended to travel alone, on horseback. The ride would be an excellent reminder of why she had bargained away three months of her life and placed herself in the hands of a man like Mark Foxwood. Nothing symbolized her desire for freedom like galloping across the field on Artemis's back.

Cassandra, darling, you have no idea how much danger you are in. Mark's words echoed in her mind throughout the afternoon. She supposed he would be dangerous if she were younger or less hardened by her choices in life. Unlike her husband, Mark would never hurt her physically. Some instinct born of studying her husband and his friends told her that. Now that she knew how easily he affected her with his touch, she could brace herself. She would take pleasure from him, but her heart would remain her own.

He would be a danger to her reputation to be sure, but that was in tatters already simply by her marriage to Reddington. Besides, who would learn of her affair? She intended to remain in Devon, and Mark had agreed to discretion.

He might be dangerous to other women, but for her, he was simply a means for gaining her independence. And a chance to explore her desire for adventure, which had always been overshadowed by duty. As the firstborn, she had protected and defended her sisters at all costs, even agreeing to a marriage akin to a trip to hell.

She took one last look in the mirror. As usual, an array of tight curls had worked loose from the combs in her hair. Several of them bounced against her forehead and along the side of her face. She wished her hair could be tamed, but if no one—not even the most expert stylist hired by her mother—had managed it in twenty-two years, she wasn't likely to fix it now.

She wore her blood-red riding habit. Thick, silver braid sparkled at her shoulders and along the lapels of the jacket. The ensemble was too flashy for a young wife, and it had gained her many a disapproving look in Hyde Park. But when she'd seen it in her seamstress' design book, she had to have it. It was as unconventional as she.

On her way to the stable, she stopped to say good-bye to Loring. "My lady, I wish you would reconsider," he said as he walked her to the stables.

"I appreciate your concern, Loring, but I will not let Reddington best me from beyond the grave." She handed him an envelope. "Please ask Mr. Jenkins to deliver this to my sister. She is staying with my aunt in Grosvenor Square." She had no intention of telling anyone else what was going on, but she kept nothing from Amanda. She hoped her younger sister was up to the shock.

"I will see to it, my lady." Cassandra placed her foot in the stirrup, but Loring took the liberty of laying his hand on her arm to stop her. "I stand ready to rescue you at any hour."

She started to tell him there would be no need for such heroics. Instead, she simply thanked him and mounted her mare.

The sinking sun had turned the landscape pink. Still she decided to take the longer, more scenic route to Northamberly. She wanted time to take in the crisp air. She didn't know how often she would get to feel the wind on her face in the coming weeks. Would Mark permit her much time for riding? A shiver of anticipation ran over her when she thought perhaps he would not.

She couldn't help remembering the overwhelming heat that poured off Mark when he kissed her. What would it be like to feel his hands on her body? Only one word came to mind. Delicious. She smiled at the thought but dismissed it quickly, admonishing herself to enjoy the scenery and her last moments to herself.

Artemis flew over the stone wall that marked the border of her family estate. As the mare landed and kept her vigorous pace, cold air slapped Cassandra's face. She shut her eyes against the icy sting.

A shot echoed across the field, magnified by the silence of the afternoon. It was close, too close. Artemis reared. Cassandra clung to the reins, but the horse panicked. She slipped from the saddle and came crashing to the ground.

Unhurt, she righted herself and raised her fingers to whistle for Artemis when a second shot cracked. She stumbled backwards, but her body refused to be easily felled as if she couldn't accept that she'd been hit. Then, ever so slowly, she slumped to the ground.

When she once again became aware of her surroundings, disorientation held her in its grasp. Was she dead? Was all the white she saw the cloudy floor of heaven? She reached out a tentative hand. Wetness and cold penetrated her thin glove. No, it was only snow.

A red stain marred the snow by her head, but she didn't feel much pain. She struggled to sit up. Her head throbbed, and a wave of nausea rolled over her. She ignored it and brought her hand to her temple to examine her injury. When she touched her head, her fingers came away red and sticky. Fortunately, the bullet had only grazed her. A straight on hit would have rendered her as dead as her husband.

Her mind was fully alert though her hands shook and blood dripped from her wound. She gathered her wits and focused on standing without being sick.

What had happened? Had some hunters' bullets gone astray? One shot in her direction would be easy to dismiss as such, but two? Still, who would want to harm her? The only person who ever intended her physical harm was her husband, and he was dead. Loring had seen his body.

It was an accident, she told herself. It had to be. One she was quite fortunate to have survived.

The shots must have come from the woods on the far side of the meadow. That was the only place a hunter could have concealed himself. She tried to discern any sign of human presence, but night was fast approaching. She saw nothing but a black mass of trees. All she could do was pray that the shooter was gone.

A few deep breaths of cold air worked to calm her stomach and ease the spinning in her head. She wiggled her feet to bring feeling back to her nearly frozen toes and whistled to Artemis. The horse quickly joined her from where she had cowered at the edge of the woods.

Cassandra's head swam when she tried to mount, but she succeeded on her third try. Each step the horse took sent a bolt of pain through her head, but she was too far from Northamberly to walk, even if she could stay on her feet. She would have to endure the ride.

By the time she approached the entrance to Mark's home, her fingers ached from her tight grip on the reins. When she dismounted, the footman who met her caught her arm. Her body swayed wildly, but he helped to steady her. Once she no longer feared collapsing, she turned to face him. His loud gasp let her know he saw her wound despite the darkness.

"It's only a scratch. I'll be fine." She tried to smile.

"Let me help you to the door." She started to protest, but as her knees began to give, she grabbed his arm for support.

A loud thud drew her attention. She looked up to see the front door swing open. Mark stepped onto the porch wearing nothing but a shirt and a pair of form-fitting buckskin breeches. Even through the haze of pain, she appreciated the thick muscles of his legs.

"Ah, you didn't change your mind after all. I had begun to suspect I would never see you again."

"I—"

He cut her off before she could explain. "I'd hoped to have more time to…get acquainted before we dined."

The footman started to explain. "Mr. Foxwood, I think—"

"That will be all, Nicholas." Mark tried to wave him away.

"But, Mr. Foxwood—"

Cassandra released Nicholas's arm. "Thank you for your assistance. I assure you I will be quite fine."

The young footman frowned, but he took Artemis' reins and began to lead the mare toward the stable.

As they stepped into the foyer, Mark turned and saw Cassandra in the light for the first time. His eyes grew wide, and his hand lifted to her face.

"My God, what happened?" He cupped her chin, turning her head to examine her.

"I was shot."

Before she knew what he intended, he scooped her up and carried her into his study, shouting for Andrews and directing him to bring the necessary supplies.

The heat of Mark's body penetrated all the layers of Cassandra's clothing. The wave of dizziness that hit her had nothing to do with her injuries. She needed to get away from Mark long enough to catch her breath. "I'm fine. I only need to clean up."

He proceeded as if he had not heard her. After sitting her down on the supple leather sofa, he knelt in front of her and bent to look more closely at her wound. "The bullet only grazed you. You should recover quickly once this has been cleaned."

"That was precisely my assessment."

Once again he ignored her. "You could have died."

The genuine look of concern on his face made her forget his high-handedness. "I know."

When Andrews came in with water and a towel, the man offered to send for a maid. Mark insisted on taking care of Cassandra himself.

Mark wet the cloth and lifted it to her face, marveling at the whiteness of her skin and boiling with anger as he lightly touched the red gash that marred its perfection. "I'll try not to hurt you."

He ran the cloth over her wound, trying to soften the dried blood before attempting to rub it away. He hated the thought of how tender her ragged flesh would be. She flinched but made no sound of protest.

"You're allowed to complain, you know. It must hurt like hell."

She smiled slightly, her eyes still closed. "I'm tougher than I look," she said, her voice a low whisper.

His body reacted fiercely to the husky sound, but he forced himself to continue his work until all the blood was washed from her face. The cut was ugly, but not too deep. He didn't think it would scar.

"This won't be pleasant, but we need to keep it from getting infected."

She opened her eyes and met his. He forced himself to step back. He wanted to kiss her as much as he wanted to breathe. But if he gave in, he would not be able to stop until he'd removed her wonderfully unique habit and pulled her beneath him. He intended to have his way with her, but first he needed to discover exactly what had happened.

"I promise not to scream, just do it quickly."

"Of course." He reached for the decanter of brandy on the side table and poured some of the amber liquid on the cloth. He took her hand in his. "Hold my hand and squeeze when it hurts."

Her strength shocked him. If she hadn't released him when she did, she might have succeeded in breaking a few fingers.

"Did I hurt you?"

He laughed, not about to admit the truth but ready to tease. "I may never recover. I should call for my smelling salts."

She frowned as he applied a bandage. "I was being serious."

"My dear, over the next few days, you will learn that my body can withstand a great deal of hard use."

He smiled as he watched her eyes widen and her cheeks flush. He picked up his snifter, needing something to occupy his hands lest he forget his resolve to allow her to rest.

She watched him lift the glass to his mouth. "I think I need a brandy, too."

He fought back a laugh. "Ah, of course. I should have guessed you wouldn't go in for ratafia or sherry."

"I can't say I have ever developed a taste for the sickeningly sweet drinks ladies are supposed to enjoy."

He handed her a snifter and sat facing her. "Now that you have your drink, my lady, tell me exactly what happened."

She described hearing the first shot, falling from her mare, being hit, and waking up in the snow. His fist tightened in his lap as he listened. He would find the man who dared to harm a woman on his land and see that the bastard paid for his error. The thought of Cassandra lying dead but a short distance from his house made him slam his fist against the arm of his chair.

She jumped.

"I'm sorry. I was imagining what I'll do when I catch the man who shot you." He took a deep breath to ease the tension from his body. "I can think of many reasons why someone would want to murder your husband, but what would tempt them to come after you?"

His question flustered her. He noted a look of unease in her eyes that had not been their earlier. "You truly think someone shot me on purpose?"

"Don't you?"

"I can think of no motive for killing me."

"What do you believe motivated your husband's murder?"

"It could be any number of things." The wariness in her eyes grew.

"Surely you have a suspicion."

"My husband was a predator. His abysmal luck at the tables is well known as is the way he paid his debts with gains from illegal activities."

"I see." But he didn't, not entirely. Cassandra knew more than she was letting on, and he was determined to find out what she was hiding.

"What explanation would you offer for your wound?"

"A hunter's bullet gone astray." Her voice lacked conviction. Why would she want him to think she was not in danger?

"No hunter should be on my land without my permission."

"You have only been here a matter of days. Before that, the castle was unoccupied for years. I believe the local residents have become rather…careless with regards to the boundaries."

"I shall remedy that immediately."

She started to speak again but Mark held out his hand. "We cannot be sure what happened, and we will not take chances. Fresh snow is falling and little more can be done in the dark. I will investigate in the morning. I must insist you do not to leave the house until I have done so."

"I will not be a prisoner," she said, her characteristic defiance clear on her face.

"When you made your proposal, you put yourself in my hands. I intend to see that you are well taken care of both in bed and out. You can hardly satisfy me if you are dead."

His comment brought color to her cheeks. In combination with the riotous nature of her hair, the added color made her look like a ripe wood nymph. His cock hardened.

"How are you feeling?" A poor attempt to distract himself.

She brought her hand to the bandage he'd placed on her temple and winced. "A little sore, but much better."

He raised his brow and studied her face. "I would bet a fortune you have a hell of a headache, and I am certain that cut still stings. But I suppose you are recovered enough to join me for dinner. I will have Andrews show you to your room so you can change."

Mark smiled as he studied the swish of her exiting backside, but his smile quickly turned to a frown. Everything he had learned of her indicated she was far too intelligent to believe her wound an accident. There was more going on here than he was being told, and worse Cassandra was creating feelings in him—affection, protectiveness—he thought he would never be foolish enough to feel again.

His mind began sending warning signals the moment his body reacted to the feel of her in his arms. He intended to heed them. He would never repeat the mistake he'd made with Katryn. What heart he had left belonged to him and him alone.

ର ର ର

"I will send a maid to help you dress," Andrews said as he began to shut the door to Cassandra's chamber.

"No, thank you." At his raised brow, she added, "I prefer privacy in which to recuperate."

"As you wish." He still wore a look of disapproval. "You may ring if you require assistance later."

As soon as she was alone, Cassandra allowed herself to sink into the chaise situated at the end of her bed. She laid back, closed her eyes, and attempted to release the tension she had been holding since the first shot.

Her mind would not cooperate. Soon she found herself studying her accommodations. Gray stone walls surrounded her, but the fire roaring behind the grate kept the room adequately warm. The linens on the canopied bed were ecru with a pink and yellow floral print that was small enough not to be garish but feminine enough to soften what would otherwise be a rather stark room. The furniture was lighter and more intricately carved than what she had seen in the rest of the house. Cassandra wondered if she had been given the chambers intended for the lady of the house.

She stood, entered her dressing room and noticed a door at the far end. A door with no apparent lock. She took a moment to listen with her ear pressed against the door before trying to open it. Nothing but silence. She turned the knob and slowly cracked the door. As she had suspected, the room on the other side was a man's dressing room. Mark would have access to her at any time of night.

Quickly, she pulled the door shut, and returned to her bed chamber. Her trunks had been unpacked while Mark had tended her wound. She opened the wardrobe and selected the gown she had chosen for the evening. She had grown used to doing without the attention of a maid since Reddington had refused to waste good gambling funds on a lady's maid. She quickly and efficiently stripped off her habit and donned her evening attire.

When she inspected her reflection in the cheval glass, she noted that bandage at her temple barely marred her appearance. Her dress was fashioned from lavender silk and a deep purple satin ribbon wrapped around the high waist and tied in back. Its long tails streamed down, directing the eye to her behind. She had tightened her stays until her breasts were so elevated they threatened to spill over the square neckline.

She felt indecent, but knowing the company a man like Mr. Foxwood kept, her dress was likely too tame. Still, she hoped he would think her attractive. She had no desire to delay the inevitable. The longer he waited to take her to his bed, the more nervous she would become. After pinning a few errant curls, she pulled on her gloves and headed toward the dining room.

When she entered the room, Mark was waiting for her. He'd added a buttery waistcoat and a black jacket to his ensemble. Next to the coat's shiny black fabric, his hair shone like burnished gold. He stood by a window, looking out into the darkness. She remembered how he'd been seated at the window in his study when she'd arrived that afternoon. In both poses, he looked like a lion contemplating his way out of his cage.

A moment later, he turned and looked her over from head to toe. His eyes widened and he smiled. "Your dress is perfection itself. The cut and color are exactly what I would have selected for you. I hope the other things you packed are equally daring. If so, I shall truly enjoy peeling them off you."

Cassandra wished she could cool the heat in her cheeks. "You consider yourself a connoisseur of women's clothing?"

"Indeed I do. One becomes well-acquainted with dress-making while outfitting one's mistress." Mark gave her a wicked smile as he walked toward her. "You should be flattered. I had not planned to take a lover while I was here, but I found myself far too curious. Are you as lovely without your clothes as you are in them?"

Cassandra had no appropriate answer for him. But his comments raised many questions. Why would such a virile man voluntarily retire to the country and forgo his pleasures? It went against everything she knew of him. *Was* he still hurting from Katryn? No matter what his birth, what woman would throw over a man like him for a bore like Southwood? Katryn was a fool.

After seeing Cassandra to her chair, Mark lowered himself into the neighboring seat with feline grace. "I have always detested the custom of sitting at the far end of the table from a woman. It makes conversation difficult. I can only feed my companion if I am right beside her."

"You intend to feed me?"

"I do. Dining together will be our first sensual experience."

She raised her brows.

"Don't tell me you have never experienced physical pleasure biting into a superior piece of steak or sipping a hot cup of chocolate on a cold morning?"

Cassandra had but was embarrassed to admit it. Not wanting to lie, she said nothing. Instead, she concentrated on the consommé in front of her.

Mark reached for his spoon, dipping it in her bowl rather than his own. "Close your eyes and breathe deeply," he said, lifting the spoon to her mouth.

To her annoyance, she found herself obeying without question. His words lulled her, made her want to do anything he asked. She wondered how many young women he'd seduced with nothing but his rich voice.

When he pressed the spoon against her lips, she opened and let the warm broth soothe her as it ran down her throat. The simple soup held layers of flavor unlike any she'd ever tasted. "That's delicious."

"Yes, I don't require a large staff, but I am insistent about the quality of my cook."

"How delightful. My husband refused to waste money on his staff when he could spend it on gambling and women. Therefore, I have grown accustomed to mediocre fare."

Mark trailed his fingers along her cheek. "I am sorry you have been neglected. I assure you, you will have everything you need during your stay with me. I take very good care of my women."

"I am not one of your women."

He lifted a brow. "Do you wish to dissolve our bargain?"

She frowned. "You do not own me, not even for these three months."

His lips curled in a smile that would charm the devil himself. "After tonight, you will wish I did."

"How do you get away with such arrogance?"

He lifted her hand and pressed his lips to the back of it. "My dear, it is not arrogance when it's true."

Cassandra held his gaze in spite of the fire in her cheeks. He was infuriating, but a secret part of her hoped his words were true.

His body promised pure delight, but men were not often what they appeared. Reddington *looked* handsome enough on the surface. Inside, however, he'd been thoroughly rotten.

Still, some women reveled in bedsport with men of their own choosing. How delightful it would be to experience physical pleasure even for this short time. Of course, if she liked it enough, she could take lovers once she was established as a widow. But for all her boldness and flouting of convention, she did not want to be involved with men for whom she cared nothing.

She would get through these three months, hopefully enjoying Mark's attention and refusing to answer his provocations. Then she would have her freedom, and she would settle down in the country by herself. She would not be lonely. She would have her child, and she would be free.

Why didn't her vision of the future please her as much as it had a few days ago?

"Tell Cook the consommé was superb," Mark said to the footman who stood by his chair.

His words drew Cassandra out of her reverie. She realized she had not even noticed the next course being laid.

"I trust you have studied me sufficiently, and you can now give your food ample attention."

"I'm sorry. I didn't mean to stare, really. I...I am simply tired." As soon as the words were out, she wished she had said nothing at all. Now she looked like a babbling fool. Why did he have the power to fluster her when no one else did?

"I see. I suppose since you are...tired I'd best let you feed yourself. Feeding two takes much longer. I don't want you falling asleep before supper ends."

They said little as they consumed the next few courses, but when Cassandra picked up her spoon, eager to delve into her crème brulée, Mark laid his hand on her wrist.

"Dessert is the most seductive of all. I cannot resist watching you enjoy it." Continuing to hold her wrist, he placed his other hand over her eyes. "Close them. Concentrate on smell, taste, touch." At this last word, he ran his fingers along her cheek and down the side of her neck, not stopping until he was barely an inch from the neckline of her gown. "Think about your body. Enjoy what you feel."

Cassandra bit her lip to suppress a moan as he traced her neckline. The sensation of thick, callused fingers, skimming the top of her breasts sent shock waves through her entire body.

"Open your mouth," he commanded.

She realized he'd let go of her hand. She expected a spoonful of the sinful concoction. Instead, his cream-covered finger swept into her mouth.

"Lick it clean."

Her lips closed around him involuntarily. She sucked the sweet egg cream from his finger then ran her tongue down its length. Mark groaned. She was lost in sensation. The taste of him was as good as the dessert. As she

39

sucked his finger, sensations rioted between her legs. She longed to move her hips but managed to keep still.

"Look at me." Mark's voice grew more sensuous with each command. Part of her bristled at his assumption of her obedience, but she was caught in his spell.

Her gaze focused on him, and she saw the promise of things she'd only heard mentioned in veiled tones. Green fire burned in his eyes. She panicked. He'd trapped her like a jungle cat stalking prey. She pushed her chair away from the table and rose.

His hand on her arm stopped her from walking away. "We're not done yet."

"Yes, we are." She pulled her arm free and stood. "There is no need to seduce me. I need to have a child, so I will go to bed with you. I would prefer to move ahead with our...relations."

Mark shook his head. "We will not have any *relations,* as you so colorlessly describe them, if you cannot view this as more than a business transaction. I intend to do more than perform a duty, and I expect you to as well."

"That is not what I agreed to."

"You agreed to pleasure me whenever I required it. I will decide what form that pleasure takes."

Her head swam, and all moisture disappeared from her mouth. Her body thrummed with a restless need she couldn't quite describe. She gripped the back of her chair to steady herself. "I never agreed to be your servant."

"Agree to it now or leave."

"I will do no such thing."

"Won't you?"

He stood. She backed away, but he grabbed her arms before she took two steps. He pulled her close. "Tell me what you feel. Tell me how your body reacts to me."

She said nothing, but her gaze remained locked with his.

"You feel hot, don't you? Hot and restless."

To her horror, she nodded her head.

"You don't want to leave. You want me to awaken the desire you've buried deep."

She couldn't move.

"You have access to my chamber through your dressing room. I will join you shortly. I expect you to be in bed waiting for me."

She turned to leave, but he called for her to wait. He reached out and skimmed his fingers along her cheek. "Is your head still hurting?"

She paused for a moment, thrown by the question. She touched her hand lightly to the bandage on her head, realizing she'd forgotten it. "No. It is much better."

"Good, then do as I said."

Chapter Four

As she sprinted up the stairs, Cassandra gasped for air as if she were drowning. Why had she thought this would be simple? Why had she thought the most difficult part would be the pain of losing her virginity? Surely that couldn't be worse than this loss of control.

If she had to endure night after night of a man's attention in her quest to have a child, then she wanted it to be as pleasant as possible. Mark Foxwood appealed to every one of her senses. But she feared she had made a grave error in choosing him. He was too seductive, too alluring, and worst of all, too commanding.

Even as she considered leaving, she laid out her nightgown and began taking down her hair, sure signs that she intended to stay. She could find someone else willing to help with her problem. Or she could give up all together. That would be the sensible thing to do. She needed to be in control of the situation.

Her body thrummed with indecision. Should she stay? Should she go? She walked to her washstand, poured icy water into the basin, and splashed her face. The shocking cold did nothing to cool the fire Mark had started in her. No, she wasn't going to leave. Making a bargain with Mark might turn out to be her worst decision since marrying Reddington, but she refused to back down.

෮ ෮ ෮

Mark ran his hands through his hair and poured himself another drink as he listened to Cassandra's footsteps pound up the stairs. He hadn't meant to frighten her. He'd meant to make her admit how much she wanted him. Her strong need threatened to reach out and grab him.

He didn't have to seduce her. She was right about that. She was the one who had propositioned him after all, not that he wasn't used to it. At every party he attended in London, he'd collected enough invitations to fill his bed for weeks—though admittedly none as direct as Cassandra's.

Still, he wanted more than acceptance of what she must do to have a child. He wanted her to surrender to the desire he saw in her eyes.

He'd lost the upper hand with Katryn. No woman as inexperienced as she'd claimed to be could have manipulated him so. Katryn had known exactly how to touch him, exactly what to say to make him beg to have her again and again. He'd been as wild as a beast with her, but she'd made him tame. She'd leashed him with her touch and her false protestations of love.

Never again. He'd seen fear in Cassandra's eyes, but he'd also seen a spark of desire, one he intended to fan into an inferno. She was strong and determined. He couldn't allow himself to be gentle with her. There was too much risk involved. If he let his heart go again, he might lose his sanity all together.

CR CR CR

Cassandra peeled back blankets and sinfully silky sheets. Using the stepping stool, she hoisted herself into Mark's bed and snuggled under the covers. A servant had kindled the fire, but the blaze was still small. The wind whistled through the cracks in the stone walls. She shivered and pulled the blankets tight around her.

She longed for something to soothe her fears. If she wasn't so cold, she would've gotten out of bed to pour herself a brandy from the decanter she saw across the room. She remembered the commanding tone Mark had used when he sent her up and shivered more. His voice had carried desire for something dark and elemental.

She'd told Mark she wasn't the cause of Reddington's impotence, but she wasn't as confident in her assessment as she'd pretended to be. How many nights had she lain awake wondering what was wrong with her? Mark seemed to find her attractive, but what if the sight of her body rendered him unable to perform? What if she was repellent after all?

Her thoughts were ridiculous, of course, yet only Mark's appearance in the doorway served to banish them from her mind. She sat up when she saw him, gathering the sides of her nightdress which threatened to slide off her shoulders.

His gaze perused what he could see of her body. "What are you wearing?" Mark asked.

"A nightrail. It's what I always wear to bed."

"When I asked you to wait for me, I expected you to be naked."

Her heart hammered. He looked positively feral.

"Stand up."

She did as he asked but feared her legs would not hold her. The strangest rush of fear and need dizzied her. How could he show such concern one moment and such violence the next?

Her stared at her breasts. Her nipples were painfully hard from a combination of cold and desire. The heat in his eyes told her he saw them plainly through the thin material of the gown. She fought the urge to cover herself, not wanting him to know her embarrassment.

He surveyed the rest of her body. Then his hand gripped the lace-trimmed neckline. In one smooth gesture, he pulled the two halves apart, sending buttons flying.

She shrieked.

When he pushed the torn garment from her shoulders, she was completely naked. "That's better."

Heat radiated from her face. "Mark, I—"

"Turn around." His voice was low and harsh.

She stepped back, almost hitting the bed.

"I want to see all of you. Turn for me."

Biting back another protest, she did as he asked. She stabbed her nails into her palms to distract her from fear and something else, some wicked feeling that made her want to display herself for him.

"You are sinfully beautiful." His compliment served to lessen her fear, reminding her of his gentle touch that afternoon.

When she faced him again, he cupped her breasts. "I may keep you naked for the next week at least. It would certainly take me that long to tire of feasting on you."

Cassandra tried to swallow, but her throat was too dry.

Mark's gaze moved from her heavy breasts to her eyes. "You will not cover yourself when you are in my bed. Your body is mine to enjoy, and I intend to explore every inch."

She took a step back, unable to keep her hands from shaking. His expression softened and he caressed her face with the back of his hand. "You have nothing to fear from me. I will only push you as far as you want to go."

"Wh-what do you mean?"

"I can see desire in you. Desire for things you cannot name." He breathed the words more than said them as he placed his lips against her neck. "Trust me." His tongue traced the line of her collar bone. "I will fulfill all the fantasies you have buried inside your mind."

She started to speak, but he bent his head and ran his tongue over her nipple. She gasped, and her hands tangled in his hair. By the time he sucked the bud all the way into his mouth, her breath came in pants.

"Mark. Stop. I feel so strange. I…" He sucked harder. She lost the ability to speak.

Mark couldn't stop. He had to have more of her. Her low whimpers made him realize how intensely he was pulling on her. He switched to her other nipple, not wanting to make them sore so early in the evening.

Her moans grew louder, and her fingers pulled at his hair, trying to stop the sweet torture. When her knees gave way, he caught her with an arm around her waist and scooped her into his arms. Keeping his mouth locked to her breast, he laid her on the bed and lowered himself on top of her

She pressed his head against her. Her hips bucked, rubbing against his cock. He wondered if he could bring her to climax just by playing with the rock hard buds, but he decided to answer that question another time. He was desperate to find out if she was as wet as he thought.

He released the nipple he was suckling and supported himself on his hands. As he gazed down at her, her eyes flew open. When they met his, she turned away, trying to hide her face against the sheets.

"Cassandra, you are beautiful, and your response is all I had hoped for. Never be ashamed of your desire."

She didn't move. He grasped her chin and forced her to turn her head. "Look at me."

Slowly, her eyes opened He had to force himself to keep his gaze on her face when he wanted to watch her full breasts rise and fall.

"What have you done to me?" she asked.

"Exactly what you wanted. I've awakened your hunger for me."

He knelt by the side of the bed, positioning himself between her legs. She resisted his attempt to push her thighs apart. "Open to me, Cassandra. I want to see you."

"I can't."

"You can. Within a few days, we will know everything there is to know of each others' bodies. You can hide nothing from me."

Her legs moved apart an inch or two. "Wider." He pressed gently on her thighs. Finally, she relaxed and opened to him.

Her pussy was beautiful, pink and full and dripping with cream. He breathed deeply. Her scent intoxicated him. His cock throbbed. He longed to bury his face against her and taste her essence. But she wasn't ready for that yet.

He had no intention of treating her like a fragile flower, but he wanted to introduce her to the delights of the bedchamber slowly so she would savor each one. He wanted her surrender, but he would not push too hard and make her fear his touch.

He gripped her hips and pulled her closer to him. He moved his thumbs across her mons and down along the sides of her outer lips.

She tensed.

He looked up and saw distress on her face. "Trust me."

She smiled and nodded.

He pressed one finger against her damp core, sucking in his breath when her heat surrounded him. Suddenly, he wasn't sure he could hold back long enough to ready her. It was all he could do not to rip his pants off and plunge into her right then.

He rubbed his finger back and forth through her wetness. Finally, when the thrusting of her hips told him she was ready to beg for relief, he pushed his finger inside. The walls of her channel gripped him fiercely and he groaned.

She was wet and slick, but God, she was tight. He pressed his thumb against her clit. She jerked, her eyes flying open. He increased the pressure. She tried to protest, but he began to move his finger in and out before she spoke any coherent words.

Cassandra tore at the sheets with her hands. An intense need built in her, like a thirst she had to quench or die. She couldn't explain it, but her body knew Mark could give her what she needed.

She cried out involuntarily as he pressed another finger inside her, widening her even more. His thumb never stopped moving against her clit and made her lose her ability to think. Her whole body squirmed, wanting escape, release, something more.

He curled his fingers upwards, touching a spot inside her that sent her soaring. "That's it, Cassandra. Surrender. Ride it."

She heard the words but didn't understand until a wave of pure pleasure hit her. One so strong she tried to draw back as it crested.

Mark forced himself to close his eyes. The sight of her reaching climax was the most exquisite thing he'd ever seen. He feared he might embarrass himself by coming in his pants.

He'd detected her natural passion in the way she moved, the way she spoke. He'd expected to make her sizzle with desire, but the intensity of her response dumbfounded him. The next few months were going to be a hell of a lot of fun.

Her breathing slowed. Gradually, she came down from her peak. Mark kept his fingers inside her. He had never been with a virgin before, but he decided the best strategy for not hurting her was to have her so passion-drugged by the time he entered her, she would not be able to think.

She stirred, and he pulled his slick fingers from her and gripped her clit with them. He squeezed gently, and she cried out. "Stop!"

He smiled down at her. "Not until I bring you again."

"No, please. I can't. I—"

Her words became whimpers as he began to stimulate her again, forcing her to begin a second climb toward release. He slid his fingers inside her, adding a third one.

Cassandra needed a chance to breathe, to recover, but he didn't give it to her. Why was he insisting on drawing this out? She wanted to know what it would feel like to have him inside her.

She opened her eyes to watch Mark. His gaze was fixed between her legs, and his look of wonder surprised her.

A hard thrust of his fingers made her grab the covers again, as if she could keep herself from falling. Then he pressed his thumb firmly against that place where all of her restless need centered, and nothing could prevent her fall. She thought she screamed, but she didn't know if Mark heard it or if the sound only echoed in her head.

When she was capable of opening her eyes again, Mark had removed his coat and waistcoat, and he was unbuttoning his shirt. She was fascinated by the thickly-muscled chest he revealed. Her gaze swept across his abdomen as he removed his shirt, casting it onto the floor. She couldn't help but observe the large bulge in his breeches.

She didn't think it possible for desire to build in her again, not after the way he'd pushed her to that nearly painful peak twice already. But watching him made her want to lift her hips off the bed and offer herself again.

Mark looked up and caught her staring. "Do you like what you see?"

She started to answer, but she choked on her words when his hands went to the buttons that would release his breeches and bare him completely. As he pushed them over his hips, she gasped. Mark's shaft was enormous, and it jutted upward in a way that demanded attention.

His size made her understand why so many women found only pain in the marriage bed. His fingers had delighted her, but she did not feel confident this other part of him would fit. "I don't think you will fit."

"As hot and wet as you are, I assure you, I'll fit."

Her cheeks burned, but his sexy voice only increased her longing. "May I touch you?"

He groaned and closed his eyes for a few seconds. "Next time, yes, but I'm on the edge as it is."

He climbed onto the bed and grabbed her by the waist, yanking her toward him until she felt his shaft press against her. She was torn between arching up and trying to scramble away. She tried to remind herself why she was doing this, but the animal glint in his eyes disturbed her. Despite his earlier tenderness, he was not accustomed to being gentle, and he had already stolen most of her wits with his caresses.

He must have noted the fear in her eyes, because as he caressed her belly, he said, "I haven't hurt you yet, have I?"

"No." Her voice came out in a breathy whisper.

He laced his fingers through hers and stretched her arms over her head. "There will be some pain when I pierce your maidenhead. I can't prevent that, but I will make it as easy for you as I can."

She nodded, not trusting herself to speak.

He kept her arms imprisoned as he pressed the tip of his shaft against her opening. He entered a fraction of an inch. No longer able to keep still, she arched her hips up, trying to take more, but he pulled away.

"Please." The part of her mind that remembered where she was cringed at her desperate tone, but the rest of her didn't care. All that mattered was feeling those riotous sensations he had shown her again and again.

Mark's breath came in pants. He gripped her fingers so tightly they ached. "I…have to go slowly at first…or I will…hurt you."

She whimpered. He pressed forward again, entering her further. She bucked against him. This time, he didn't hold back. With one fierce stroke, he pierced her, entering to the hilt.

She cried out, and he stilled. He fought for control as he waited for her body to accommodate him. Her muscles clamped around him like a vise. It was all he could do not to come right then.

After what seemed like an eternity, Cassandra began to relax. He opened his eyes and saw her looking up at him, her eyes wide and fiery. "Please, tell me there's more."

Her breathless words made him lose all the ground he'd gained by holding still. One tiny movement would have put him over the edge.

He sucked air into his lungs and tried to find the breath to answer her. "There's more. I'm…waiting for you to…adjust."

She pressed against him, letting him know that she was more than adjusted. Something snapped in him then. He forgot about holding back. He forgot that she was a virgin, and he should go slowly. Instead, he began driving into her with long, full strokes, going deeper each time.

He let go of her hands and grabbed her thighs, pressing her legs back until they were doubled on her chest. He wanted to get as deep inside her as he could before he spilled his seed.

He realized she was screaming. He prayed it was from pleasure, because he couldn't stop. All he wanted was the release his body had been crying for since he had first seen this beguiling sprite.

Her body went rigid beneath him, caught by the tremors of her orgasm. The rapid contractions of her muscles tossed him into the abyss. He screamed as he hammered against her and emptied his balls.

Chapter Five

A heavy weight lay against Cassandra's waist. Slowly, she pulled herself far enough from the depths of sleep to realize it was Mark's arm. She vaguely remembered Mark leaving her to blow out the candles and retrieve the covers they'd flung to the floor. Unfortunately, everything that had come before stood out vividly in her mind, including the utterly abandoned way she had reacted to him.

She needed to get back to her own room. Lying in bed with him, she felt suffocated, and the feeling had nothing to do with his arm pressing on her ribs. His very presence was enough to keep her from breathing properly. She needed time to think, to consider her reaction to him and whether her fear of its intensity was justified.

Mark was far too dominant and aggressive, the sort of man she would have avoided like the plague during her Seasons in London. Had her desperation to thwart the strictures of Reddington's will so clouded her mind she had not fully grasped how much he would demand of her?

After successfully disentangling herself from Mark, she tried to sit up. Her body protested violently. She was sore everywhere, but the worst ache came from the delicate region between her legs.

She wanted to blame Mark, but she couldn't. As he had pounded against her, somewhere in the back of her mind, she had known it would hurt later. But she had dismissed the thought and begged for more. Not for one second had she wanted him to stop. She had been as wild for him as he apparently had been for her.

Gritting her teeth against the discomfort, she slid off the side of the tall bed, unable to locate the steps in the dark. As she bent to retrieve her torn nightdress from the floor, a hand closed around her arm.

"Where are you going?" Mark's low voice sent a shiver across her.

"I thought it was customary for a lady to return to her chamber after fulfilling her duties."

"It is, if the woman is a wife. You, however, are my mistress. It is a mistress's duty to stay with her lover. She never knows when he may grow hungry for her again in the night."

"But I am not your mistress in truth."

He propped himself up on his elbow and studied her. "Yes, you are. Until you are with child, you exist to service my appetites. Come back to bed."

Cassandra shook her head, forcing herself to ignore his insulting words. "Surely there's no reason for me to stay. I mean you couldn't possibly want me again tonight."

"Oh, you are quite wrong, my lovely Cassandra." He sat up and pulled her closer so she felt the hard ridge of his arousal. His other hand delved between her legs.

She winced when he made contact with her abraded flesh, and he abruptly withdrew his hand.

"Damn…I'm sorry. I should have realized you would be sore."

He pulled her into his arms and stroked her back. "I should have been more gentle with you."

"Don't worry. I enjoyed what we did. But I can't do it again right now."

"Lie down. I'll be right back."

"Where are you going?"

"I'm getting a wet cloth. The cold water will take away the sting. In the morning, you can have a long, hot bath to ease the deeper ache."

She did as he asked, once again confounded by the change in him. Which was the real Mark—the gentleman who wanted to see to her every need or the savage who could shatter her with his touch?

Despite his warning, Cassandra yelped when he pressed the cloth between her legs, but the cold did feel delicious after the shock subsided. The stinging heat friction had stirred melted away.

Moonlight shone through the window, enabling Cassandra to see Mark's outline clearly, but his features remained masked. It was easier not to be embarrassed in front of him when they were in the shadows. She relaxed against the bed and gathered the courage to satisfy her curiosity.

"Was my response to what we did tonight typical of the women you have bedded? You seemed to enjoy what we did, but—"

Mark leaned forward and silenced her with a kiss. "I assure you your reaction was exactly what I had hoped for. The pleasure a woman finds in bed depends on how considerate her lover is. Not all men care enough to see that their partners enjoy bedding them, but all women's bodies are designed to feel what you did. Any man who cannot bring a woman to such devastation is no real man at all."

She smiled at his reassurance. "Thank you. I was only concerned that I had reacted with too much vigor."

"Your *vigor* is what most men dream about. Some men want wives who will lie still and take what is given to them. They believe it is only a mistress's place to enjoy the sex act, but I would never willingly couple with a woman who had no passion in her."

"So you enjoyed tonight in truth?"

"Cassandra, words cannot describe the pleasure you brought me. I shudder to think what you will do to me when you become more experienced."

His words were low and husky. Desire stirred in her as his hand pressed the cloth against her body. She pulled away, needing him to remove his hand before she became aroused again. "I think I'm better now."

"Good." He sat back, folding the cloth in his hands.

Mark took a deep breath, but he continued to stand by the bed. "If you would be more comfortable in your own chamber, you are free to go. I will order a bath for you in the morning and await you at breakfast."

"I do believe I would sleep better there." She was able to stand with less discomfort than before.

He caught her arm before she could leave. "Enjoy your time alone. When you are recovered, we will test the true limits of your endurance."

His words made her shiver. She barely managed to say good night before scurrying across the room and pulling the door shut behind her.

ದ ದ ದ

As had been his pattern all his life, Mark woke long before dawn. Even when he had stayed out most of the night in London, he enjoyed the quiet of the morning hours.

He stretched and sat up. Andrews would be up soon with water for his bath, and Mark would order hot water for Cassandra. Mark winced when he thought of how sore she would be. What kind of beast was he not to have restrained himself? He had taken her like he would the most experienced Cyprian. He would consider himself more than fortunate if she hadn't run for Reddington Abbey as soon as she escaped his bed.

Her response had sent his mind reeling. He had always enjoyed his bedsport on the rough side, but he had never been so out of control with a woman as he had with Cassandra. Not even with Katryn.

Katryn. Every time he had been with a woman since that bitch had laughed at his proposal, he had thought of her. No woman had been able to make him forget, until last night. But he was only now remembering she existed. Not once had he thought of her while Cassandra was in his bed.

He felt more alive than he had in the last six months, but he wasn't sure that pleased him. He'd thought he hated the cold, deadness inside him, but now he thought it preferable to this reawakening of feeling. If he could feel, he could be crushed again.

Perhaps the wisest thing to do was stop this madness. There was only a small chance Cassandra would have become pregnant after one night. It wasn't too late for her to find someone else to help her. Was it?

He shook his head at his foolishness. He could no more let her go to another man's bed than he could erase the last day from his mind. For the next three months, Cassandra was his.

ଔ ଔ ଔ

A clanging sound woke Cassandra. She opened her eyes and sat up with a start. The tension in her body relaxed when she realized the noise had been caused by a young, blond-haired maid attempting to bring the dead coals back to life.

The girl didn't look a day over sixteen. Her hands were covered with soot, and she had apparently dropped the poker into the fire as she tried to stoke it. She now seemed to be trying to figure out how to retrieve it without burning her hand. Cassandra immediately felt sorry for her.

Cassandra picked up one of the extra blankets from the foot of her bed. "Try wrapping this around your hand."

The young woman gasped and whirled around. "My lady, I'm sorry. I didn't mean to wake you. I mean I did. I was supposed to, but I wanted to room to be warm for you first."

"That is quite all right." Cassandra glanced at the sun peeking around the edges of the curtains. "I do not usually sleep this late." Of course after being shot and then bedding Mark, she might have slept until noon if left undisturbed.

The maid took the proffered blanket and used it as Cassandra had suggested. "Thank you, my lady. Please don't tell Mr. Foxwood about this. I only started here yesterday and this is my first position. I came to help my sister with her baby. Then she insisted I apply. I was so happy when they hired me. I'm trying. Really I am."

"I am sure you are, and I will not say a thing. Tell me your name."

The girl smiled. "Mary."

"All right, Mary. You said you were supposed to wake me."

"Yes, my lady. Mr. Foxwood wanted you to join him for breakfast. He asked that I wake you and offer to run you a bath."

"A bath would be much appreciated." The longer Cassandra sat up, the more her muscles protested.

"Yes, my lady. The water is already heating." Mary drew the curtains and scurried out of the room, presumably to tell the footmen to bring the water.

Cassandra blinked against the bright light and snuggled down for a last few delicious minutes in bed. But all she could think of was the prospect of facing Mark again.

Last night he had succeeded in making her hunger for him like a starved woman. She had ceased to care how exposed she was or how wantonly she behaved. But now, she would have to face him in daylight. He would see every reaction, every bit of color in her cheeks.

And she would know exactly how beautiful his hard body was under his conservative clothing. She would see his hands and remember how they had moved across her body. She shivered at the thought. A small part of her worried she might succumb to desire and suggest he take her right there in the breakfast room.

The dressing room door opened, and Mary reappeared. "Your bath is ready, my lady."

The warm water felt delicious. Cassandra wished she could soak in it all morning but she could not prevent the inevitable. She would have to break her fast with Mark sooner or later. There was no point in letting the food get cold.

The air seeping in around the windows was bitterly cold, so she chose a thick beige muslin. After applying the salve Mary had brought for her wound, she covered it with a fresh bandage. The jagged cut looked much improved. She only hoped the scarring would be minimal. Her unmanageable hair could take an hour to tame, so she simply tied it back with a green ribbon. Wearing her hair down was hardly as scandalous as her reason for staying at Northamberly.

She asked Mary to inform Mark that she would be down shortly. She needed to compose a letter to Loring, but she wasn't sure what to tell him. If she let him know she had been shot, he would likely bring the carriage to collect her before he finished reading the letter

In the end, she settled for a brief paragraph saying things were going according to plan with Mark, which was entirely true. Mark had bedded her, and that was what mattered.

As she sealed the letter, she took a deep breath and steeled herself to confront Mark. She needed to settle the matter of his attempt to confine her to the house. He might be able to dictate when and how they were intimate, but he would not control her entire life.

Chapter Six

The breakfast room was in a wing of the castle that had been added within the last hundred years. Tall windows looked out on the park, and their light bounced off the blue and yellow-striped silk covering the walls. Cassandra was so mesmerized by the beauty of the sun streaming in the sound of Mark's voice made her jump.

He chuckled. "I do hope you slept well."

She turned to see him standing by the sideboard, which was loaded with eggs, bacon, scones, oatcakes, and bowls of exotic fruits. The catlike expression on his face unnerved her.

"Tolerably well, yes." She had no intention of telling him how long she lay awake analyzing what had passed between them.

He gestured for her to take a seat. "Obviously I did not exhaust you sufficiently. I'll do better tonight, or perhaps later this morning."

He smiled again in a way that made her blood run hot. She tried to ignore the melting sensation in her legs. She refused to let him know how easily he flustered her. "I have no complaint with how you fulfilled your duty."

He took two plates and began filling them from the steaming trays. "I am glad to know you approve, but you have only begun to learn my skills."

As Mark sat her plate in front of her and joined her at the table, Cassandra fought not to fidget in her chair. The mere thought of the things Mark might do made her want to beg him to show her right then and there.

Mark gave her another wicked smile as if sensing her distress. They ate in silence for a few moments. After polishing off an enormous serving of bacon, Mark said, "I sent a few footmen to search the area where you were shot. I'm going to join them when I finish eating."

"Excellent. I'll go with you."

He froze, his fork halfway to his mouth. "You most certainly will not."

"Since I am the only one who knows exactly where the incident happened, I would be quite useful in the investigation."

His fork hit his plate, and he pierced her with his sharp green gaze. "You will stay in this house until we discover whether or not this was an accident."

"I am not going to sit here like a prisoner. Besides, Artemis needs exercise."

"One of the grooms can see to that. I will not have you risking your life."

"You are overreacting."

He stood and hauled her out of her chair. The roll she had been eating fell to the floor. "You will obey me on this. I will not have you hurt again."

His face was only inches from hers. She smelled his unique scent, leather and fresh spring grass. His hands gripped her arms, and her breasts brushed against his chest as she breathed.

"Why does it matter to you?" Her voice came out far breathier than she had intended.

He let go of her arms as if they had scorched him. His eyes were wide. He looked startled, almost panicked. "Is it so hard to imagine that I wish to protect you, that I should not like to see an innocent woman die?"

He turned and stomped out, leaving her to finish the meal alone.

CR CR CR

Even with her heavy habit and her warmest cloak, the wind cut her. Steam poured from Artemis' nostrils, and the mare seemed none to pleased to be out on such a cold morning. Artemis was usually as agile and obedient as

Cassandra could wish, but this morning, the mare was reluctant to move faster than a walk.

Perhaps Artemis sensed her rider's tension, not to mention her discomfort. The split skirt of Cassandra's riding habit allowed her to ride astride. While this was her preference, the pressure of the saddle on her most intimate region made her only too aware of the places Mark had touched her and how vigorous he had been.

When she approached the wooded area bordering the field where she'd been shot, her heartbeat accelerated. What if Mark was right? What if it wasn't an accident? She couldn't be lucky enough to take a mere grazing a second time.

She heard voices as she approached the trees and pulled on the reins until Artemis stilled, and listened carefully. The next words came from the footman who'd helped her the night before. Nicholas. She thought that was his name.

Now if she could only stay hidden while keeping close enough to hear what the men were saying. Dropping down from Artemis' back and looping her reins around a low limb, she whispered to the mare to keep silent and prayed she would obey.

Cassandra moved in the direction of the voices, taking slow, careful steps. She heard a hushed voice, which she recognized as Mark's, but she could not make out his words. She moved a few feet closer, stopping behind a tree and straining her ears. Nothing. Had they moved on to continue the search? She hadn't heard anyone move.

An arm closed around her neck and hauled her away from the tree.

"I told you to stay in the house." Mark's breath was hot against her ear, but his voice was eerily calm.

She struggled against him, but he held her as if she weighed nothing. His firm body pressed against her back. One arm imprisoned her waist. The other remained about her neck. She could breathe if she stayed still, but her air supply dwindled when she struggled.

"I told you I wasn't going to be ordered around." She refused to let him know she was frightened.

He tightened his hold, and she gasped. "Do you want to die?" He squeezed until she could hardly breathe.

"N-No."

Still he held her.

"Damn you!" She forced the words out as she tried with all her might to kick him.

With enough speed to make her dizzy, he whirled her around to face him, holding her by the upper arms. "Then you are going to listen to me."

Her anger boiled over. She gulped in air and lashed out with her foot. Mark's keen reflexes prevented the kick from landing where it would do the most damage. But she made contact with his thigh. He grunted and stumbled back, but he did not fall.

The look of pure animal rage in his eyes made her back up. She'd made a mistake. She no longer needed to worry about the shooter coming back. Mark was ready to kill her himself.

She stepped back again, but she bumped into the tree she'd been hiding behind.

He was almost on top of her.

Her heart raced. She swallowed a scream.

He put a hand on either side of her head, trapping her against the tree. Fire burned in his eyes. His body radiated such heat, she expected steam to rise from it.

"Never. Do. That. Again."

She nodded to show she understood.

He didn't move.

"You scared me to death and you think you can—"

His mouth came down on hers and cut off her words. His kiss was brutal as if he wanted to pour his anger into her. His tongue thrust into her mouth, and a stab of lust ran through her, nearly making her knees give.

He pressed her back against the tree, giving her no chance to escape. He was rock hard where he pressed against her belly, and she had the sudden wild urge to lift her skirt and let him take her there in the woods.

The friction of his tongue on the roof of her mouth made her moan and press her hips to his.

His hands reached under her cloak and massaged her breasts. The fabric of her shift rasped against her nipples, and they tightened. She wanted to feel his mouth on them again.

She slid her hands along his back until she cupped his firm buttocks, kneading them as he did her breasts. He groaned and pressed his shaft against her. Instinct made her open her legs and tilt her hips, rubbing against the center of her need.

The crack of a twig brought them back to reality. Mark pulled away, and Cassandra turned to see Nicholas standing in the clearing, his mouth hanging open.

"What is it?" Mark growled.

"W-we found some tracks, sir."

"Show me." Mark grabbed Cassandra and pulled her along with him. "Don't even think about leaving my sight."

Mark gave his stallion his head as he and the animal flew across the meadows. The tall grass slapped at his boots, and his greatcoat whipped around his legs. When horse and rider reached the rocky hills marking the coast, Mark nudged the stallion toward the path that would bring them safely to the coast. They descended to the spot Mark had come to think of as his own. He dismounted and sat on the jagged outcropping of rocks while he tried to sort through what he had learned of Cassandra's attack.

He had spent the early afternoon hours visiting some of the older villagers whom he had met when his father brought him to the castle as a child. He'd hoped they might have seen a stranger or heard some rumor about Reddington and what he was involved in. But he had not turned up a single clue.

He ran his hands through his hair as a vision of Cassandra entered his mind. At least she hadn't followed him to the village. He had told her he was in need of exercise and would be taking a long ride, alone. He told Nicholas and another footman to keep watch over her and see that she stayed in the house.

Every time he thought of Cassandra's presence in the very woods from which she had been shot, a red fury closed over him.

For all he knew she might never come to his bed again after his display of temper. He shouldn't have treated her so roughly. But if scaring her was what it took to save her life, he wanted her scared. He kept imagining her being shot right in front of him while he stood by, powerless to help.

She was the stubbornest woman he had ever met. But as infuriating as she might be, he was determined to keep her safe. If he had to tie her to his bed to protect her, then he would do so.

All his instincts told him Cassandra's injury was not the result of an accident. Someone wanted her dead. The footprints they found in the woods told them nothing. They fit the pattern of boots belonging to most farmers for miles around.

With no leads and no evidence, he didn't know how to continue the investigation. All he could hope for was that one of the villagers he alerted would overhear something in the next day or two. He feared he *would* have to tie Cassandra up to keep her inside longer than that.

જી જી જી

Andrews called to Cassandra as she ascended the winding stone steps, intent on writing a letter to her sister. "I'm sorry to disturb you, my lady, but a letter came for you earlier. I was unable to find you after breakfast. The messenger came from Reddington Abbey, and he indicated it was important."

"Thank you, Andrews." She met him at the landing and took the letter.

"Do you require anything else, my lady?"

"No, I intend to be in my chamber until supper. I assume Mary will call me at the correct hour."

"I will see she does." He bowed and turned to go back to the foyer.

Cassandra opened the letter as soon as she closed the door to her sitting room. When she read its contents, she almost sank to the floor. Instead, she forced herself to take the few steps required to reach the chaise.

She closed her eyes, took a deep breath, and read it again, hoping to find the words changed.

Dear Lady Reddington,

I regret to disturb you, but I needed to inform you that Reddington Abbey was burglarized last night. The family chambers were ransacked. I do not know if any of your personal effects were taken, but all your bureau drawers and your wardrobe were ransacked. The footmen and I searched the grounds but found no trace of anyone nor any indication of forced entry. I pray this is unconnected to the events which transpired in France, but I am uneasy.

Sincerely yours,

Mr. Arnold Loring

Until she read those words, Cassandra had convinced herself her injury had been an accident. Now, she no longer held that conviction.

Should she tell Mark about this development? He would become even more insufferable and controlling. Yet, she *was* scared. She wasn't truly reckless with her safety, no matter what Mark thought. She was simply used to solving her own problems.

A chill passed over her as she remembered the look in Mark's eyes as he had pinned her against the tree. Would he have taken her right there if Nicholas hadn't found them? Her heart fluttered at the thought.

For the rest of the morning Mark had remained cold and aloof. He made certain she stayed near him, never letting her stray further than an arm's length away, but he hardly spoke to her. When his gaze touched hers, the spark of passion was gone.

When they had arrived back at the castle, he informed her of his plan to go for a ride after taking a solitary lunch in his study. He had not sought her out since then. Had she pushed him too far? Would he decide she was too much trouble and send her away?

She hoped not. She still needed to be in his bed. And now, she had to admit, she needed his protection.

Chapter Seven

If frost had formed on the table in the dining room, Cassandra would not have been surprised. The evening meal was as unlike the previous night's as it could be. Mark hardly acknowledged her presence except to offer her more wine or inquire if she was ready for the next course. When a footman sat a plate of berry pie topped with cream in front of her, Mark did not glance her way, much less offer to feed her.

When Mark excused himself shortly thereafter, Cassandra sat at the table fuming. If he wanted her gone, he needed to say so. Otherwise, she expected him to fulfill his part of their agreement.

After a brief search, she found him in his study. He was bent over his desk, writing so fast his pen flew over the page. She wondered what correspondence could be so urgent. Reluctant to interrupt him in mid-thought, she stood in the doorway, watching and considering what she was going to say.

"If you will not leave, at least come in and sit down. It is rather hard to concentrate with someone hovering on the threshold."

He never looked up, nor did his writing slow. How had he known she was there?

She sank onto the leather sofa and pulled her legs under her, positioning herself so she could see him over the back of her seat. She watched him seal the letter and lay it aside before he stood and began to approach her.

He smiled but with none of his characteristic teasing or the heat he had shown the night before. "I suppose you have come to berate me for my coldness, remind me you are in charge, and force me to bed you."

"I suppose I have." She held his gaze even as she sensed color rising in her cheeks.

"I imagine you will be successful with the latter. I *have* given my promise after all. I never believed to escape it."

Fury swelled in her. "If taking me to bed is so odious, then I will pack my things and leave immediately."

He lifted his hand and stroked her cheek with his knuckles. His gaze grew heated. She couldn't have looked away for anything. "Touching you could never be anything but delightful. I am more concerned it will be too pleasurable. I might forget my anger when I feel your heat again."

She frowned. "You are only angry because you cannot control me."

"Perhaps that is part of it, but I am far angrier that you show no concern for your own safety. How can I protect you when you throw yourself into danger? Your willingness to approach me with your proposal should have shown me how reckless you are. I don't have the strength to protect you from me. But I will not allow anyone else to hurt you."

She started to ask why she would need protection from him, but he placed a finger against her lips. "Stand up."

Her body obeyed without thought, as if for that moment it did belong to him.

He walked around the sofa so they both stood in front of the fire. "Turn around."

She did.

He began to undo the buttons on her bodice. As each one opened, he kissed the newly exposed flesh before moving to the next one. He progressed with agonizing slowness.

The light brush of his lips made her long for more. Heat built in her body and rushed toward her center, making her aware of the secret place between her legs which Mark had so thoroughly awakened the night before.

When Mark pushed her dress from her shoulders, his hands brushed against the sides of her breasts. She groaned, wanting to force him to touch her nipples, to give her the same shooting sensations of pleasure he had before.

He loosened the tapes of her petticoat and let it fall to the floor. Then he gathered the fabric of her chemise and pulled it upward. She stretched her arms up so he could remove it completely. Suddenly, she was naked except for her stockings.

She turned to face him. "I want to see you too."

"You will have your chance to explore. But first, I intend to give you something special. I saved it for tonight."

Her heartbeat accelerated. "What?"

"I would rather demonstrate than explain. Sit."

He gestured toward the sofa. She backed up until the backs of her knees hit the edge of the seat, and she had no choice but to sit. Her heart pounded wildly.

He knelt before her and pushed her legs open. "Lie back." Once again, she obeyed without a thought, letting her head come to rest against the velvet cushion.

He supported himself on his hands and leaned over to kiss her. She met his lips eagerly, opening her mouth and letting his tongue tangle with hers. His mouth moved to her throat, and she twined her fingers in his hair while he licked, kissed, and nibbled his way across her breasts.

She whimpered when his tongue made contact with one of her nipples, lapping at it, then licking with long hard strokes. The room grew warmer.

He made growling noises as he slid his lips further down her body. Mark inhaled as he looked up at her. "I can smell your desire, Cassandra. Tell me what you want."

"I don't know."

"Don't you?" He ran his tongue from her navel to the top of her curls.

"I want what I had last night. I want to explode."

Mark closed his eyes and drew in a few shallow breaths. His hands tightened against her waist. "You will, Cassandra. You will."

He lowered his head toward the juncture of her thighs. Was he really going to kiss her there? "Surely you're not, you can't—"

But then he did, and she could no longer speak. At first he used only the lightest touch with his tongue. The tiny flicks tickled her like the swipe of a feather. She tried to press his head against her, but he refused to give her the pressure she wanted.

"More, please."

He laughed, the sound muffled by the closeness of her flesh. He sucked her tight bud into his mouth, and her hips bucked sharply. She cried out, begging him to stop and not to stop, so dizzy she knew not what she said.

Mark couldn't get enough of her. Her honey was an aphrodisiac to him. The more he tasted, the more he wanted. Her fingers twisted painfully in his hair, and her hips pressed against his face. He sensed the tension building in her body. It would only take a little more to push her over the edge and give her the explosion she craved.

He thrust his fingers into her passage, groaning as her internal muscles squeezed him. Her whimpers grew louder as he nipped and tugged on her clit while he worked his fingers deep.

Her body convulsed. The contractions of her release milked his fingers. It was all he could do to hold his control as he imagined her squeezing his cock.

Once again she had pushed him to a point beyond his usual detached control. He had intended to stir her, to enflame her, to her make bold. Then he could let her explore his body, get to know him as he had her, but now he couldn't endure it. If he wasn't inside her within seconds, he would combust.

He fumbled with his pants, like a clumsy lad of fifteen about to couple with an overeager village lass.

Finally free of all clothing save his shirt, he pulled Cassandra to the floor and laid her out on the thick fur rug. Still caught in a web of sated passion, she smiled at him drunkenly.

"Look at me." He positioned himself above her.

"Mark, please, I need you!" she panted.

"I want to look in your eyes as I enter you."

She looked at him then. Her eyes had darkened from golden brown to rich chocolate. They shone like polished marble.

"Tell me again. Tell me you want me."

She lifted her hips to him, and the head of his cock slipped inside her. He saw the pleading in her eyes, but he wanted her confession. He wanted her to want him because her body cried out for it, not because it was a duty she had to perform.

He pulled back. "Tell me."

Cassandra opened her mouth to speak but her words were lost when one of the huge windows shattered.

Mark leapt up.

Cassandra screamed as a man leapt through the window with a pistol trained on them.

Mark lunged toward him and caught him in the chest, forcing him back against the wall. The pistol cracked, but the shot went wild.

Mark grabbed the man's wrist, slamming it against the wall. His weapon clattered to the ground.

The intruder pushed back, throwing Mark off balance. They both fell to the floor, rolling and grappling with one another.

Cassandra sat paralyzed, watching the struggle as if in a dream. Fleetingly she thought how beautiful Mark looked, how graceful his movements, how his near nakedness did not slow him down.

Then she spotted a large, ivory figurine on the mantle. Her mind cleared and she leapt into action.

The intruder momentarily gained the upper hand, rolling on top of Mark. She leapt forward and brought the figurine down on his head. He slumped against Mark, who stared at her with wide eyes.

She held up her makeshift weapon until Mark saw it. He smiled as he shoved the intruder off of him.

Mark pushed the man onto his back and removed his mask.

Cassandra gasped and took a few steps back.

"I assume you recognize him."

She nodded. "He's one of the groom's from Reddington Abbey. His name is Henry." Shock overwhelmed her. Henry had been the one to saddle her horse for the ride to Northamberly. Had he tried to kill her?

Mark cursed then looked up at her. "You're pale. Why don't you get dressed and have a seat?"

She looked down and blinked in amazement. She had completely forgotten her nakedness in her haste to protect Mark.

"Cassandra? Are you all right?"

"Yes, I'm fine, just shocked I think."

"I'll pour you a brandy as soon as I tie him up. I hope you don't mind donating your stockings to the cause."

"Stockings?" He held up the articles in question. "Oh, fine. Yes." Shaking all over, she walked to the settee and located her chemise and her dress.

By the time she was dressed, Mark had finished tying Henry's wrists and ankles. He poured two drinks, handed her a snifter, and slipped his pants and boots on before sitting down next to her. "As soon as he wakes, I'm going to question him. I need you to tell me everything about him and his connection to Reddington."

"Loring sent me a note this afternoon." She should have told him earlier. Now the information was vital.

"Loring?"

"Reddington's valet. He's been my greatest ally since my marriage. I think he only kept his position to protect me. He knows my true reason for being here."

Mark's eyes narrowed. "What did the note say?"

Cassandra swallowed and trying to still the shaking of her hands. "I was going to tell you at dinner, but then you behaved so insufferably I decided not to and then I—"

"What did he say, Cassandra?"

"Someone ransacked mine and Reddington's rooms at the Abbey. Loring couldn't tell if anything had been stolen. He and some of the footman went after the intruder, but the man escaped."

Mark's face turned a deep shade of red. "When did you receive this note?"

"It came this morning, but I didn't read it until mid-day."

"You could have told me any time since I returned from my ride."

Cassandra was saved from having to respond by a groan coming from Henry.

"He's waking. Tell me what you know about him. We will discuss your appalling judgment later."

"There is nothing more to discuss. You know everything I do now and—"

"Cassandra." Her name came out as a growl.

"Henry came to work at Reddington Abbey about a year ago. Reddington took him on in London and brought him to the country when we returned there after the Season. Henry has always seemed a trifle odd to me, but I have never seen him harm anyone "

"Odd how?"

"Unsure of himself. Too distracted to be good as this job, jumpy around me. I thought he was simply inexperienced and nervous."

Mark stood, but she grabbed his arm. "He knew I was riding out yesterday. He saddled my horse"

"And he could have followed you?"

"Yes."

She watched Mark shake the young groom, trying to wake him. It sickened her to think Henry could have shot her. She constantly wondered what the staff knew or didn't know about Reddington's nefarious dealings, but she'd never suspected any of them of being deeply involved.

Henry groaned again and opened his eyes. He immediately began to struggle. Mark put a booted foot on his abdomen, pressing down until he stilled.

"Who sent you here?"

The young man's eyes widened with fear, but he shook his head. "I ain't got to tell ya nothin'."

Cassandra gasped when Mark pulled a knife from his boot and pressed the point against Henry's throat.

"I would like very much to kill you. However, I might refrain if you cooperate."

"My boss'll kill me anyway when he learns what I've done."

"Who do you answer to?"

"I ain't telling ya."

A small trickle of blood ran down Henry's throat where Mark pressed the knife in harder. "I think you will."

Henry began to shake. Mark didn't move.

Finally, Henry spoke again. "Some Frenchie. I don't know his name. Claims he killed Lord Reddington, and he's come for his cargo. Said I best work with him if I knew what was good for me."

"What cargo?"

"I don't know."

More blood flowed from Henry's throat. "Something about girls. I'm guessing he meant some whores. Reddington runs some whorehouses up in London."

Mark turned to face Cassandra. She simply nodded in acknowledgement. She knew Reddington owned at least one brothel, but what would that have to do with transporting women to France?

"Why did you come here? Did you think I had this cargo?"

"No."

"Then why are you here?" Mark pressed harder with his boot. "Tell me!"

Henry remained silent. Mark dropped the knife and wrapped his hands around the man's throat, squeezing until Henry struggled for air.

Mark let go as Henry began to turn purple. The groom sucked in air and rubbed his throat.

"Ready to talk now?" Mark asked.

Henry's looked at Mark as if he were a monster. "He told me Lady Reddington knew too much." Henry paused to gasp for more air. "He told me to get rid of her and to search her room for information."

"Did you find anything?"

"No."

"Do you know anyone else who might know about this cargo?"

"No."

"Did you shoot Lady Reddington yesterday."

"No."

Mark's hands closed again.

"Yes, damn it. Yes."

Mark punched him then. Once. Twice. Three times. Henry fell unconscious.

Cassandra watched with a combination of awe and horror. Mark sank to his knees and took a long, deep breath.

"Is he dead?"

Mark reached out and touched the young man's throat. After a few seconds, he shook his head. "No, but I could arrange for him to be."

"Mark, we can't murder him."

"Why not? He wanted you dead."

When Mark turned to face her, the anger in his eyes frightened her even though it was not directed at her.

"What would you have me do with him?"

Panic rose. When her life should be improving, her whole world threatened to crash around her. "I don't know."

"He'll hang for attempting to murder a lady."

"But if we tell the authorities, we'll have to reveal Reddington's death."

"You would let him go free to preserve your precious secret?"

It sounded so wrong when Mark said it that way. Perhaps she was a fool, yet she knew she could not waver. She could not risk losing everything she had worked for. "Mark, please try to understand what my life has been like. With Reddington's money, I won't be at anyone's mercy."

"So you would rather die than remarry or go back to your family."

She paused to think. Would it be that bad? If she married another man like Reddington it would be, and her father had sold her away, she could never take his money again. "Yes, I would."

He looked at her with fire in his eyes. "Fine. We'll play this your way for now. Andrews will turn Henry over to the authorities, mentioning only the break in and assault—"

"But Henry may talk, he may tell people Reddington is dead."

"I'll have Andrews make sure he does not."

"Can he do that?"

"If you don't believe he can, you are welcome to kill Henry instead." Mark picked up his knife and held it out to her.

Was he serious? Would he sit by and watch her kill a man? She studied his face. Yes, he would.

She sat down again, shaken. Mark put the knife back in his boot. "You're going to have to trust me to handle this. But understand—whether you wish it or no, your life comes first. If I must reveal your secrets, then I will do so before I let you die."

She looked up at him. His shirt was only half buttoned, and his hair stood out wildly. He looked like a predator, ready and eager for the kill. She wanted to ask again why he cared, but this was not the time to push him any further.

He gathered her shoes and the petticoat she had omitted in her haste to dress and held them out to her. "Go on up to bed. I will join you as soon as I can."

She turned and fled.

•

Chapter Eight

Cassandra pulled her nightgown over her head and unbraided her hair with shaky hands. She stood near the fire, but even its blazing heat could not take away the chill Henry's appearance had given her.

Henry had worked at Reddington Abbey for over a year. How could she have misjudged him? What other servants were involved?

Henry's words took her right back to what had previously been the most terrifying night of her life. The night she learned her husband kidnapped young women and forced them to pleasure the male guests at his parties. She could still see the frightened faces of the girls she'd seen auctioned off to an odious elderly man.

It came as no surprise that Reddington sold women to his friends for their pleasure, but why would he be sending women to France? Whatever the reason, those responsible had to be stopped. She did not know whether Mark would agree to help her or not, but one way or another she was going to put an end to their operation.

The creak of the door connecting her apartment to Mark's made her jump.

"Cassandra! Where the hell are you? I thought I told you to—" He stopped speaking when he saw her. His hands clenched and a furious fire came into his eyes. Suddenly, she feared he intended to rip the gown from her as he had the last one.

She stepped back. "This is the only other gown I brought. I will not have you destroy it too. Surely you do not wish to take me to bed after what has happened."

"I have, against all I feel is right, let a murderer live. I did this because you wished to give your precious plan a chance to succeed. Now you act surprised that I intend to follow through with this plan?"

She took another step back. "It's only that…after what happened, I did not think you would be in the mood. You seemed rather angry and…"

"I assure you my anger in no way prevents me from wanting you. In fact, anger and passion are closely linked." He took a few more menacing steps toward her. "You have put me through hell today. Now I intend to take some pleasure in compensation."

He walked until he stood close enough to touch her. She forced herself to stand still, keeping her hands folded across her chest.

He smiled wickedly. "If you are serious about keeping your lovely garment intact, you'd better remove it immediately."

Cassandra was startled to the thrum of desire. The sight of Mark looking at her with such lust, moving toward her like he intended to devour her sent fire racing through her belly. She gathered the gown in her hands and, in one movement, pulled it over her head and dropped it to the floor. Mark smiled. She was utterly naked underneath.

"Are you still sore?" he asked, clasping her waist with his hands and pulling her to him. His hands were firm but gentle.

"No." Lying would have gotten him to leave or at least to take her gently, but no matter how the force of his desire unnerved her, she did not want that.

"Good, I can't hold back tonight."

His words made her shiver. Did he mean to imply he had held himself back the night before? If so, she wasn't sure she could handle the full force of his lust. She swallowed hard, trying to regain the ability to speak. Before she could, he took her hands and brought them to the lapels of his coat. "Undress me."

She slid her hands across the silky fabric of his shirt and pushed his coat from his shoulders. He hadn't bothered to put his waistcoat on, so she tackled the buttons of his shirt next, but they would not cooperate.

Mark grew impatient, pushed her hands away, and freed the buttons. The shirt joined his coat on the floor.

When he was naked to the waist, she ran her hands over his chest, reveling in the feel of hard muscle there. Breathing deeply of his musky scent, she leaned forward and let her tongue play over one of his flat nipples. It hardened as hers had, and she suckled it before licking the surrounding skin.

He groaned, and she smiled. The crisp golden hairs of his chest tickled her face, and the salty taste of his skin made her want to bathe his whole body with her tongue. She sucked and nibbled her way up to his throat.

"You were born to seduce a man, weren't you?" He pushed her hands down his abdomen to the laces of his breeches. "Tell me you are not a witch come to enslave me."

"I rather fear it is I who am enslaved." Later Cassandra would regret revealing her vulnerability, but at that moment, she floated in a dream world where nothing she said was real.

Her hands slipped lower and made contact with his hardness. "You speak and I obey though I have never taken orders easily. You make me feel as if I am starving for you, as if I can never have enough."

She ran her hands down the length of his shaft, and his eyes closed. He pressed himself into her hands. When she freed him from his breeches and touched the silky skin covering his shaft, he growled.

He grabbed her hands, gripping them so tight her fingers throbbed. "That's enough."

Startled by his harsh tone, she looked up. "Did I do something wrong?"

"No, my little witch. Feral desire shone in his eyes. "But I will spill my seed in your hands if you don't stop. Climb on the bed."

He followed her, grabbing two pillows and pulling them to the center of the bed. "Turn over." As she did so, he pulled her hips up and placed the pillows under her belly.

Then he leaned over her. His chest brushed against her buttocks as he nipped at the skin of her back. His bites created spirals of pleasure that ran down her body to coalesce with the fire at the juncture of her thighs.

He pulled her hair back and whispered against her neck. "Tell me if I hurt you, and I'll try to stop. Though God knows if I can."

Before she could ask him what he intended to do, he sat up and pulled her hips back to meet his. After testing her with a finger and finding her passage well lubricated, he pressed slowly into her.

Shock had her gasping for air when he began to move. She whimpered and pressed back further, gripping the bedclothes to keep herself from sliding forward with the force of his thrusting. Her surprise was quickly forgotten. The pleasure was too intense for anything else to matter.

This position allowed him deeper access than he'd had the night before. Never had she imagined feeling so filled, so stretched.

Her hips pressed against the pillows, and the silky fabric rubbed against the place where all her hungers commingled. She squeezed his shaft with her internal muscles, trying to draw him even further into her. At the moment when he reached the top of his thrust, his sac slapped against her, teasing her swollen lips.

Mark groaned, and his thrusting grew furious, making him pound against her.

She levered herself onto her hands and clutched at the thick bedspread. Her fingers ached from her effort to keep herself from falling, but she met every stroke with the push of her hips.

Their coupling was even more wild and primitive than the night before. Desire controlled her completely, leaving her unable to speak, unable to do anything but concentrate on finding her release.

Mark sensed how close she was. Her body clenched him fiercely, trying to hold him inside. She thrust against him so hard, he struggled to stay on his knees.

He reached around her, forcing his hand between the pillow and her belly to find her swollen clit. With only the smallest pressure from his hand, she exploded, shrieking and pressing wildly back in a staccato rhythm.

Mark nearly bit through his lip in an attempt to keep himself from finishing. Simply breathing made him nearly lose control. The air was filled with the scent of her lust. He forced himself to remain still until her body quieted, and she lay limp across the pillows.

Then he began to slide in and out at a painfully slow pace. "Remember when I touched you earlier, in my study? Remember how you begged for more?"

Her only answer was a moan.

"I intend to give you much more."

She moaned again.

"Feel it building again? You already need more of me, don't you?"

"Yes," she whispered, her face buried against the bedspread.

"Don't be embarrassed. Your need intoxicates me. It's beautiful."

He pulled out of her long enough to turn her over. He'd loved taking her from behind, but he wanted to watch her face the next time he made her shatter.

He sat back on his heels and pulled her to him until her hips were elevated on his lap. As he slid into her, he teased her clit with his thumb. He knew exactly how to torture her by using less pressure than she needed. She tossed her head back and forth, reaching for him with her arms, unable to get to him.

"Look at me."

She kept her eyes closed.

He moved in her, making the small stroke their position allowed him. "Look at me, and I'll give you what you want."

Her eyes opened. They sparkled, making him think of cinnamon sprinkled on warm chocolate. Her face was flushed and her teeth made indentions in her swollen lower lip. Damp curls lay against her forehead in tight spirals, and the tangled mass of her hair spread across the pillows.

He thrust slowly, and her eyes began to close. He froze. "You're not watching me."

She opened them again, and he began to stroke her as his thumb rubbed circles on her clit. She pressed against him, moving faster and faster. Her back arched as her body sought what it needed, but her gaze never left his.

He let himself drown in her gaze, never wanting to leave the warmth of her body. She was perfection. "That's it. Let go. Let go."

She thrust hard against his hand, and her body stiffened. She held herself still for the space of a breath. Then she fell back against the mattress with a sharp cry. Her body spasmed against his shaft.

Her cry of ferocious delight did him in. He pushed himself over her and began thrusting deeply. Once, twice, three times and he flew into oblivion. His seed poured into her, and he collapsed against her body.

Chapter Nine

Cassandra lay face down on the bed, her body heavy, loose, and thoroughly relaxed. She wasn't sure she could move, and she didn't want to. Not when she could enjoy a few moments of peace.

Heat crept across her cheeks when she thought of her display of animal passion, but far worse was her embarrassment at doing so little to stop Reddington. She realized she would have to explain everything to Mark but she feared what he might think of her. It would serve her right if he turned her out before she could finish her story.

She took a silent breath, deciding to spend a few more delicious minutes in his arms before she had to face her harsh reality.

Moments later as she was drifting back to sleep, Mark sat up and began running his fingers up and down her arm. "Cassandra, we need to talk."

"I know." She took a deep breath. With her hands, she massaged her temples, trying to stave off the headache she knew would come when she thought of her husband. "I think I could handle this better if we dressed and talked in your study. I know it sounds silly, but I don't want to talk about my husband while I'm in bed with you."

He reached out and ran his hand along her cheek. Then he stood and pulled on his pants and shirt. "I'll wait for you in my office. Come find me when you are ready."

"Thank you." Once again she was struck by how easily Mark moved between gentleness and ferocity.

After closing the door behind him, she leaned her head against it. Unbidden, an image of Reddington pawing at her as he tried to rouse himself filled her mind. She placed her hand over her mouth as if it could keep the bile down. Several moments passed before she was sure she could stand without vomiting.

As her strength returned, anger replaced the nausea. Why did Reddington still have power over her? As long as his memory made her sick, she would never have true freedom.

At least now, she knew she was capable of having relations with a man. Even though she would have to relive some of her worst memories, she reminded herself of what had just happened between her and Mark. It had been beautiful without any of the taint Reddington had placed on the act.

She pulled on her nightdress and dressing gown and brushed the tangles from her hair. She wanted to take more time to compose herself, but the longer she put off talking to Mark the harder it would be to confess what she knew about Reddington.

When she reached his study, Mark was seated in chair by the dying fire. A tea tray sat on the table behind the sofa, and he held a bite sized tart in his hand. "Would you like a cup of tea or perhaps a brandy to fortify yourself before we talk?"

She looked longingly at the teapot but her stomach churned. "I'm afraid I couldn't eat or drink anything right now. Maybe later."

Mark crossed the room to where she stood. He circled her waist with his arms and pulled her back against him. "Cassandra, I want you to know I hate the thought of what Reddington put you through. If someone had not beaten me to it, I would consider it an honor to call him out and avenge you."

The solidity of Mark's body anchored her to the present. And his gentle, touching words reminded her that if she found the man who wanted her dead, the horror of being Reddington's wife was over. Even if her scheme to become pregnant failed, and she did not gain financial freedom, she would no longer have to fear being hurt by her husband or his minions.

But in order to catch the man who wanted her dead, she had to tell Mark everything. She squeezed her eyes shut and let words tumble out. "During the first two years of our marriage, I knew little about what Reddington did in London. He only allowed me to accompany him to town at the height of the Season."

She looked down and realized her hands were shaking, resentment welled up inside her. Why couldn't she be stronger about this? She squeezed her hands into tight fists. "Damn him!"

Mark pulled her hand to his mouth and placed kisses across her knuckles then folded both her hands in his. "Cassandra, I'm going to make sure no one hurts you anymore."

She tried to make herself smile, but only managed the slightest curving of her lips. "Thank you. This is hard, but I'm going to get through it."

She closed her eyes and began telling Mark secrets she wished she could hide. "Reddington often held parties at a special house he rented solely for that purpose, parties I was not allowed to attend." She stopped and wiped away tears from the corners of her eyes. "I began to hear rumors. Sickening rumors. Finally, I disguised myself as a maid and snuck into one of his gatherings. I discovered that the rumors were true. He was auctioning off women to the highest bidder. The men who won them could force them to do anything."

She clenched her fists and dug her nails into her palms, trying hard not to cry. "Reddington and his friends drugged their victims so they would be unable to resist. Sometimes they were beaten. I wanted to believe the women came there freely, that they shared Reddington's twisted desires. But they didn't, at least not all of them."

More tears came, and she paused to swipe at her cheeks. "I wanted to stop them. I wasn't sure what to do, so I wrote a letter to my cousin Edward. As an MP, he has some measure of influence in London. I thought he might be able to put an end to Reddington's actions, but Reddington found the letter before I posted it."

She couldn't hold back the tears anymore. They coursed down her face faster and faster, until she was sobbing so hard she had to force her words past the lump in her throat.

"Reddington had never hit me before. I think I was too far beneath his notice for him to expend that much energy on me. But that night, he confronted me about the letter. Then he beat me." Mark's arms tightened around her. "I…I thought he would kill me."

Mark sat on the sofa and pulled her onto his lap, letting her sob against his chest.

"I should have tried again to stop him. I wanted to, but I knew if he caught me again, he *would* kill me."

Mark lifted her chin, forcing her to face him. "Cassandra, you did what you could. I'm sure he watched you closely after that. I don't doubt that he would have murdered you." He caressed her face. "Now I'm here and I'm going to help you. We're going to put a stop to this once and for all."

She couldn't look at Mark any longer, but neither could she pull away. Tucking her head against his chest, she clung to him. He held her while the rest of her tears poured out, stroking her back and placing feathery kisses against her temple. When her sobs subsided, she leaned back and looked down at his face.

"Feel better?"

She nodded.

"Whom would Reddington work with on a plot like this?"

"I suspect his closest friends, the Linton twins. They were supposed to go to France with him. Apparently they changed their minds at the last minute. Maybe they knew something had gone wrong."

"I've only met them once, but I found their company nauseating."

She hugged herself. "The way they stare at me gives me chills."

"I imagine you are not alone in that sentiment. Do you know of anyone else?"

"A few months before Reddington left for France, I overheard him conversing with Oscar Linton. They kept mentioning someone called The Cat. I didn't think much of it, plenty of their acquaintances used code names. However, I remember them saying The Cat always brought them the best women. It probably means nothing, but—"

"It's worth investigating. Anything else?"

She thought for a moment recalling the last conversations she'd heard before Reddington left. Finally, she shook her head. "No, that's all. But Mark?"

"Yes?" He brushed her hair back from her face.

"You do not have to help me. Our agreement doesn't extend to investigating Reddington's murder and I—"

He placed a finger against her lips. "I don't want to hear another word. I have freely offered my help. I will not be satisfied until everyone who wants to harm you is dead or imprisoned."

Once again Cassandra had to fight back tears. "Thank you."

Mark stood and tugged on her hands. "Let's go back upstairs."

When they reached her chamber, Mark followed her in and pulled her into his arms. His lips met hers, and his hands stroked her back. His touch sent warmth spiraling from her core out through her limbs. Even the tips of her fingers and toes melted. But the memories of Reddington were too fresh in her mind, she didn't want to lay with Mark when she was thinking of her husband.

She pulled back from the kiss. "I'm tired."

He sat on the bed and pulled her onto his lap. "We will have to work on your stamina. I intend to spend hours enjoying you each night."

"Mark, please." She tried to stand, but he held her firmly in place. His thick arousal pressed against her hip, and she had to work to keep her breath steady.

"What's wrong?"

"Nothing. I just need to get some sleep."

"Did I hurt you earlier?"

"No! Not at all." She smiled to reassure him, unable to bear the look of intense concern on his face. "It was very nice."

"Nice?" His brows lifted.

"More than nice, wonderful, superb. I've never felt anything like it. I never imagined such pleasure existed."

Neither did I. For a moment Mark was afraid he had said the words out loud. But when he looked down at her, he saw no reaction on her face. No other woman, not even Katryn had affected him in such a way. When he reached his peak, he poured all of himself, body and soul, into Cassandra.

The crazy thing was that it should have terrified him. He had come here to seclude himself, not to risk his heart again. But there was no turning back. He wanted nothing more than to be inside her again.

Propping himself on one arm, he lifted his other hand to touch her face. He brushed her hair back and let his fingers trail across her cheek. "If you are thinking of Reddington then I must stay and erase those memories."

She looked up and studied his face. "How did you know?"

"You look fearful. You have never been afraid of me before, not even when you should have been."

She smiled. "You don't scare me, even though I've been warned numerous times that you should. But I can't stop thinking about Reddington, about what he did to me and all those other women. I don't want that to taint anything we do."

"Give me a chance to help you forget."

His voice was hot in her ear, and she shivered. If anyone could end Reddington's power over her, it was Mark. But would she be giving up one man's power for another's? Of course any woman would rather be in Mark's thrall than in Reddington's, but Cassandra wanted independence. She feared the intense feelings Mark stirred in her. "Not now. I need to be alone."

"You need a man's warm hands to rub away the chill that bastard has left on you." As Mark spoke, his hands massaged her hips then slid up over her ribs to lightly brush across her breasts. After teasing her nipples to peaks, he pulled her toward him.

"You need to feel a man's hard body sliding all over yours to remind you how very alive you are, how no matter what else happens you have defeated Reddington by surviving." Mark pressed so close, Cassandra's breasts flattened against his chest as she fought to suck in air. "Let me prove how free you are. Let me make you fly."

She meant to say no, but all that came out was a sigh. Mark bent to run his tongue along the line of her throat. She didn't have the strength to fight. Her whole body needed Mark, from the top of her head down to her toes and every inch of hot, tingling skin in between.

"Lay down."

She obeyed Mark's command, settling herself on her back.

Mark knelt between her legs. He gave her teasing, tickling caresses on her belly. Then he slowly worked his way down her legs, avoiding the part of her that throbbed more insistently with every brush of his fingers.

His caresses were sweet torment. On another night, she might have forced herself to endure them, to let him show her everything he had in mind to enflame her. But she realized with a sudden certainly that the only way he could erase her fears of Reddington was to take her swiftly and relentlessly, to thrust so hard and so deep she thought of nothing else.

Her cheeks burned with embarrassment at her crude thoughts but she gathered the courage to tell him. "Mark?"

"Mmmm?" he murmured as he began to use his tongue instead of his fingers.

"I need you."

"I know."

"Right now. Inside me."

He looked up. His eyes had taken the predatory gleam he got when he was highly aroused. "Tell me more."

"I need it fast and hard to make me forget."

"God, Cassandra, you're killing me."

"I—"

"Hush. More talk and I won't last until I'm deep inside you."

Cassandra smiled. Baffled once again by the effect mere words had on him.

After testing her readiness, Mark covered her body and thrust to the hilt in one stroke. She gasped.

He gave her no time to recover before he pistoned her harder and harder with each stroke. As she had hoped, she forgot everything but the sensations building in her body. When they reached a fever pitch, she clung to Mark and let herself fall into total oblivion.

ରେ ରେ ରେ

Mark jumped down from Sentinel's back and reached the door of Reddington Abbey in a few long strides. He knocked insistently, despite the early hour. When a perfectly polished gray-haired man answered the door, Mark presented his card and explained that he had come to speak with Loring.

The man studied the card for a moment. "Good morning, Mr. Foxwood. I am Mr. Loring. I expect your visit has something to do with Lady Reddington."

"Yes, and also with one of your stable lads, Henry. You have no doubt noticed his absence."

"Yes, sir. Please come in. I believe it would be best if we spoke in the privacy of the library."

"Whatever you think best." Mark followed Loring through one of the doors leading away from the circular foyer.

Mark surveyed the floor-to-ceiling shelves filled with leather-bound volumes. He doubted Reddington had ever touched them, but he smiled when he thought of Cassandra curled by the fire with a book in her hand. Then he shook his head to clear it of the image. What was he doing having such domestic thoughts?

"Would you care for tea or other refreshment?"

"No," Mark took a seat in one of the cane-backed chairs flanking the small fire place. "I prefer to finish our conversation as quickly as possible."

"Certainly. What do you know about Henry?"

"He broke into Northamberly last night, intent upon murdering Cassandra." The color drained from Loring's face. "He confessed to having been the man who rummaged through her rooms. He's also the man who shot her."

"Shot her?"

"Don't tell me she neglected to inform you that someone shot her as she rode to Northamberly."

Loring exhaled in a rush. "Oh course she did not inform me. I would have come to see her if I'd known. Was she badly hurt?"

"A bullet grazed her temple, but she is quite recovered. I've tried to keep her indoors, but she does not listen to reason."

Loring still looked wan, but he smiled. "Lady Reddington is not an easy person to persuade."

"Difficult to persuade is kind in its mildness."

Loring's smile widened. "Did you learn anything else from Henry?"

Mark summarized what he knew and explained that he intended to go to London to investigate Reddington's brothel. "Cassandra may want to return home while I am gone. It is imperative that she remain inside and under guard at all times. I have my butler, Andrews, and two footmen watching her now. They will watch her every more if she prefers to stay at Northamberly."

Loring studied Mark intently. "I will do everything I can to protect her. For all her stubbornness, she is a very special woman. I have no intention of letting *anyone* hurt her."

Mark caught the meaning behind Loring's words, but he ignored the implication that he might harm Cassandra. She was far too practical to let her heart get involved in their liaison.

"I will send word of Cassandra's plans as soon as I have spoken with her. This card gives my London address. Contact me if you learn anything new."

"Of course, sir. I will have my eye on the other servants. If Henry was working for Lord Reddington, chances are good that there are others."

Mark thanked the man and left. As he galloped back toward home, he tried to decide how best to tell Cassandra that he was leaving for London.

ભ ભ ભ

Cassandra dressed for the day in a pale green dress with minimal decoration and a neckline that hid all her cleavage. She and Mark had to construct a plan for finding Reddington's killer and she needed to prevent distractions.

For further security, she added a fichu and pulled a dark blue shawl around her shoulders. Since she had arrived they had not spent more than a few minutes in each other's company before Mark's lips were on her and she lost the ability to think.

Despite her attempts at modesty, Mark's gaze raked her hungrily as soon as she entered the dining room. She shivered involuntarily when his eyes met hers, and he smiled a particularly feline smile. He looked as if he'd like to eat her for breakfast.

"Good morning, Cassandra." His seductive smile transformed into a smirk. "I took the liberty of preparing your plate when Mary informed me you were on your way down."

She looked at the large serving of eggs, meats, and fruit. Before she could protest that she would never eat that much, he spoke again, using his sexiest voice. "After last night, I thought you would need a large breakfast to restore your strength."

"You would." She gave him a sarcastic smile. But once she began to eat, she realized she was quite ravenous. "So what is our next step in tracking Reddington's killer?"

"There isn't much more to be done here. I'm going to London this afternoon."

"I shall I pack as soon as I finish eating."

"There's no need. You will be staying right here."

His pronouncement sent the tender feelings he'd stirred the night before fleeing before her anger. "If you think for one moment you are going to go to London while I sit quietly in your house and wait for your return, you are sadly mistaken."

"You are welcome to return to Reddington Abbey if you would prefer. I spoke to Loring this morning, and he assures me that he will see to your safety."

"You spoke to Loring? How dare you go behind my back and make arrangements for me?"

"Loring needed to be told about Henry. I did not think you would enjoy being woken before dawn, so I rode to Reddington Abbey myself."

"Don't pretend you didn't know I'd be angry."

"I did what needed to be done. Now, I am going to London, *alone*."

"No, you are not." She tucked her loose curls behind her ears. "We will discuss our travel plans later. First, I want to know what Loring said."

"I see no reason to divulge the contents of our conversation."

"If you won't tell me, I will go ask him myself." She stood from her seat, but Mark grabbed her arm, holding her still.

"Sit down. I will tell you what you need to know."

"What I *need* to know, not what I want to know?"

"Damn it, Cassandra. Sit down"

His commanding tone made her furious. If Mark and Loring had concocted some ridiculous plan Mark did not want her privy to, she had a better chance of making Loring tell her. She pulled free of Mark's grasp and headed for the door once again.

He caught her before she escaped, turning her to face him and pressing her against the wall by the door.

"I've had enough of your childish behavior. You will listen to what is best for you and do as I say."

"Perhaps if you did not treat me like a child, I would not react with such anger." She struggled to escape him. "Unhand me. I no longer wish to stay here. Nor do I wish to have your assistance."

He kissed her then. His lips crushing hers as he pinned her to the wall.

She wanted to fight him, but fire raged in her body. She couldn't prevent her impassioned response to his touch. Before her mind registered her body's actions, she'd unbuttoned his waistcoat and pulled his shirt free of his pants. She was desperate to feel his skin under her hands.

He gathered her skirts in his hands, pulling them up until he bared her thighs. She wrapped one of her legs around his waist and pressed against his hand as it slid between her legs. An electric jolt ran through her when he found her entrance.

He continued to kiss her ferociously as his fingers slid in and out in an ever-quickening rhythm. Pressure built between her legs. She spiraled upwards rapidly, but she wanted more. She needed to feel him inside her.

He sensed her urgency. His free hand slid to the back of her thigh and lifted her other leg. He pressed her into the wall, and she locked her ankles behind his back. Her fingers dug into his shoulders to keep herself steady while he worked the buttons of his pants.

The sound of a door opening down the hall brought Cassandra to her senses.

"Mark, the servants," was all she managed to say, but it was enough. He held her waist and pulled away from her, letting her legs and her skirts drop.

He raked a hand through his hair and took a few more steps back. "Go to my study. We will finish our conversation there."

Cassandra stood still, trying to catch her breath, rather enjoying how flustered Mark appeared.

He scowled at her. "Now."

She kissed him on the cheek as she swept by him. "It's nice to know I'm not the only one overwhelmed by desire."

Little minx, he thought as she left the room.

She was right though. His need for her hit him like an unexpected storm. One minute he had been angry enough to throttle her. Then suddenly he was kissing her, and he couldn't get enough. If she hadn't stopped him, he would have taken her right against the wall.

He didn't care what the servants thought. It wasn't their place to judge what he and Cassandra did. What did worry him was his loss of control. He'd had no intention of touching her at all.

If he was going to keep the upper hand in this relationship then he had to be in control of all his emotions, including the nearly painful lust that consumed him every moment he was around Cassandra. He could not let his emotions take over. He'd done that with Katryn, and it had sent him straight to hell.

He pulled the bell rope, summoning a servant and requesting tea and scones be brought to his study. Cassandra had not finished her breakfast and neither had he. They both needed more sustenance after their nocturnal exertions.

A picture of her as she lay basking in the afterglow of pleasure came unbidden to his mind. As soon as he returned from London, he intended to see how long they both could last. Maybe in the process he could quench his unrelenting hunger for her.

He arrived at the door of his study as a maid entered with a tray. Cassandra stood next to the window, staring across the lawn, her back rigid.

She turned to face him as he approached her. "I will not stay here while you go to London."

"I already told you I would be perfectly happy to escort you to Reddington Abbey."

"I intend to go with you."

"You will do no such thing."

"How are you going to stop me? Will you lock me in my room?"

"If I must."

"Then I will climb out of the window and follow you anyway."

"Are you always this difficult?"

"Of course. My father has three daughters. Why do you think he chose *me* to sell to Reddington?"

He heard the pain underneath her words, and it tore at his heart.

She looked out the window once again, but he grasped her shoulders and turned her to face him. "I know what it's like not to be wanted." His fingers trailed down her cheeks and traced the outline of her lips. "I want you to stay here because I care about your safety, not because I wish to abandon you."

She pushed his hands away. "I don't need a champion. I can solve my own problems. Your job is to—" She stopped speaking suddenly. Her cheeks grew red, and her eyes widened.

He didn't have to guess what she'd been going to say. "My job is to fuck you."

She sucked in her breath. "Mark!"

His words were cold. He almost regretted them, but she'd cut him. Once again, he was nothing but a plaything.

She leaned against the windowsill. Her shiver didn't escape his eye. "I'm sorry. I did not mean to be so insensitive."

Her words were so quiet he almost didn't hear them. Did she really think of him as only a body to use? He wished that was all he felt when they came together.

He took a deep breath. She didn't know women had been using him all his life or how much it hurt him to be seen as a toy. She probably thought his myriad of meaningless affairs were all he wanted from life. For many men, they would be more than enough.

Unfortunately, a man with a faulty bloodline, no title, and only a modest income was not marriage material. Katryn had made that abundantly clear. He supposed he should consider himself lucky he found lovers so easily. Before Katryn, he had longed to feel more from a woman. Now he wished he couldn't feel at all.

"Apology accepted. I'm tired of arguing with you. I should be on the road to London. Will you stay here, or do you require an escort to Reddington Abbey?"

She turned to face him. Anger in her eyes once again. "I'm coming with you. You have a contract to fulfill, and you cannot do so if we are separated."

"I will be back in a few days."

"I refuse to waste any of the precious time I have. I'm coming with you."

He studied her. Tight curls hung in disarray about her face. The rest of her hair spilled down her back, restrained only by a ribbon. Deep color infused her cheeks, and her eyes were wild and alive. She looked thoroughly unrestrained, and he didn't want to go an hour, much less several days, without touching her. Perhaps she would be safer where he could keep an eye on her. Neither Andrews nor Loring stood a chance at restraining her.

"You have one hour to prepare yourself for the journey. While we are in London you will obey my every command, and you will remain in my house where I can fulfill my part of the contract. Otherwise, I will be working alone. Is that understood?"

She looked at him quizzically as if she could not believe he had agreed. Then she rushed for the door saying, "Half an hour is all I need."

He noted that she never agreed to his stipulations.

Chapter Ten

By the time their carriage rolled to a halt at Mark's London residence, Cassandra's legs were so stiff she feared they would fold under her when she attempted to stand. But even if she had to crawl, she would get into the house and see that a bath was drawn immediately. Then, she would let Mark know exactly what she thought of his ridiculous plan to make her stay trapped inside while he unraveled the mystery of Reddington's death.

She had intended to use the journey to convince Mark that she would be assisting with the investigation, but Mark spent most of his time riding his stallion alongside the carriage or feigning sleep in the seat across from her. The one time they had stopped for more than the minimum time required to consume a meal, he had taken her into a room and rendered her incapable of thought much less speech.

Her hot bath was like a slice of heaven, but by the time she emerged from it and dressed for dinner, Mark had escaped. Andrews had come up to London with them, and he informed Cassandra that Mark had gone out for the evening. Andrews cautioned that she would not want to wait up for Mark.

She wasn't going to let Mark get away that easily. After she finished her evening meal, Cassandra selected a book from the library and curled up in a chair in Mark's personal sitting room. Each time the clock in the hall chimed, her anger grew.

Suddenly, a hand was shaking her awake. "Why aren't you in bed?"

As the cobwebs in Cassandra's head cleared, she realized the speaker was Mark. She rubbed her eyes and looked around the room. She remembered hearing the clock strike two only moments before, why was the sun streaming in the windows? And why *wasn't* she in bed? Oh yes. She was waiting for Mark to come home. Except apparently he'd been out all night.

"Why aren't *you* in bed? What have you been doing all night?"

"I asked Andrews to inform you that I would be late."

"This isn't late. This is morning."

"We are in London, now. This is the time most fashionable rakes return home."

"Were you investigating my husband's activities or were you engaging in the expected behaviors of a fashionable rake?"

Mark massaged his temples as he sat on the edge of a chair. "I would rather discuss my evening after I've had some sleep."

"I waited all night to talk to you. I am sure you can spare a few moments now."

"Fine."

Cassandra smoothed the wrinkles from her dress and sat up straighter. "Where have you been?"

"The location would mean nothing to you. I needed to find out who among my acquaintances were in town."

"Were your mistresses in residence?"

"Why should it bother you if they were as long as I continue fulfilling the terms of our arrangement?"

Cassandra wondered the same thing but refused to consider the possible answers. "I do not need you getting distracted from your duties to me."

Mark raked his hands through his hair, heightening his disreputable appearance. "Damn it, Cassandra. I have not been wasting my time visiting women I would be perfectly happy never to see again. I left London for a reason. I was sick of my life here, and I have no desire to return to it."

"Then go back to Devon."

"I am not going to leave you here to die."

"I can take care of myself."

Dark anger flashed across Mark's face. "I may not be a gentleman, but I can be counted on to protect you, even from yourself."

Cassandra forced herself to ignore the pain coming through in his voice. "Fine, but I will not be confined to this house. As soon as I can dress and pack, Mary and I are taking up residence at Reddington House. I refuse to hide my presence in town."

Mark shook his head. "Cassandra, if we are seen together, everyone will assume we are lovers."

"Society can assume whatever it wishes. I am not sitting at home while you solve my problems for me. If I were going to do that, I could have stayed at Northamberly."

"I allowed you to come to London, so I could fulfill our bargain. I will not expose you to greater danger."

"I came to London to investigate my husband's death and the threat against my life. I will do that with or without your help."

"Cassandra."

The warning growl in his voice was clear. She fought to keep her words civil. "I understand your concern for my wellbeing. Like it or not, I'm not as physically strong as you. Therefore I am not as well prepared to defend myself from attack. However, I know more about Reddington's acquaintances than you do. I may recognize someone whom you would never think to suspect."

"Cassandra, you were the one who insisted on discretion when you made your proposal."

"That hardly seems important now. Other women of the *ton* take lovers, why shouldn't I?"

"If we are seen together, and you start increasing, it will be assumed the child is mine. Others must know Reddington has been in France."

Mark was right, but she couldn't let him sway her. She wasn't some delicate flower who sat at home while others risked their lives. "The will only said I needed to have a child. It did not specify that Reddington had to be the father."

"That's a hell of a risk to take."

"I will visit my solicitor later today and inquire."

"Do not bother. No matter what he says, I will not risk your reputation."

Cassandra took a long slow breath. Fighting to stay calm. "Then I will have to find the killer on my own."

"I cannot allow a lady to go to the places I will need to go."

"I can handle myself."

"No, you cannot."

"I *will* visit Mr. Jenkins, and we will continue this discussion this afternoon. I expect to see you at Reddington House by teatime."

Mark grabbed her upper arms and jerked her against him. "You will not leave this house without guards to protect you. Andrews will introduce you to the men I have hired. After I have gotten some sleep, we will discuss your role in this investigation, but you are not to go anywhere alone. Is that clear?"

"Perfectly, now let me go."

"Not until you promise to do as I say."

Cassandra wanted to refuse him, to tell him she would be safe in the crowded, day lit streets of London, but something in his eyes stopped her. Along with the anger, she saw fear. "I promise."

"Thank you." He released her arms. "I have a meeting midday with a friend who may be able to help us. I will call at Reddington House when I return."

CR CR CR

Cassandra left Mr. Jenkins's office, satisfied she'd been correct about the wording of the will. Afterwards, she went straight to her aunt's townhouse, followed closely by her guards. When her aunt's butler, Sanders, opened the door, she saw her sister making her way down the stairs.

Amanda gasped. "Cassandra, is that truly you?"

"It is I. I'm sorry I could not warn you of my arrival in advance."

Amanda rushed to the door and flung her arms around her older sister, forgetting all sense of decorum. "That hardly matters. I'm thrilled to see you." Amanda leaned in close to Cassandra's ear. "Are your plans moving along nicely?"

"I've been in such a whirlwind, I hardly know," Cassandra said.

Amanda's smiled and her eyes sparkled as she took her sister's arm. "Let's find a private seat, and you can tell me all about it."

Cassandra nodded her acceptance though she dreaded the conversation. When her sister said she wanted to hear all, Cassandra knew she truly meant it. Her cheeks heated at the thought.

Amanda turned to her aunt's butler. "Sanders, please see that tea is sent to the conservatory."

"Certainly, Miss Amanda. Should you care for any other refreshment?"

"I had a tray in my room, but Lady Reddington may."

"No, thank you, Sanders. I breakfasted before I left home."

Cassandra followed her sister to the conservatory. The room was an excellent choice. If anyone else was about, they would not want to sit there since the tall windows let in cold air. When they were seated together, close to the fire, Amanda implored Cassandra to tell her more about Mark.

Cassandra struggled against her desire to censor her story for her sister. Amanda was no longer a little girl. In fact, she'd never behaved like one. She was the most serious young woman Cassandra knew, yet she managed not to be dull. Her curiosity made her want to learn about everything the world had to offer. Relations between men and women were no exception. In fact, Amanda was quite eager to learn as much about men as she could, though more as a defense against them than because she longed to be involved with one.

Still, sometimes her practical sister could be quite romantic. There was an underlying passion in Amanda that Cassandra hoped would someday be brought to the surface. Thus far, it was only evident in the expressiveness of her exotic eyes that contrasted so completely with the conservative clothes she chose. All three girls in their family looked quite similar, but each also had one distinctive feature. Cassandra had gotten an excess of curls, while Amanda had eyes a deep shade of gray which appeared lavender in soft light.

"I did not shock you with my letter?" Cassandra asked, pausing to study Amanda's reaction. Her sister smiled. "No, it rather looks like I've delighted you."

"I *was* delighted to hear that you were rid of Reddington. Now, I no longer have to fear for your safety."

Cassandra fought to keep her face blank. She would eventually tell Amanda why she had come to London, but first she wanted her sister to enjoy a few girlish moments of curiosity. "I can take care of myself, Amanda. You don't need to worry about me."

"You have never fooled me with the brave front you affect. I know how difficult this marriage has been." Amanda reached up to push an errant curl off her sister's face. "I know what you sacrificed for all of us."

Cassandra sighed. She had tried to shelter her sisters from the worst of what she'd experienced, but Amanda was particularly intuitive.

Amanda placed a hand on her sister's arm. "Please tell me about Mr. Foxwood. I've seen him at a few parties, but I've never been introduced to him."

"I should think not. He's hardly an appropriate acquaintance for an innocent."

Amanda laughed. "All the more reason I need you to tell me about him. So what is it like to…I mean how is he…oh, tell me everything."

"He's overbearing, controlling, infuriating, and even more stunning without his clothes than he is in them."

At this, Amanda burst into giggles. "So it is enjoyable, not just painful?"

When Amanda had inquired about how she had fared in the marriage bed, Cassandra had been forced to tell an abbreviated version of Reddington's problem, so her sister knew she had never experienced relations with a man. "It hurt a bit the first time, but yes, I can emphatically say it is enjoyable. I don't think it would be with every man though. I am guessing that Mark is quite skilled."

A deep shade of red crept into Amanda's cheeks. "I am glad you no longer have to suffer. Do you still believe you are doing the right thing?"

"The only thing I have doubted is my choice of Mark as my co-conspirator. He is he's too powerful, too overwhelming."

Amanda's mouth hung open. "Oh, my God. You're in love with him."

"No!"

The vehemence of Cassandra's answer made her sister jump.

Cassandra placed a hand on Amanda's arm. "I did not mean to frighten you, but I can not possibly fall in love now, not when I finally have the chance to be free." This was the thing she'd feared most. The name she had refused to give the flip-flops her heart made every time she was near Mark.

"In that case, forget I said anything." Amanda lips curved upward a bit.

Cassandra had the horrible feeling her sister was laughing at her.

"Tell me why you've come to London."

Cassandra wished she didn't have to tell her sister about the danger she was in, but she forced herself to be honest. "The people who killed Reddington wish to eliminate me as well."

"What?" The color receded from Amanda's cheeks.

"Someone—a groom from Reddington Abbey—shot at me. Fortunately, the bullet only grazed my temple."

Amanda reached out and lifted her sister's curls to reveal the thin scar. "You should not be out alone when you are in such danger. Where is Mr. Foxwood? Why isn't he protecting you?"

Cassandra gave an exasperated sigh. "He has been doing nothing but protecting me since this happened. He tried to make me stay in Devon while he came to London, but I refused. He's hired two men to follow me at all times. I'm sure if we look out front we will see them in the street."

"Why would Reddington's enemies be after you? What do they want?"

The last thing she wanted to do was tell her sister the ugly truth, but keeping Amanda in the dark would be unfair. That was exactly what Mark wanted to do to her. She gave Amanda a summary of Henry's break in, the things he had revealed, and the conclusions she and Mark had made.

"So Mark is trying to find out about Reddington's business interests?" Amanda asked.

"Yes, he and I are working to track down the killer."

"It's like one of the books you read. Mark is the hero whom the heroine would marry in the end."

Cassandra groaned as she registered Amanda's smug smile. She should never have let her sister borrow her Gothic novels. "I will pretend you never said that. And I would charge you to remember that while it may be an adventure, I would never have chosen it. For all that it may seem romantic, the people we must confront are as depraved as my husband was. I do not relish the thought of spending even a few moments in their company."

Amanda frowned. "I'm sorry, Cassandra. It's just that I so dislike London. I'm tired of dinners and balls and card-playing evenings. Any adventure, even one so dangerous as this, sounds exciting to me."

Cassandra smiled. Her sister had made little attempt to befriend other debutantes during the Season, and Cassandra imagined she was both bored and lonely. If only Cassandra could thwart Reddington and receive her inheritance, then she would be able to invite Amanda to stay with her in the country where her sister would be happier.

"I understand, dear. I didn't take offense."

Amanda gave her a tight hug. "Please be careful. I know how stubborn you can be, but Mark's right, you should not go out without someone to protect you."

"I won't. I promise." Cassandra stood, taking Amanda's hands and pulling her up as well. "I should be going."

"What about Aunt Claire? What do I tell her when she asks about your visit?"

"Tell her the truth, but as little of it as you have to."

"I am sure she will wish to hear everything, but she is good at keeping secrets."

"Can you make her understand that I cannot call on her frequently and that she should not call on me?"

"Yes, I've learned over the last year that she can be very understanding and indulgent. I hope you will have more time to spend with her once you are safe."

"I hope so too."

They walked to the foyer and Sanders brought Cassandra her cloak. As she pulled it around herself, Amanda asked if she would be allowed to call on her sister.

"As much as I long to see you, I do not think it would be wise."

"Perhaps not, but I am ever so eager to meet Mr. Foxwood. I need an opportunity to size up the man my sister has chosen as her companion."

"In three months, we will cease to associate with each other. It is hardly worth your time to begin an acquaintance."

Amanda raised her brow and smirked. "As you say. Still, I would like it very much."

Cassandra shook her head. "I will see what I can do."

෧ ෧ ෧

Mark's head still throbbed when he woke in the early afternoon. He'd downed quite a lot of whiskey the night before, but the splitting headache was more likely induced by Cassandra than his overindulgence.

Thank God his servants were trustworthy and stayed far from his rooms at night, or she would have embarrassed and exposed them both. When she was angry, she gave no thought to propriety. In fact, she behaved much as she did in the throes of passion.

She was open, honest, and thoroughly unconcerned with letting her raw emotions show. When they fought, he found it infuriating. But when she was laid out under him in all her naked glory, it sent sparks of lust exploding through his body. It also scared him half to death.

He'd never been with a woman who was so authentic. Until he met her, he'd been unaware that his other bed partners had been holding something back. Now he knew the truth, and he almost wished he didn't.

A knock on his door interrupted his thoughts.

"Yes?"

A footman stepped into his room. "Your bath is ready, sir."

"Thank you." His room was still ice cold. If he hadn't been desperate for a bath, he would have hidden in the warm covers for a few more hours.

When he entered his dressing room, he smiled at the sight of the steaming water. The heat would improve his headache, and it would feel delightful to be clean again. In his haste to re-immerse himself in town life, he hadn't gotten the chance to properly wash away the grime left by two days of travel.

When he and Cassandra arrived in London late the day before, his first priority had been to see Cassandra settled and give strict instructions to the men he had chosen to guard her, men sent to him by his solicitor whom he trusted implicitly. He'd have to remember to thank the man for performing yet another minor miracle. Once he knew Cassandra was well guarded, he set out to discover who among his acquaintances were in town.

Though he had been out of the city for a short time, he was out of contact with society. During his last months in town, he'd shunned all *ton* gatherings and immersed himself in a lifestyle that hardly fit his station. Of course it was in such places that rumors of Reddington's most depraved activities had filtered down to him. He should be grateful for what knowledge he did possess.

He'd known he wouldn't be able to move quickly. He could not afford to arouse suspicion with too many questions. He'd learned nothing definite, but he did have a few good leads. Most importantly, he'd run across Rhys Stanton, one of the few friends he had not dropped while attempting to rid himself of Katryn's taint.

Of all his acquaintances, Stanton was situated to know the most about Reddington. He was also one of the handful of people Mark trusted. Stanton had always moved in faster circles than he. While Mark enjoyed spending an entertaining evening with a woman, particularly one who was quite skilled at giving pleasure, he had never gone in for the more exotic delights available to those who knew where to search.

Only with Katryn had he explored that world. She had taken him to a few country house parties more properly described as orgies. She'd insisted that one of her friends, a young widow who was notorious for spreading her favors far and wide, had begged her to come. She'd giggled girlishly and acted as though she found it deliciously wicked.

Against his better judgment, he'd decided to indulge her. He was certain now that he wasn't the first man Katryn had accompanied to such a party. She'd been perfectly willing to couple with other men while they were there. He'd struggled to convince her that sharing her did not appeal to him.

He shuddered at the memory and realized his bath was growing cold. After pulling himself from the water, he began to dress quickly, not wanting to be late for his appointment with Stanton. They'd spent hours drinking together the night before, but Mark had not wanted to ask too much where others could listen. He also wanted to be sober when he questioned Stanton, lest he inadvertently reveal more than his friend needed to know.

When Mark entered his favorite club, Stanton was there leaving his coat and hat with the doorman. His skin had the sickly pallor of one severely hungover. His paleness was amplified by its contrast to his thick, black hair and his ludicrously bright yellow waistcoat. Stanton insisted on dressing like a consummate dandy despite the fact Mark knew he was nothing of the kind.

Despite his haggard appearance, Stanton's eyes were bright and sparkling like the sapphires women so often compared them to. And he was walking straight, not a mean feat for a man who six hours before had been completely unconscious.

He clapped his friend on the shoulder and said, "You're looking better than I expected. I wasn't at all sure you'd make it out of bed in time for our engagement."

Stanton scowled. "That was dastardly of you to keep ordering drinks. You knew I'd feel obliged to keep up with you. I should have learned my lesson years ago. Why can't I accept that you drink me under the table every time?"

Mark laughed. "For your own sake, you shouldn't try to compete, but I would miss the entertainment."

Stanton shook his head. "I'm sure you would. Now what was it you wanted to talk to me about, and why wouldn't you explain it last night?" He frowned. "You didn't tell me, did you? I remember things up until dawn, but everything after that is a blur."

"As well it should be. You insisted we walk outside to see if the sun felt as warm as it looked. Then you passed out on the sidewalk. I practically carried you to a hack and had to tip the driver an enormous sum to ensure he'd take you all the way to your door."

"I didn't make it much farther. I woke up on the floor in the foyer." They laughed so hard Stanton had to hold his head and lean against the wall for support.

"Come. Let's find a private spot." Mark gestured toward the tables at the back of the dining room.

"I thought you meant to stay in the country at least until the Season began."

"Too boring. I need more excitement. I'm hoping you will bring me along to some of the more exotic events you like to attend."

Stanton stared at him with disbelief. "If I do, you'll run into Katryn."

Mark hated lying, but he thought of Cassandra and did what he had to do. "I'm tired of running. It hasn't worked. Maybe confrontation is exactly what I need."

Stanton sunk his teeth into his lower lip and stared at Mark for several long seconds. "You're certain?"

"Absolutely."

"If you insist. Maybe you do need something more adventurous. After a while, a man gets bored with the usual arrangements, grasping young widows, light skirts who never deliver as well as they promise."

Mark laughed. "If even half the tales of your exploits are true, I'm sure you've had your share of run-ins with every type of woman in existence."

Stanton smiled. "*All* my tales are true. How could you doubt it?"

How could he indeed? Mark had never lacked for female companionship, but he worked for it, flirting, playing the game, stalking until his prey gave in. Stanton, on the other hand, had only to enter a room and women flocked to him. Mark often feared he'd have to beat the women off his friend in order to safely extract him from a party.

Stanton slapped his hand down on the table then winced at the effect of the loud noise. "I've got just the thing for you. Langley is hosting an entertainment tonight. I'll see that an invitation is sent to you straight away. You're welcome to bring a woman with you, of course, if you've got one who would be so inclined. If not, I'm sure Langley will have provided some fine specimens for the gentlemen who are in need."

"Perfect. Langley's parties are legendary. I can't believe I've waited this long to attend one." Thankfully, while he would be able to meet men who would have associated with Reddington, everything he'd heard indicated that Langley was an honorable man.

"Neither can I. I'm positive you'll find it keenly arousing."

Mark nodded. "I also wondered if you could recommend an establishment where one might contract a girl for something very special. Wasn't Reddington connected to such a place?"

Mark waited for suspicion to cross his friend's face, but all he saw was a devilish grin. "I'm not sure if Reddington has an interest in it or not, but the place you want is Miss Caroline's. Ask for Simone and tell her I sent you. She'll provide *any* service you require." He winked at Mark then checked his pocket watch. "I'm afraid I have to shove off. I've been summoned to my aunt's house."

"Best of luck. She isn't trying to marry you off again, is she?"

"I fear so, but I shall hold firm." Stanton drew himself up and gave a stern look.

Mark laughed. "It's good to see you again. I'll be looking for the invitation to Langley's affair."

"I'll be sure you have it," Stanton said as he turned toward the door.

Chapter Eleven

Mark approached Cassandra's house braced for another fight. His stomach churned at the thought of going to Langley's party and the memories it would dredge up. The last thing he wanted to do was argue with Cassandra. But a fight was inevitable as soon as he informed her that he was going to Langley's tonight, alone.

He wanted to forget about Reddington and his depraved business arrangements, sweep Cassandra off her feet, and carry her upstairs to bed. He would not stop fucking her until he was too exhausted to move. Then they could order a hearty dinner tray, revive themselves, and start the process all over again.

As soon as Reddington's killer was found, that was exactly what he intended to do. He thought they could keep up such a schedule for at least a week.

He let the knocker fall. A maid answered the door almost immediately.

"Your card, sir?"

"Lady Reddington is expecting me." He pushed past her, calling for Cassandra.

"Sir! Sir!" the maid called, but she made no serious attempt to stop him.

Cassandra emerged from the drawing room, no doubt having heard the commotion. "Don't worry, Rebecca. Mr. Foxwood is permitted entrance at any time."

"Beggin' your pardon, ma'am." The young woman curtsied. "I didn't realize—"

"It is of no consequence. You can hardly be blamed for his abominable rudeness." She frowned at Mark.

"I see you are in your usual spirits."

Indecision showed on her face. Mark could imagine her thoughts. Did she answer him with a feisty retort, or would she try to be civil a little longer? She chose a middle path. "Whatever made you come barging in here like that?"

"I see no reason to exercise formalities when I come to see you."

"Why are you in such a foul temper?"

"There is nothing wrong with my temper. I simply see no reason to present a card at your address."

"Do refrain from frightening my staff in future."

"I will do my best."

She pursed her lips. "See that you do."

She indicated that he should take a seat in the small drawing room. "I saw Mr. Jenkins, my solicitor. I had indeed remembered correctly. No matter what rumors circulate about us, I will still receive my inheritance if I am with child at the time Reddington's death is announced."

He took a deep breath. "Your news changes nothing. You will be stay here tonight and every night we remain in London."

"I do not like flaunting our association any more than you do, but I will not be left behind. This is my problem, not yours. I cannot allow you to do all the work for me."

"Once Reddington's death is known you will need to think about your reputation for the sake of your child or need to find a respectable position to support yourself. Either way, you cannot afford to earn the scorn of respectable society."

"We have discussed this already. I'm only asking to follow along as your escort, not to couple with you in the middle of the Season's first ball. If taking a lover brought such scorn on a married woman, there would be few women left in *ton* circles. One is far more likely to see men out with their mistresses and wives with their lovers than anyone accompanying his or her own spouse."

Ignoring her words completely, he said, "I refuse to be responsible for ruining your reputation."

"I would hardly think it's intact now. Going about town with her lover is nothing less than people would expect from the woman who married Reddington. Besides, if we go to respectable parties, we will be discreet. I only—"

Mark interrupted her. "Hold it right there. What do you mean *if* we go to respectable parties? Please don't tell me you've gotten it in your head that I am going to take you to the entertainments Reddington frequented."

"That is precisely what I expect. How else am I going to help with the investigation? If the party is like those given by Reddington, the guests will be masked so my reputation is hardly in danger.

Langley's invitation had indeed specified that he and his escort wear half masks and use pseudonyms. Still, taking Cassandra there was not an option. "Such entertainments are not suitable for a lady to witness."

"You didn't mind taking Katryn."

Shock had Mark reeling. "What?"

"I saw you when I spied on Reddington. You were there with Katryn. If you escorted her then you can damn well escort me."

Mark stepped back as if he'd been slapped.

Cassandra's eyes widened and her hand came to her mouth. "I...I am sorry. I should never have mentioned her."

The thought of Cassandra seeing him at such a place, behaving as he had with Katryn made him feel sick. The knot in his stomach tightened and his head throbbed.

For a few seconds, he stood frozen, unable to speak. Then suddenly the anger and horror burst inside him. He grabbed her shoulders and shook her. "What the hell were you doing risking yourself like that?"

"I followed him to London. I had to know if I truly had married a monster."

He stared into her eyes, knowing she told the truth but unable to let go of his fear and anger.

She struggled to free herself of his hands. "Please, you're hurting me."

He looked down and saw rather than felt his fingers digging into her shoulders hard enough to bruise. Stunned, he released her and walked to the far side of the room. "Forgive me. I do not like to think of the time I spent with Katryn." He ran his hand through his hair, tugging on it and making the ends stand up. "Why did you come to me for help after seeing me in such a place?"

"You weren't participating in any of the particularly lurid or violent activities. Then I saw you again at Katryn's engagement ball, and I understood. I'm sorry she hurt you."

This is not happening. But the sick feeling in his stomach assured him he was. "I am sorry you had to witness such a…low point in my life."

"If you ever want to talk to me about it, I would be glad to listen. I know what it's like to be hurt."

He studied her intently. A few moments ago, she had been spitting fire at him. Now concern was clear on her face.

When she smiled, the knot inside him loosened a bit. "You are a most perplexing woman."

"My sister, Amanda, says I'm an acquired taste. I'm sure you will get used to me in time."

He crossed the room to stand in front of her and traced the line of her jaw, lifting her chin to look in her eyes. "Any man who does is a fool."

Her eyes narrowed. "If you don't wish to take me for granted, then stop holding me back. Let me help you."

"Do you truly understand what will happen if you appear in public as my lover? Masks are no guarantee of anonymity. Someone is bound to recognize you. Then the ugly rumors will begin."

"I know, but it's not as if I am worried about losing friends. I've never received invitations to respectable parties or vouchers for Almack's. I would be a fool to even make an inquiry. Marrying Reddington ruined my chances for social success."

Her words reached into Mark's chest and squeezed his heart. He longed to erase her pain. How could her father have given her to Reddington? How could any man do that to his daughter?

He knew he was going to give in. She was right. As Reddington's wife she was already ruined in the eyes of society, simply by association. She was willing to risk herself, and he would not let her out of his sight.

He reached out and caressed her cheek. "I will be back in a few hours. We will dine together. Then we will go to a party hosted by Viscount Langley. Did you pack the dress you wore the first night you stayed with me, the lavender silk?"

"Yes." Triumph lit her face. "I remembered how much you liked it."

He would give her the option of coming with him, but if she were to be convincing, she would have to dress like the other women. "Wear it tonight with nothing but your thinnest chemise."

"No stays?"

"Nothing. The chemise is merely a concession."

"But the dress is too thin. Everyone will be able to see—"

He smiled. "Yes, they will. If you would rather stay at home…"

"I will be ready when you return." With that, she turned and left the room.

Mark stood frozen in place, mesmerized by the sway of her hips. Thinking of her in that beguiling dress with nothing underneath made his cock harden painfully. He doubted she would couple with him at the party with other guests in earshot, but he wasn't sure he could wait until they returned home.

ख ख ख

Cassandra was sitting at her vanity when a rap at the front door drew her attention. She assumed it was Mark and decided he could wait while she gathered her wits.

She looked at her reflection again. *You can do this.* She had gone to such a party before when curiosity and anger had gotten the better of her, but now the stakes were higher. *Mark will be with you.* For all that he drove her crazy and tested her very sanity, he made her feel safe.

Studying herself in the mirror, she frowned at the ensemble Mark had instructed her to wear. Thankfully, it was cold, and she could wear a thick cloak going to and from the carriage. But once she was in Lord Langley's house, all the guests would see her as she was now. Her gauzy silk chemise hid nothing. Embarrassment made her cheeks heat, but she knew Mark would refuse to take her with him if she was not dressed as he'd ordered.

She suspected the outfit had been a gamble. He'd hoped she would refuse to wear it, and she had no intention of letting him win. Still, her appearance was beyond a scandal. If she stared at her reflection long enough, she could make out the pink tips of her nipples through the two layers of fabric. And with the light behind her, the lines of her legs showed plainly.

She looked like a courtesan, and while a part of her thrilled at the idea of Mark seeing her like this, she did not want her husband's friends evaluating her like one of their playthings. Despite her protests to the contrary, she was afraid of being unable to confront the world her husband had moved in. What if one of her husband's friends thought he had the right to touch her? Mark would kill him. She did not doubt it. But where would they be then?

"I hope you plan to wear a pelisse to dinner. If not, we will never make it to the party."

She looked up and saw Mark reflected in the glass. "What the hell are you doing in here?"

"Your maid took you quite seriously when you told her I was to be admitted at any time. She made no protest to my coming to retrieve you."

He opened the door of Cassandra's wardrobe and removed a thick pelisse. "This will do," he murmured more to himself than to her. Then he walked toward her and held it out.

She refused to take it. "You are the one who requested this outfit. I have no intention of further altering my appearance to please you."

"Fine. Don't say I didn't warn you." He moved to stand behind her and leaned down. His warm breath caressed the back of her neck. "Look at us," he said, his voice low.

She could not refuse him. Glancing up, she saw herself in the mirror. Her wild eyes and flushed cheeks betrayed her high arousal, and Mark looked ready to give her what she needed. The golden highlights in his hair flashed in the candlelight, and his green eyes glowed. He was a lion, and she his prey.

Her body tingled with the now familiar gathering of warmth that always preceded the wild desire he could stir in her any time, any place, no matter how annoyed she was. Her gaze met his in the mirror, and the power reflected there made her shiver. He pulled her to her feet and kicked her stool out of the way. When he drew her against him, his shaft felt like an iron bar at her back. Her gaze fell to his hands as they slid up her body, over her ribs, to her breasts.

When his thumbs brushed her nipples, they hardened. The peaks stabbed against the fabric, and Mark rolled them between his fingers. The feel of the silk sliding against them made her shudder. She tried to break free of his hold, but he would not let her.

"Watch." His words were more of a caress than speech.

One hand released her breast and began to gather her dress and chemise until he had access to the bare skin above her stockings. His fingers stroked her inner thigh. "All the men at Langley's will want you. They will want to touch you, to possess you, possibly even to hurt you." As he spoke, his hand moved closer to the place where a fire burned hotter every second. "They will want to watch you in the heat of passion. You would mesmerize them the way you become so free in that moment."

Panic rose in her. "Mark, I can't—"

"Shhh." He stroked her hair, pulling her head back onto his shoulder. "No one but me will ever touch you."

The significance of his words hit her, penetrating the sensual haze surrounding her. Ever? Of course she had told him she intended to stay in the country after their association ended, but could he possibly think she would never take another lover? Or did he mean…no, that was not a possibility to be considered.

"Lean forward." He pulled her hips back, forcing her to brace herself against the vanity. He pushed her skirts higher, exposing her buttocks to his caresses.

Her sex throbbed, and she couldn't stop herself from arching her back, tilting her hips to give him greater access. She looked over her shoulder and saw that he was opening his breeches. "Mark, what—"

"Shhh!"

Before she could respond, he slid one of his hands between her legs, feeling the damp heat that proved she wanted this as much as he did. And he wanted it so much he could hardly force himself to slow down and test her readiness.

The sight of her standing there, admiring herself in that lethal dress had done him in. He'd come upstairs to admonish her for not being ready. Then he had seen her in the soft candlelight, the curve of her buttocks and the lines of her thighs visible through the thin fabric, the hint of dark pink nipples taunting him through her bodice.

He watched her in the mirror as he sank his cock into her. She leaned further forward so she could take him deeper. He watched her bite her lower lip.

"Don't hold it in." He began to increase his rhythm. "I want you to scream for me."

And she did. Her cries, moans, and words of encouragement filled his head as he moved harder and faster with every stroke. At the end, when he could no longer hold back, he used his fingers to tease her swollen bud until she clenched him tightly and screamed in truth, arching sharply and pushing against him with great force. It was the most beautiful thing he had ever seen.

When he had recovered enough to move, Cassandra had her head down on top of her folded arms. She had yet to catch her breath. He reached out and stroked the curls which had worked loose from her top knot and tumbled down her back.

"Mmmm," she said as his hands stroked her head and her back. "That was amazing."

He smiled. "Yes, it was." Every time he exploded inside her, it was better than the last. He would never get enough. Never.

Suddenly panicked, he had to get away from her, to halt the rush of feelings their coupling sent spiraling through him. He buttoned his breeches and checked his appearance in the mirror. "We should eat before our dinner gets cold." He stopped to survey her. "I hope I haven't wrinkled your dress beyond repair. See if you can arrange it and meet me downstairs."

She looked dazed as she stood in front of the mirror, straightening her dress with shaky hands.

"Cassandra, did you hear me?"

"What? Oh, yes. I'll be down in a few minutes. The wrinkles should fall out while we eat."

He started to leave, but then he thought of what he'd said about the other men at the party. Hot rage swirled in his head. "Put on some stays and a different chemise before you come down."

"What?"

"I've changed my mind. I'm not letting other men see you like that."

"The hell you're not. This is how the other women will be dressed."

"Damn it, Cassandra."

"No."

He'd been a fool to challenge her with the outfit, but he accepted his defeat and closed the door quietly.

Cassandra took several deep breaths, trying to calm her nerves and still the fluttering in her stomach. Mark sat across from her in the carriage. A deep line creased his forehead, and he kept shifting position. He looked ready to pounce at any second, like a caged lion ready to devour the first thing in sight.

The carriage turned onto a street bordering the edge of an elegant neighborhood. One block down, the houses showed signs of wear. The tenants were not people a lady would wish to confront at night. It was the perfect location for an event like Langley's, safe enough to appease the guests, but far from busy thoroughfares used by the *ton*.

Mark exited first and held out his hand to Cassandra. "Your mask," he said as she started to exit without it.

"Thank you." Mark had brought her a lavender half mask decorated with feathers and sequins. He had a matching one in black.

He pulled her into his arms when her feet touched the ground. "This is your last chance to turn back."

Her heart slammed against her ribcage, and perspiration dampened her palms. She was tempted to flee, but instead she pulled her cloak tightly around her. "Let's go in."

A liveried servant showed them inside and told them their host would be with them shortly. Cassandra looked around and noted the understated surroundings, which were nothing like she expected. The foyer's unpapered beige walls were decorated with a few simple prints. A small table holding a sculpture of two people entwined in a lovers embrace and a bench were the only furnishings.

A maid came to collect their outer garments and Langley appeared as Mark removed Cassandra's cloak. Their host had not yet donned a mask, and he paused mid-greeting, letting his gaze rake over Cassandra's body. He paused far too long for comfort on her nipples, which were puckered from the cold.

"I must say you've brought a most intriguing companion," he said to Mark, never taking his gaze from Cassandra.

"Thank you. I do believe she will be most entertaining." Mark's words were spoken in a pleasant tone, but tension radiated from him.

Langley took her hand and brought it to his lips. "Find me later." He spoke almost too softly for her to hear.

It was all she could do not to jerk her hand back, but Mark stepped forward, taking her arm and pulling her toward him. "I would hate for any misunderstandings to arise. I am not inclined to share this evening."

Langley looked Cassandra over once again. "I can only hope the evening's entertainment encourages you to change your mind."

"It won't." Mark's voice was so cold Cassandra would not have been surprised to see frost exit his mouth.

Langley smiled. "Refreshments are available in the salon." He gestured to the door that stood open across the foyer.

As they entered the salon, which was as plainly decorated as the foyer, a tall woman with artfully-styled blond hair drew Cassandra's attention. The woman stood directly in front of Cassandra, but her back was turned. The white toga-like dress she wore dipped so low Cassandra could see the upper curve of her buttocks. Cassandra was grateful she wasn't *that* exposed. As she watched the woman pay court to three men who hung on her every word, Cassandra tried to determine where she had seen the woman before.

But it was only when the woman turned around that the realization hit. Those full, lush lips and perfectly rounded breasts could only belong to one woman. Lady Katryn Wentworth.

Chapter Twelve

One of the men in Katryn's entourage noticed Cassandra. He leaned over and whispered something to his companion.

Cassandra looked at Mark, wishing his mask did not obscure his expression. His eyes had darkened, and his arm was as cold and hard as marble.

Katryn sent them a dazzling smile. The front of her dress dipped below her navel. Her nipples were clearly visible through the thin fabric. Their color was unnaturally deep. Cassandra suspected she'd rouged them.

Katryn walked their way. After the briefest glance toward Cassandra, her gaze focused on Mark. "You've finally finished brooding over me, I hope? I knew you'd eventually be back for more."

"I'm sorry. I believe you must have mistaken me for someone else." Mark's voice was even colder than it had been when he'd warned off Langley.

Katryn's eyes said she did not believe him for a second. "Aren't you going to introduce me to your companion?"

"I can hardly introduce someone I do not know, and asking your name would render our masks ineffectual. Would it not?"

Shifting her gaze to Cassandra, Katryn studied her closely. "Oh my. I do believe it *is* you. I thought at first I must be hallucinating, but that hair, you never were able to keep it contained."

Cassandra barely managed to stop herself from lifting her hand to touch her errant curls. Katryn's smile deepened. "I wonder what your darling husband will have to say about this?"

Finally, Cassandra found her voice. "I do believe you are mistaken in my identity. I am not married." Cassandra forced herself to smile.

Katryn's eyes narrowed. "So you say. Enjoy the party, but don't get too attached to your dear escort. A woman like you hasn't a prayer of satisfying him, especially when he remembers how I used to make him beg."

Katryn slid her hand down Mark's chest. He grabbed her wrist as she reached his waist. "You presume far too much."

Katryn only laughed and walked away.

Mark pulled Cassandra in the direction of the refreshment table. "I think we could both use some champagne."

Cassandra tried to look at him, but he avoided her eyes. The tension in his body told her he was in pain, but if he chose to ignore what happened, she wasn't going to say anything else about it, at least not in public.

"I'll wait for you here." Cassandra wanted a moment to sort through the emotions stirred by Katryn's appearance.

She expected him to protest. But apparently he was too shaken by his encounter. Instead, he said, "Do not leave this spot," and walked in the direction of the refreshment table.

As her eyes followed his broad shoulders, a hand closed on the back of her neck. "I could not resist your curls," a male voice said from behind her. His breath on her neck told her he was too close for comfort.

"I have not given you leave to touch me, sir." She tried to sound annoyed rather than afraid.

Ignoring her request, he slid his fingers down her neck to caress her shoulder.

She stepped away, forcing him to let her go. But he grabbed her hand and attempted to force it against the bulge in his breeches.

"Release me now." Cassandra struggled to get away. Finally, the man complied and she stumbled, almost bumping into a footman carrying a punch bowl.

The man stepped forward until he was only inches away. "Do you like men to force you? Do you wish to pretend you don't want what we all came for?" The man licked his lips and curved them into a particularly self-assured smile. "I'll be glad to play any game you wish."

Cassandra wanted to tell him exactly what she thought of him and his suggestions, but she stopped herself in time. If she and Mark were going to learn anything, they could not alienate the people in this set. She tried to force herself to smile though her stomach churned. "I am afraid I will be quite busy tonight. My companion has requested all my attention. He would not appreciate defiance."

"I will have to convince him to share." As he spoke, the man focused on her breasts rather than her face. "I'm generous, you know. I would let him watch."

"I am afraid you will be disappointed. He's rather possessive."

"We'll see about that."

Cassandra thought he was going to press the issue, but he bowed and walked off. The air in the room was stale and smoky. She noticed a door leading out into a courtyard. Mark would be highly displeased if she went outside without him, but she feared she would faint if she didn't get a breath of fresh air.

She stepped out, and the biting wind immediately eased the nausea that had risen higher every second the stranger's hands had been on her. After a few deep breaths, Cassandra was ready to return to the drawing room. But as she turned toward the door, a man she didn't recognize entered the courtyard.

"Good evening, Cassandra."

She almost responded to his use of her name, but she stopped herself in time. "Excuse me?"

"A mutual acquaintance pointed you out as you left the room. I could not resist taking the opportunity to speak to you privately."

"I'm afraid your acquaintance was mistaken in my identity."

His lips curled upward, and Cassandra cursed the way his mask kept her from seeing his eyes clearly. "My friend said you might protest. But that matters not. I still wish to have a taste of you."

He leaned into her, pressing her against the low wall lining the brick patio. His hands gripped her waist and forced her body against his erection.

Her heart pounded. She took hold of his wrists and tried to push his hands away. "I am sorry, sir. I am already spoken for this evening."

He glanced around the courtyard. "I see no one about."

She detected a slight French accent. He was covering it well, but it was there. Icy pins stabbed her neck, and cold beads of sweat trickled down her back.

She tried to keep her voice from shaking. "I asked my companion to fetch me some champagne. He will return shortly."

"There are plenty of beautiful women inside. He can make do with them."

Cassandra's mind raced. If she could get the man to take her back inside she stood a better chance of escape. "Perhaps you are right. Why don't we go back inside and find a room where we can be alone?"

"I prefer to take you out here. There's nothing like hearing a woman's screams floating on the wind."

Swallowing her fear, she thrust her breasts out and pulled her mouth into a pout. "Please, it's too cold. Wouldn't we be more comfortable in one of the bedrooms?"

"I am not interested in your comfort," he snarled.

She wrenched her hands free and made an effort to push past him. He caught her and pulled her against him so hard the air whooshed from her lungs. He clamped one hand over her mouth and used the other to drag her toward one of the shadowy corners.

"Unless you have a death wish, I suggest you let her go." The sound of Mark's voice made Cassandra's struggling limbs go limp with relief.

When her assailant released her, she swayed and gripped the wall for support.

"Forgive me," the odious man said to Mark, "the lady and I were indulging in a bit of fun while you were occupied."

"I do not believe the lady thought it fun."

"I assure you she did. I told her how a woman's struggles excite me."

"How dare you—" She stopped when Mark looked at her and shook his head.

The man turned to her and laughed. He let his fingers trail down her arm. "It's all right, darling. He won't be angry. Everyone comes here with the intention of sharing their partners."

Mark grabbed the man's arm and pulled him away from her. "Never touch her again."

The man struggled, but Mark's grasp held firm. "Unhand me."

"I will not share this woman with anyone." Mark pushed the man toward the drawing room doors.

The man turned back around and smiled. "Such possessiveness is a liability." Then he disappeared inside.

"Are you all right?" Mark asked.

Cassandra paid no heed to his question. "His accent. Did you notice? I think he's French. He knew who I was."

Mark whisked Cassandra toward the door. "Do not leave the drawing room for any reason. Stay near the refreshment table. If I do not return, my friend Rhys Stanton is here. He is tall with black hair and blue eyes. He is wearing a brocade mask with silver feathers. Trust him and no one else."

When they reached the door, Mark dropped her hand and pushed off through the crowd. Cassandra made her way to the refreshment table.

Her heart pounded and prickles of fear ran up and down her spine. What if Mark never came back? If he caught her assailant, she had no doubt there would be a fight to the death. Mark had the advantage of size, but that was no guarantee he would survive.

Trying to keep her mind off the possibility that she would never see Mark again, Cassandra contemplated what she knew of her attacker. Was Katryn the mutual acquaintance he referred to? She had known Mark and had seemed certain of Cassandra's identity as well.

Long minutes passed, and she saw neither Mark nor anyone who fit his description of Mr. Stanton. She sipped a glass of champagne and tried to look inconspicuous. A few men approached her, but having far better manners than the other men she had encountered, they took their leave when she told them she was waiting for someone.

She was close to panic when she finally saw Mark striding toward her. He took her arm and drew her into an empty room, the breakfast room from its appearance. His eyes were wild, as though a fire burned inside him. He pulled her into his arms and held her close. "Did that son of a bitch hurt you?"

"No. Did yo—"

He gave her no chance to finish. "What the hell were you doing out there? I told you to stay where I left you. If I hadn't gotten there when I did, he could have—"

"I needed some air, a man made advances to me inside. I thought I was going to be ill."

Mark looked back toward the drawing room. "Where is he?"

"It doesn't matter. Your calling him out won't help our situation. Unlike the man from the courtyard, he is not a serious threat."

Mark turned back to face her. He ran his hand through his hair, knocking his mask askew. He exhaled slowly as he righted it. "I looked everywhere. I couldn't find him. I'm sorry."

She reached up to cup his chin, turning his head so he had to meet her gaze. "I thought you'd been killed. I thought you were never coming back for me."

He wrapped his arms around her and crushed her to his chest. She fought the tears she wanted to shed.

After several moments, he released her. "Tell me what happened."

She explained the man's use of her name and his attempt to first seduce and then attack her.

"I should never have let you out of my sight. I won't make that mistake again. How did he know who you were?"

"Possibly from my hair." She frowned and twirled one of her loose curls. "He said a mutual acquaintance pointed me out. Could it have been Katryn?"

"Katryn's a cold bitch who thinks of nothing but her own pleasure. Still, I cannot imagine her being involved in kidnapping and murder."

"Reddington never mentioned her, but that doesn't tell us anything. He rarely shared the names of his female companions."

Mark took her arm. "Let's go back. But this time, you will not leave my side."

When they re-entered the drawing room, Langley was announcing the commencement of the evening's entertainment. "What does he mean?" Cassandra asked in a whisper.

"Men and women will perform in order to…inspire the audience to move on to the evening's true purpose."

Cassandra stomach flip-flopped. Surely she would not be forced to watch a scene like those her husband had provided for others. "Mark, I don't know if I can…"

He must have seen the fear on her face, because he pulled her into his arms and leaned down to whisper in her ear. "No one will be harmed. I'm certain all the participants are willing. Langley enjoys many forms of pleasure, but he's an honorable man, unlike your husband. I would never have brought you here if I thought otherwise."

The guests left the drawing room and entered the ballroom. It no longer looked like a space for dancing, though. Langley had re-designed it to accommodate his own pursuits. Plush chairs and sofas covered in rich fabrics had been placed along one wall. There were large pillows scattered about on the floor which was covered with thick, soft rugs. Cassandra longed to take off her shoes and let her toes sink into the silky pile. The far ends of the room were sectioned off by thin walls and curtains.

Mark pointed out a man standing to the side of the crowd. "There's Stanton. We were at Oxford together. His conquests are legendary, but he would never harm a woman. He is one of a handful of men I truly trust. If you will give me permission, I will enlist his aid in our quest."

Cassandra tried to assess Mark's friend, but she registered nothing besides his flamboyant clothes and raven black hair before other guests stepped in front of him and obscured her vision.

Could she let Mark share her secret with someone she didn't know? "How much will you tell him?"

"Only that Reddington is dead and you are being pursued. I will stress the need for secrecy, and I will not reveal the true nature of our relationship."

"You truly trust him?"

Mark nodded. "He's the one friend who tried to warn me about Katryn. I treated him abominably when he did, but he was right, more than right."

Cassandra hated the pain she saw on Mark's face. "Tell him what you must."

They took a place along the wall with the rest of the guests. Cassandra turned her attention back to the center of the room. A masked woman entered through a side door and approached the satin-covered mattress that lay on a low platform. She wore a white, feathered mask, a matching corset and a diaphanous skirt that swirled around her hips and legs, concealing nothing. Several of the men whistled and cheered.

A man, also masked but dressed all in black joined the woman on the platform. He carried several long pieces of thin rope and something that looked like a small whip, like a riding crop with long tassels dangling from the end. He laid his implements down and instructed the woman to remove what little clothing she had on.

Slowly, while swaying her hips, she began unlacing her corset. As she revealed the dusky brown tips of her nipples, the crowd applauded. Cassandra's heartbeat accelerated. Despite her discomfort with the scenario, wetness pooled between her legs.

When the woman was completely naked, the man gestured for her to lie down. She did so, stretching her arms over her head and spreading her legs, giving the audience a clear view of her sex. The man knelt by her head and threaded one of the long strips of velvet through a ring embedded in the platform. Cassandra had not noticed it before, but now she saw that rings lined the edge of the mattress.

He took hold of the woman's wrists and tied one of the ropes around it. The woman arched her back and wiggled her hips sinuously while making a low purring sound. Cassandra didn't breathe as she watched the man tie the woman's other arm and her ankles. When he finished his work, the woman laid spread out like a sacrifice.

The naked woman struggled a bit, testing her bonds. Her eyes were wide and her breathing rapid, but Cassandra did not think she was frightened. Instead, she looked thoroughly aroused. Her hips moved up and down restlessly like Cassandra's did when she was so ready for Mark it hurt.

Cassandra meant to search the crowd for the man who had attacked her, but she could not stop watching what was happening on the platform. The man picked up the tasseled crop and brought it down across the woman's open thighs. The woman jerked and moaned but made no serious protest. Instead she raised her hips toward her tormenter, silently begging for more.

Then the man shifted his focus to slap at the woman's breasts, catching the tassels on her hard nipples. Cassandra gasped. The woman whimpered, but she continued to smile at the man.

Warm heat flooded Cassandra's body. Her arousal embarrassed her, but she couldn't prevent her response to the erotic scene unfolding before her.

Mark looked down at Cassandra and hardened instantly. Her eyes were wide, her face was flushed. Her breasts rose and fell quickly, all evidence of her intense arousal. Damn, he wanted to haul her off to one of the private alcoves and sink into her wet heat.

He forced himself to look away from her and scan the faces of everyone in the audience, but the man who had accosted Cassandra was not there. Katryn looked back at Mark as she stood between two men, both of whom freely ran their hands over her body. He looked away from her and noticed several men watching Cassandra, taking in her obvious enjoyment of the performance. He thought it likely their interest lay only in her sexual charms. Nevertheless, he would ask Stanton their names later.

He turned his attention back to the platform where the man worked his way across the woman's belly, slapping the crop across her skin. Several men and a few women continued to cheer and make suggestions.

The woman's body was striped with light red lines, but the man had clearly done no real damage. She struggled against her bonds, but she also arched toward the lash every time it came down. Mark was quite certain the only thing she wanted more than the brush of the crop was her lover's cock.

He had been afraid the entertainers would disgust Cassandra. He should have known better. A woman as passionate as she could hardly watch such a scene without receiving some stimulation, even if she told herself she should not.

He looked at Cassandra again. Her lips were slightly parted, and her hands clutched at the fabric of her dress. He could not resist taunting her. "If we were alone, I would take you right now. You're wet and ready for me, aren't you?"

She gasped and turned to him. He hadn't intended to touch her where others could watch, but the fire he saw in her eyes did him in. He captured her lips and his hands cupped her breasts. Cassandra made no attempt to pull away, instead she melted into him. He kissed her far longer and far more passionately than he should. By the time he pulled away, he was so hard he feared his cock would burst through his pants.

They turned back to the platform as the man undid his pants and positioned himself to enter the woman. She lifted her hips to him and pulled at her bonds. Mark couldn't help but watch. Cassandra leaned into him and rubbed her bottom against his erection. He placed his hands on her hips and forced her to be still. "Not here," he whispered in her ear.

She gasped. "I'm sorry. I didn't mean to. "

He took her arm. "We need some place private."

The man and woman on the platform screamed out their release as Mark drew Cassandra along. Other couples and small groups headed toward the curtained alcoves at one end of the room. But many of the guests did not mind an audience. They began to shed their clothing and arrange themselves on the pillows and sofas lining the ballroom.

Cassandra's mind raced as Mark swept her toward the far end of the room. She was ashamed by the feelings the woman's restraint had stirred. If Mark hadn't stopped her from touching him, she feared she might have coupled with him right there. *What is wrong with me?*

"Please." She tugged on his arm, trying to halt his progress. He ignored her until he had pulled open the curtain of the closest alcove and drawn her inside.

He pulled her against him and brought his lips to hers, but she pushed at his chest. "I can't do this here."

Despite the semi-privacy of the alcove, Mark knew others could hear them if they spoke above a whisper. Even if he made Cassandra forget her embarrassment, they could not afford to lose control when her attacker could return any time.

Mark closed his eyes and took a deep breath. "I know. I got carried away out there. You are so wickedly beautiful when you are aroused."

Cassandra turned to leave the alcove, but Mark pulled her back. "We need to talk."

He pulled her down on the chaise that took up most of the space in the tiny room. He leaned down so his lips were against her ear. "We need to stay here long enough that people think we've made proper use of the room. In a few minutes, we will go back to the drawing room. I saw Stanton after I'd given up on finding the Frenchman. He will meet us there.

His voice was calm and steady, but she saw the thick bulge pressing against his pants. When she brushed a lock of hair from his face, his skin scorched her fingers. For a moment she considered changing her mind. No one would see them, and everyone else was occupied.

No! What was she thinking? She was here to investigate, not to become involved in this lifestyle. Was she as depraved as Katryn?

She knew she had not said the words out loud, but Mark spoke as if to answer her. "Do not be ashamed of your desire. You would have to be made of stone to feel no reaction to what you saw."

"But the man whipped that woman."

"Only lightly. And her enjoyment was quite evident."

"You said these parties disgusted you."

"The way the guests treat each other disgust me. Most of the men view the women like inanimate playthings. The women who are too strong to accept such treatment are typically cold and heartless like Katryn. Most of the guests are here for power games, not pleasure. The scene we saw aroused me as much as it did you. At some of Reddington's parties, I can assure you, the man in black would have drawn blood, and the woman wouldn't have been willing."

Cassandra shut her eyes to block out the image of the frightened young woman Reddington had auctioned off. "It is still wrong of me to long for—" She brought her hand to her mouth, horrified at what she'd almost revealed.

Mark guessed her words anyway. "Do you? Do you long for me to do that to you?"

"No! I didn't mean that. I—"

He placed his finger on her lips. "I saw how it aroused you, and I want to fulfill all your fantasies. We can consider it later."

Her cheeks burned with embarrassment. "I think we'd better leave now. If we don't, I will not be able to wait."

His low laugh echoed against her throat where he traced circles with his tongue. "You were wise to make us stop. If I took you here, it would be hard and fast. I don't want to rush tonight. I have many things planned for you."

She tried to get away, unable to bear the feel of his mouth on her any longer. But he held her against his chest and rolled her nipples between his thumb and forefinger. She moaned, writhing against him, unable to keep quiet.

"Should I bring you to release or leave you in need?"

Her only reply was a whimper. She did not know what she wanted more, for him to stop so others would not hear her cries or for him to lift her skirts and thrust into her as he had in her bedroom.

He nipped the back of her neck then lifted her upright with his hands on her waist. Her knees gave as if made of mush. He laughed and steadied her.

She wanted to be angry, but the world seemed unreal. As if she were in dream. How could this night be real?

Mark stood and wrapped her hand around his arm. "Come. Let's look for Stanton."

She pushed back an errant strand of hair and looked at him. "Everyone will know how aroused I am, won't they?"

"Of course they will, but that is the point. We are all here to be aroused and to be pleasured. They will assume you need far more pleasure before you are satisfied. And they will be right."

Before she could protest, he opened the curtain and led her out. They exited the ballroom quickly. But before they did, she saw bodies in positions she had not known the human form could take.

Once they were back in the drawing room, the atmosphere was like that of any London ball with the exception of the scant attire of the women and the fact that most of the men had discarded their jackets and waistcoats. Mark and Cassandra located Mr. Stanton near the refreshment table. From a distance, his green and blue waistcoat made him look the part of a peacock, but when they got closer, Cassandra realized he had far more strength of presence than the lazy, useless young men she had met in droves prior to her marriage.

He did a good job of hiding his physical strength with the cut of his clothing, but he had rolled back his sleeves, and she saw the well-defined muscles in his arms. He was not what he appeared to be. She should have known better anyway. Mark was not likely to befriend someone who spent his entire morning devising new ways to tie his neck cloth.

Mark tapped his friend on the shoulder, and Mr. Stanton turned to face them, smiling when he looked at Cassandra.

"Do forgive me for not having made your acquaintance." He bowed low. "I should have taken notice of a woman of your superior beauty long before now."

Mark frowned. "Cut the act. We need to talk."

Mr. Stanton sighed. "You could at least introduce me."

Mark exhaled sharply, his annoyance evident. "Not here. We need to find a private room.

They entered the breakfast room again. Mark closed the door and braced it with a chair. Then he insisted they all remove their masks, saying he wanted Cassandra to be certain she could recognize Stanton later.

Looking at Cassandra, Mark said, "Lady Reddington, may I present Mr. Rhys Stanton."

When she smiled at his friend, Mark scowled. He obviously did not want her to appreciate Stanton's charms. Cassandra was unable to suppress a wicked desire to taunt Mark, especially after he had deliberately aroused her to the point of madness and given her no relief. "Do forgive Mark. He is a trifle overprotective. I am delighted to meet you." She offered her hand to Mr. Stanton.

Stanton laughed. "I will be happy to rescue you if his attentions become too odious." He touched his lips lightly to the back of her hand like the most studied gentleman.

Mark cleared his throat, and Cassandra turned to face him. "Are you two quite finished?"

Cassandra smiled. "We are for now."

Mark made a sound that was close to a growl. "Stanton, I have to confess that I was not completely honest this afternoon. I will call on you in the morning and explain all you need to know. For now, please indulge me.

Have seen or talked to a short man with light blond hair and a very long nose tonight? You might have noted his French accent."

Stanton's brow creased. "I believe I saw such a man when I first arrived. I didn't speak with him though, and I haven't seen him in quite some time."

"I think the bastard left." Mark clenched his fists. "Do you have any idea who he is?"

"I don't know his name, but I have seen him before in the company of," he paused and looked at Cassandra, "Lord Reddington."

Cassandra felt the color drain from her face. The heat Mark had stirred in her turned to cold fear. Once again, she had come very close to death.

Stanton looked back and forth between her and Mark. "What is going on?"

Mark shook his head. "I will tell you tomorrow. You said you weren't sure if Reddington owned Miss Caroline's? Do you know the name of any similar establishments he does have an interest in?"

Stanton looked uneasy. His gaze darted toward Cassandra. She quickly spoke up. "Mr. Stanton, let me put you at ease. When one is married to a man like Reddington, one quickly becomes accustomed to discussing topics not normally mentioned in front of a lady."

He smiled. "Thank you. I suppose it sounds ridiculous considering where we are, but I would not normally admit the existence of such an establishment to a lady of your caliber."

"I could hardly be considered a true lady after appearing here."

He smiled. "I do not think you came here for the same reasons I did."

"No, Mr. Stanton, I am quite sure I did not." Overcome with the desire to tease him, she added, "I must say you would not find yourself in this dilemma if you did not frequent places that cannot be mentioned in front of a lady."

Mark laughed. "Unfortunately were he that wise, he would be of no help to us. Answer the question, Stanton."

Mr. Stanton looked from Mark to Cassandra and smiled. "There are several men who have an interest in Miss Caroline's. It is likely Reddington is one of them, but their leader is referred to as The Cat." Cassandra gasped and Stanton turned toward her. "I take it you have heard of him?"

"My husband mentioned him in connection to...well, Mark will explain more tomorrow. Do you have any idea who he is?'

"No. Despite what Mark may have told you, I do not go to Miss Caroline's frequently." Cassandra smiled as color infused his cheeks. "I've never seen this man or heard him called by any other name. Langley might be able to help though."

Mark nodded. "Please see to Lady Reddington's comfort while I search for our host."

"My pleasure." Stanton offered Cassandra his arm.

Mark scowled and gave his friend a quelling look. "I hope to hear that you have behaved in a manner above reproach."

"I will do only what Lady Reddington requests of me."

His friend's words echoed in Mark's head as he walked off in search of Langley. He trusted Stanton to keep Cassandra safe. Knowing she was under Mark's protection, Stanton would do no more than flirt with her in his outrageous but harmless manner.

The thing that made him uneasy was Cassandra's obvious acceptance of his friend. Stanton was criminally handsome. He'd probably turned down four or five offers in favor of meeting with them. Would Cassandra fall prey to his spell?

Why did it matter so much? He had no real claim over Cassandra, and their relationship had an established end. If she wanted to take Stanton as a lover after that, she was certainly free to. He would do nothing to stop her. In fact, he would be glad to see her continuing to embrace her passionate side.

Perhaps if he repeated these sentiments enough, he could make them be true.

Chapter Thirteen

A short while later, Mark located Stanton and Cassandra on the balcony, standing far too close for his comfort. He began walking faster when Cassandra laughed at something Stanton said and gave a stunning smile, one Mark rarely saw unless they were in bed.

Cassandra turned to Mark before he had a chance to speak. She reached for his arm and pulled him to her. "You were gone so long I was beginning to worry. Did you learn anything?" Her obvious concern did much to alleviate his fears.

"I did. Reddington and the Lintons are part owners in both Miss Caroline's and Lucifer's, a notorious gaming hell. Langley does not know The Cat's identity, but he told me to use his name as entree to both establishments which admit only a select clientele."

As he spoke, Mark couldn't help but stumble over a few of his words. Cassandra's cheeks were flushed, and she was fanning herself despite the cool breeze rustling the trees. She twirled her hair and shifted from one foot to another, obviously restless. Apparently, the desire Langley's entertainment had inspired still rode her hard.

Stanton spoke first. "I have an engagement tomorrow evening which I cannot break, but the following night, I will visit Simone. Perhaps I can discover something useful from her."

Mark forced himself to be polite despite his eagerness to get Cassandra home. "Thank you for your assistance. I will visit Miss Caroline's myself tomorrow using your name for entree."

"Call on me tomorrow."

"I will." Mark locked Cassandra's hand around his arm and headed for the entrance, needing to collect their coats and leave as fast as possible.

As soon as the carriage door closed, Mark knelt in front of Cassandra, needing to touch her, to establish the bond their passion had formed between them.

Cassandra pushed at his shoulders. "What are you doing? The driver will hear us."

Mark ignored her concerns. His servants knew the importance of discretion. "I have many plans for us tonight, but you will not enjoy them in your current state."

"What do you m-mean?" Her voice caught as he slid his hands along her thighs.

"You have been ready to come since I touched you in the alcove. You can't wait much longer.

He slid his hands down her calves and lifted her skirt, working it toward her waist. "I intend to keep you going for hours tonight. This will take the edge off."

"But—"

"Hush."

When he had bared her completely, he bent and flicked his tongue across her clit. She cried out as he had hoped. His hands gripped her thighs, pulling them further apart and anchoring them against the velvety seat.

He tasted her again and again. Her hands gripped his head, trying to push him back. He ignored the pressure on his scalp, nothing she could do would deter him from wresting more delightful cries from her. He continued to work her, sucking, licking, nibbling, drinking her in.

He knew that once her breathing grew labored and her hips jerked up and down rapidly mere seconds separated her from gaining her release. He stopped his ministrations abruptly and shifted so he could nip the soft skin of her inner thighs.

"No. Please."

Mark smiled as he ran his tongue down her leg. He had no desire to be merciful.

When she calmed enough to stop tugging at his hair, he returned his attention to her pussy. He slipped two fingers into her while he drew her clit into his mouth. When he stretched her passage open, he pressed his fingers upward as though trying to rub the tip of his tongue as he licked her clit.

She gasped and bucked under him, trying to squirm away.

Mark vibrated his fingers against the front of her channel, and she dropped over the edge. Her spasms squeezed his fingers, and her hands pressed his head tight against her until her hips ceased their gyrations and her arms went limp.

He sat back on his heels. Cassandra's eyes fluttered open, staring drunkenly up at him. Mark lifted his fingers to his mouth and licked them clean. Her eyes widened as she watched him, and he noted her breathing accelerating once again.

He had intended to save his own release until much later, but he found himself reaching for the buttons of his pants when the carriage came to a halt.

"Damn!" He would have to wait after all. He righted Cassandra's skirts and helped her descend from the carriage. But as soon as he closed the door of her townhouse behind them, he unfastened her cloak and let it fall to the floor. His fingers skimmed the naked skin of her back. "Are you still thinking of them?"

She stiffened. "Who?"

"The man and women who performed for us." He brought her against him and held his lips inches from hers.

"I don't…I'm not—"

"Your reaction surprised you, didn't it?"

She nodded mutely. He scooped her into his arms, carrying her upstairs. When he set her down on the thick rug by her bed, he undid the buttons at the back of her dress.

She hadn't spoken either to protest or to share her fantasies. When he succeeded in removing her dress, he lifted the hem of her chemise and pulled it over her head.

He held it in his hands and let his gaze roam over her naked form. The soft silk caressed his flesh. Suddenly, he had an idea.

He began to rip her chemise into long strips. "Remind me tomorrow to buy you another one of these."

Her eyes widened. "Mark, stop! What are you doing?"

She tried to grab the garment from his hands, but he kept it out of reach. "This silk will work perfectly to restrain you."

She gasped.

"You want it, Cassandra. Play along with me."

"But I—"

"I saw your face at the party. You could hardly breathe as you watched that woman struggle for her freedom."

"I don't think I can give up control like that."

"Your surrender is a gift. You can take it back anytime." Mark stepped forward and caressed her face. "Trust me."

He wrapped the silk around his hand and caressed her neck and collarbone. She gasped when he touched her tight nipples. "Your body knows what you want."

"What if I don't like it?"

"Then we will stop."

"But—"

"Say the word 'Northamberly', and our game will end. That way you can struggle and protest all you want just like the woman at the party."

She drew in a sharp breath and covered his hands with her own, encouraging him to rub the silk against her breasts. "All right."

"Lie down on the bed." When she complied, Mark pulled one of her arms above her head, securing it to the bedpost. She tugged against it and was

143

unable to free herself. He wrapped the silk around her other wrist and secured that arm. Her breathing accelerated. The flush that had suffused her cheeks now stretched across her chest. Her nipples were taut buds, and Mark could not suppress the desire to play with her before she was fully restrained.

One hand captured a nipple while the other slid between her thighs. She watched Mark with wide eyes. When his fingers slipped inside her, she twisted frantically, wanting to get free. "Mark, please!"

He smiled. "I love that I've got you begging and you're not even fully restrained yet."

He brought his wet fingers to his mouth and slowly licked them clean, remembering how that had aroused her in the carriage. "You taste delicious."

"Then taste me more." Her seductive purr nearly did him in, but he managed to ignore her suggestion as he tied her ankles. When she was completely restrained, he paused to take in the sight. The wave of lust that hit him forced him to grab the bedpost for support.

Her dark curls lay spread out across the pillow. Her hips gyrated in small circles, and she tugged on her wrist bonds, pulling the ropes tight as she arched upward, thrusting her breasts toward him. The angle of her bound feet forced her smooth, creamy thighs open so he could see her swollen lips.

His cock begged to be inside her. He removed his waistcoat and his shirt, but he knew he had to leave his pants on lest he be enticed to finish before he'd truly gotten started.

Cassandra opened her eyes to watch him. He saw no trace of fear in her gaze. She studied his bare chest and licked her lips while moving her body in a way calculated to entice him.

"Little witch. If you think you are hot now, you have no idea how far I can drive you."

She dropped her gaze to the thick bulge in his pants. "I wouldn't be so certain if I were you. You hardly appear unaffected."

"But I know the rewards of delayed gratification."

"Why wait when I'm ready and I can't get away?"

Refusing to let her silky words test his control further, he knelt on the bed and stretched over her body until his lips made contact with one of her nipples. Her body jerked off the bed as he drew it into his mouth. As he'd hoped, she lost the ability to taunt him. He sucked hard, making her cry out. She begged him to stop, but he was relentless.

Wildness pumped through Cassandra's veins. When she'd seen the woman tied up at the party, she had wondered how it would feel to be her. Despite her fear of giving up control, part of her had wanted to find out, but she had never imagined how incredibly erotic it would be.

She'd been climbing a precipice of desire since Mark had toyed with her in the alcove. Her release in the carriage had calmed her only momentarily. She didn't know how much more she could take.

Yet, Mark spoke the truth about the delights of a delayed release. When he teased her like this, building her desire until every nerve in her body tingled, reaching her peak was even sweeter.

Mark hands roamed over her body, brushing her breasts, her belly, her thighs, everywhere but the center of her desire. Cassandra closed her eyes, allowing herself to revel in the sensations. His rough, thick fingers slid over her skin. His nails raked lightly down her sides, and the sharpness made her jump.

He replaced his nails with his teeth, nipping the skin of her throat and breasts. As his bites grew rougher, the sensations rode the edge of pain, making her crave the wildness that always exploded in her when they coupled.

Using lips and teeth, Mark traced a line along the center of her belly. Cassandra panicked as she thought of how his mouth would torment her raging body. His hands gripped her inner thighs, holding them immobile.

Cassandra arched her body toward him, pulling desperately at the bonds holding her arms. Mark lowered his mouth until it hovered over the center of her need. His warm breath tickled her mound, but no matter how hard she flexed her hips, she could not reach him.

"Tell me what your body needs."

Her breath caught, preventing her from saying the words.

"Tell me." He exhaled slowly, letting his breath caress her. Even that feathery touch made her muscles clench.

"I need you to touch me." She was writhing, trying to make contact with his mouth. "Please, Mark, I can't stand it."

"Where should I touch you?" His voice was so husky she barely heard him.

Her face burned with embarrassment. "Between my legs. Touch me. Lick me. Please!" She struggled so fiercely she broke his hold on her legs. Her hips arched up, and he brought his mouth down to her. But his tongue gave only teasing flicks before he pulled back again.

It wasn't nearly enough. She was so close to climax she could taste it.

"I...need you...inside me. Now." The last of her words came out as a growl.

Mark pulled back. A deep red flush covered his face and neck. His shallow breaths made his chest heave. She wondered how much longer he could hold out, praying it wasn't long.

"You need this too." She tried to make her voice low and seductive.

He ran his hand through his hair and stood at the end of the bed, letting his gaze move slowly over her writhing form. Ever so slowly, he loosened his pants and let them slide down his legs. "God, Cassandra. You're the one who's restrained, yet I could no more deny you than you could break free and force me to."

"Take me, Mark. Please. I'm dying to feel you inside me."

He moved over her, positioning himself to enter but he paused, and she feared he would hold back. He brushed himself against her wetness. "Is this what you want? My cock inside you?"

She nodded.

"Say it."

She had lost all sense of embarrassment. She would have said anything to have him. "I need your cock inside me. Now!"

He groaned and drove inside her. But when he was fully seated, he paused.

Cassandra squirmed, trying to force him to move. "More, please. I need more."

"Take it." He pulled out and slammed back in, deep and hard.

His rough words, and the feel of him grinding against her were all she needed to find release. Her body exploded in all directions.

She didn't know how long it took her to come back to reality, but when she did, he was riding her with short, fast strokes. His thrust should have hurt, but they didn't. The brutality was exactly what she needed. Her hips met his on every stroke. She wanted to beg him to untie her, but his pace was so fast she couldn't gather the breath to speak. All she could do was feel.

He placed his hands on either side of her head and leaned down until their faces were inches apart. A storm of emotions flashed in his eyes—lust, ferocity, and vulnerability. As she looked at him, something passed between them, something deeper than desire. "Watch me. Watch me pour my seed into you."

She could not have looked away to save her own life. When Mark cried out and stiffened against her, she watched his face as he poured his soul into her with his release. With his final stroke, she tumbled over the edge and sank into oblivion.

ൽ ൽ ൽ

Cassandra woke in the wee hours of the morning, lying on top of Mark. She vaguely remembered him untying her and rolling her over with him. She must have slept so deeply she hadn't moved all night.

Carefully, so as not to wake him, she rolled to the empty side of the bed and slid to the floor. After finding a wrapper, she curled up on the window seat and gazed out at pink clouds signaling the approach of dawn.

Conflict roared in her head. She had not thought it possible for Mark to give her more intense pleasure than what they had shared for the last week. But she had been wrong. From their first kiss, he had made her enjoy every touch of their bodies. But he had been holding a part of himself back, as if he too feared the depth of the connection between them.

That night he had dropped all barriers and opened himself to her completely. She marveled that she had the power to break down his resistance, especially when she'd been restrained. Somehow, she'd pushed his desire so high he had no choice but to let go.

Days ago, she'd wanted him to drop his barriers and show her the man he truly was. But now she realized that in making him give more of himself, she had broken a barrier of her own. She had been fighting what she knew deep inside.

Amanda was right, she had fallen in love with Mark.

She did not want their affair to end, yet it must. Even if Mark wanted it to continue, she wouldn't be free if she stayed with him.

And freedom was what she wanted more than anything. Wasn't it? Of course it was, she told herself. Why else would she have gone to such extreme measures to procure it?

From their first night together, she had been unable to hide the deep desire he awoke in her. Her natural response was more powerful than she had ever dreamed. For the sake of her sanity, she must learn to take pleasure from him without giving her soul as payment. If she didn't, she would never find the freedom she desired.

Mark stirred and propped himself on his elbow. "Are you all right?"

"Yes, I didn't mean to wake you."

Her heart hammered in her chest. How could she do this? How could she continue this affair after admitting her feelings to herself?

Mark swung his legs over the side of the bed and came to join her at the window. "Are your wrists sore? You struggled more than I anticipated." As he asked, he tugged on one of her arms and lifted it to his mouth. He kissed her wrist, and his lips sent a bolt of desire through her body.

He smiled as he let her arm go and stepped back. "Any more of that, and I won't be able to stop."

"Do you want to stop?" She lifted her arm and trailed her hand down his chest.

He smiled. "I would like nothing more than to stay here with you, but I must be going. At this hour, Miss Caroline's girls will be too worn out to talk, but I hope to catch one of the Lintons at Lucifer's."

"I assume you aren't going to let me accompany you."

"No. The only women allowed in Lucifer's are professionals." He stepped into his pants and reached for his waistcoat and jacket.

She slid from the bed and helped him adjust his clothing. Then she followed him to the door, feeling annoyingly clingy and protective. What had gotten into her? She had always been independent to a fault. Of course, she'd never had anyone worth clinging to. "Be careful." She stood on tiptoes to kiss him goodbye.

He squeezed her behind. "I will."

She feared her smile looked rather wistful. "Mark?"

"Yes?"

"Would you be willing to meet my sister tomorrow?"

"Why?"

"She wishes to be acquainted her big sister's protector."

"How much does she know about us?"

"Everything. I wrote to her before I came to Northamberly. She's been in town all through the fall and winter, and she's got a dangerous streak of curiosity. It's possible she has heard something that might be of use to us."

Mark nodded. "I suppose it wouldn't hurt me to meet her. Just tell me she's entertaining like you. I don't think I can bear to take tea with a silly deb."

Cassandra laughed. "Amanda is never silly."

"Then you can tell her to expect me."

Chapter Fourteen

An unnaturally large man with a crooked nose and a jagged scar above his left eye guarded the door to Lucifer's. "Card?" he demanded as Mark approached.

Mark handed him the requested item. After inspecting it thoroughly, the man flipped through a book that lay open on a podium. "You're not listed."

"I do apologize. Lord Langley said I should mention his name. He assured me he would vouch for me."

"Langley, eh?" The man scratched his head. "I suppose that will do." He gestured toward a curtain behind his podium.

"Thank you," Mark muttered as he pushed open the door separating the vestibule from the drawing room where patrons came to take a break from gaming. Cyprians dressed in brightly-colored, sleeveless chemises dotted the room, ready to accompany men to private alcoves should they desire a respite from the tables.

Mark had not been completely honest with Cassandra. There were a few society women at the tables, all attired in garish dresses no doubt foisted on them by seamstresses who claimed such attire was all the rage in France. Some of them had likely attended Langley's party and would now lose a few thousand pounds before retiring for the night.

Cassandra would be furious if she realized other women of standing were present, but he'd had all he could stand of watching men ogle her. The next one would have his eye blackened by Mark's fist. Even Stanton had not been immune from his jealousy. It mattered not that his friend's audacious behavior was harmless.

He scanned the room, looking for one of the Lintons. He'd only met them once, but fortunately their features were distinctive enough that he could recognize them. They weren't identical, but they both had square heads and eyes that bugged out, reminding him of a frog. In fact, he would not be surprised to discover that their bodies were covered in slime.

Neither of them was in the drawing room, but when he entered the gaming room, he saw Walter Linton, wearing a hideous yellow jacket and standing against the far wall. Linton kept turning from side to side and raising himself on tiptoe as if desperate to find someone in the crowd. Mark would have preferred to talk to Oscar, the elder brother, who had gotten the majority of the brains in the family, but Walter would do.

Even with dawn fast approaching, the room was packed with bodies. Mark lost sight of his target for a moment while working his way through the throng. When Walter came into view again, a woman stood with him. A cold sweat broke out across Mark's body when he realized it was Katryn. Did the bitch have to be everywhere he needed to go?

From the provocative way she touched Walter, it appeared she had not gotten sated at the party. Had she no limits at all? Mark's stomach churned as he thought how a few months ago this woman had held his heart in her hands.

Mark took a deep breath and continued to approach them. He wondered if Southwood knew what kind of woman he'd married? Probably not. Mark had been her lover for months and hadn't figured her out. He knew now how lucky he was she'd refused his proposal. Walking around with a stone for a heart was hell, but learning Katryn had cuckolded him would have been worse.

Katryn noticed him first. Walter appeared too taken with her breasts to see anything else. "Why Mark, don't tell me Langley's party wasn't enough for you? I would have thought you'd be in bed by now. If you wish to reconsider the wretchedly rude way you treated me earlier…"

Mark had never hit a woman, but his hand burned to slap Katryn's smug face. "If you would please excuse us, I need to speak to Mr. Linton."

Katryn raised her brows but started to walk away without saying anything else.

Walter seized her arm. "I'll find you later. Don't leave."

She pushed his hand away with the tips of her fingers as if she dreaded touching it. "You would do well to remember whom you are speaking to."

What was that about?

"I am looking forward to renewing our acquaintance, Mark." Katryn brushed past him, letting her fingers trail down his arm.

Both men watched her as she walked away. Mark burned with hatred, but Walter was obviously deeply smitten. Mark could almost pity him.

"So, Foxwood, what can I do for you?" Walter asked when he finally pulled his gaze from Katryn.

"I wasn't sure you'd remember me."

"How could anyone forget your performance at Lady Southwood's engagement ball?"

"I did my best to make it a memorable event." Mark forced his lips into a smile. He wondered what Linton had been doing there. He would not normally be on the guest list of a society matron like Katryn's mother.

Walter's smarmy smile deepened. "You certainly succeeded in that. But I take it you are not here to reminisce."

"I've been given to understand that you could assist me in procuring a woman who would submit to the attention of myself and a few friends."

"Miss Caroline's or Amelia's could provide you with the perfect girl."

"I don't want a brothel. I need a girl for a private party. Actually, I'd prefer she not be a professional. The fresher the better."

"Ahhh. Something really special." Linton eyes lit up as if the very idea stimulated him.

Mark fought against his urge to punch the man and continued to play his role. "I've grown terribly bored with the usual run of London life. I need some excitement."

"Excitement doesn't come cheap."

"The price is no matter as long as I get what I want."

Linton rubbed his chin as if considering Mark's comment. "Arrangements like this take time. How quickly do you need the girl?"

Mark had no time to waste, but he appeared nonchalant. "I haven't set a date for my party. I wanted to be sure you could provide me with the right girl before I did so."

"I might be able to help you out." He extracted a card from his wallet. "Call at this address in two days."

Mark looked down. The address was a townhouse near the one Langley had rented for his party. He wondered if the other residents of that street knew what went on in their neighbors' homes. "Thank you. I will see you then."

Walter nodded. "If that is all, I have other business to attend to."

"That is all." No doubt Linton's business was coaxing Katryn into bed, but Mark was only too glad to escape the garish decor and the desperation that hung in the air.

As he neared the arched doorway that led to the drawing room, someone grabbed his arm. He turned to find himself face to face with Katryn. "It *was* you earlier tonight, wasn't it?" She continued speaking without giving him a chance to respond. "And I am quite certain I recognized your companion. Although I must say I'm a bit amazed at her audacity and yours."

Damn! It didn't matter if Katryn knew he'd been at the party, but he had to protect Cassandra. "It is considered gauche even among your set to refer to one's presence at such an event. It defeats the purpose of being masked."

She gave him the smile that used to bring him to his knees. "I would have known your delicious body anywhere."

"You might have known me, but you're mistaken in thinking yourself acquainted with my companion."

Katryn tilted her head to the side as she always did when considering something. He remembered a time when he'd found it endearing.

"Perhaps not, but that is of no consequence. I've been denied the pleasure of your body far too long. A private room is reserved in my name. It can be ours for the rest of the night."

A red haze clouded his mind. He could neither speak nor move for a few seconds, else he would strangle her. How dare she think he would come back to her after she humiliated him as she had? "Let me assure you once and for all that your charms do not tempt me in the least."

"Don't be silly Mark. I know you remember how good it was between us. Surely you miss that."

"During the time we were together, I labored under the misapprehension that you had a heart. I learned my lesson and I've sworn off cold-blooded bitches."

She laughed, a high-pitched titter that sounded as pleasant as fingernails scratching on slate. "You are so melodramatic, Mark. When I told you I was going to marry Southwood, I never meant for us to stop seeing each other. I only wanted to explain that your offer of marriage was misplaced."

Mark dug his nails into his palms so hard he feared he'd rip his gloves. He needed to rip something, and he regretted it couldn't be Katryn's hide. "You called me a naive fool and refused my proposal. Pardon me for interpreting that as a dismissal."

"I suppose I was a bit harsh with you, but I never expected you to be so ignorant about the ways of the world. I obviously could not marry a bastard, even if you are the son of a duke."

Her words hit Mark like a knife. Of course he had known she *shouldn't* marry him. No woman of the *ton* would marry a bastard unless...unless she did it for love. But how dare she throw his status in his face now? His control threatened to shatter, but she continued talking, seemingly unaware of the danger she was in.

"I could never marry a man who wished to rule me. I need someone biddable in my home, but that doesn't mean I don't like dominant men in my bed." She licked her lips and looked up at him, catching him watching her. "In fact I love them."

"You love nothing but money, power, and your own pleasure."

"Ooh that is harsh. You have been so wickedly spiteful since I refused you. The engagement toast was a good touch. Not one of the guests has forgotten that party."

Trust her to turn his insult into a triumph for herself. "I no longer number you among my acquaintance. If you approach me again, you do so at your own peril."

He turned from the sexy pout she gave him and stomped off toward the exit.

छ छ छ

Cassandra slept restlessly that night. She could not stop wondering if Mark was safe. Questioning the Lintons was dangerous. If they thought Mark a threat, Cassandra did not doubt they would have him killed. She wished she'd stopped him from going or at the very least encouraged him not to go alone.

In the moments she wasn't imagining the dangers Mark faced, she was worrying about the intensity of her feelings for him, wondering if she should call a halt to the whole affair. At least if she found work as a traveling companion she could leave the country for awhile. She might be able to put the horror of her marriage behind her if she were elsewhere.

She sighed and rolled onto her back to stare at the ceiling. No matter how sensible it would be, she would not send Mark away. Why was she incapable of having a purely physical affair?

Between the turmoil in her heart and the fact that someone was trying to kill her, it was a wonder she did not spend all day crying. But she could count on her hand the number of times she had allowed herself to indulge in tears since she had agreed to marry Reddington, and she was not going to add to her tally now.

Feeling sorry for herself wouldn't help her one bit. She dragged herself off her bed and rang for Rebecca. When the maid appeared, she requested a breakfast tray and asked Rebecca's assistance in donning her riding habit, thinking perhaps the frigid morning air would help clear her head. While she ate, she penned a note to her sister, asking her to call that afternoon so she could be introduced to Mark.

When she'd given the note to a footman, Cassandra called for her guards and inquired whether she was permitted her to ride in the park if they followed at a discreet distance.

Corwyn spoke first. "Mr. Foxwood wouldna like it but aye, ye can ride."

Brant looked at them both like they were crazy. "Milady, do ya know there's a fine thick frost out there? It's fair freezin'"

Cassandra smiled. "I am afraid I have quite a penchant for riding in temperatures that would keep others inside. The cold air helps me think."

Brant shook his head, but Corwyn told her they would see to the horses.

As she'd expected, the park was deserted. She was able to canter, unencumbered by other riders. When she'd gone about halfway around the loop, Brant rode up beside her. "Two men are keeping you in their sights, Lady Reddington. I'm going to stay by your side while Corwyn sees to them."

"How do you know they are following me? This is a popular public path."

"Milady, I must ask ye to trust us."

She nodded her assent. It was foolish to take chances.

Following Brant's lead, she exited the park and turned onto a well-populated street. Servants carried baskets of household goods, and ladies who refused to let foul weather ruin a day of shopping rushed by with their maids. After a few moments, Corwyn rode up on Cassandra's other side. Looking at Brant, he said, "The men've turned 'round. I'm thinkin' they gave up when Brant joined you, my lady." He leaned forward to look at Brant. "Should I try to track 'em?"

156

Brant nodded and Corwyn turned his horse around.

"What did the men look like?" Cassandra asked.

"One was thin and blond with a big nose. The other looked like one of those frog-faced chaps Mr. Foxwood warned us about."

"It sounds like the blond man who attacked me last night." Cassandra shivered, remembering his cold hands on her.

"Aye, from the description Mr. Foxwood gave, it's likely him, milady."

Cassandra arrived home without further incident. Corwyn arrived shortly after she had settled herself in the library. He reported that he followed the men until they entered a tavern. Then he slipped a boy some coins to stay and watch for them to exit. He'd promised the lad more if he showed up at Cassandra's address with useful information.

Cassandra thanked Corwyn, and he returned to his post in front of the house. She shuddered as she thought what might have happened had Mark not provided her with guards. And she dreaded telling Mark about the incident. He would likely forbid her to leave the house again. At least she could have a pleasant visit with her sister before that confrontation.

ରେ ରେ ରେ

A servant showed Mark to the study where Stanton sat reclined in a chair, a brandy in his hand, despite the early hour. "Foxwood, what the devil is going on with you? Since when do you tempt fate by running around with the wife of a man like Reddington? I knew you were living on the edge, but isn't that a bit extreme."

"Reddington is dead." So much for his carefully planned explanation. Stanton had always known how to evoke a rash response from him.

"I hadn't heard this. Not that I mourn the bastard, but what happened?"

"No one knows except his wife, his valet and his solicitor. He was killed in France. The men responsible are after Lady Reddington now. Based on that and...some other reasons, his death has not been announced."

"How the hell did you get involved?"

"Earlier this week, Lady Reddington was shot on my land."

"Shot? My God."

"We have neighboring estates in Devon. She was riding and a bullet grazed her temple. The culprit was a groom from Reddington Abbey. He'd been hired to eliminate her."

"And you helped her recover by bringing her to your bed?" Stanton shook his head. "I thought you went out to that godforsaken, freezing castle to be alone."

"I did, but she is not an easy woman to resist. Besides, she had no one to protect her besides Loring, her husband's valet is a good man, but he's too old to fend off murderers."

"And you volunteered to risk your life to help her? You. The man who said he would never care for a woman again?"

"I could hardly leave her to the mercy of her husband's enemies. I hope you don't think I've sunk that far below civilized society."

"I would say you have sunk quite low, my friend, but for all your extremely rough edges, you are quite the chivalrous gentleman. I've said before that you should have been a knight."

"I did not come here to have my faults examined," Mark snapped. "I simply wanted you to understand why I needed the information I asked for."

Stanton swirled his brandy. "Is she as passionate as she looks?"

A wave of rage rolled over Mark. He had to remind himself that his friend meant no harm. They had often discussed their female conquests before. Still, he could hardly keep his voice level. "I will pretend you did not ask that. Don't make such a mistake again."

"So you *do* feel more for her than lust. I suspected as much."

"Stanton, I value your friendship. Cease this line of conversation, or I will forget my feelings and do you bodily harm."

"Do forgive me. I am only happy to see that Katryn did not wound you as badly as I had feared. I'm pleased to see you acting like your old self again. I was afraid I had lost my friend to that greedy bitch."

Mark lifted his brow and stared at his friend, willing him to change the subject.

Stanton did as he was bid. "What can I do to help you protect Lady Reddington?"

"Go about your usual business but listen for any mention of Reddington, the Lintons or this man called The Cat. We think Reddington kidnapped women and shipped them to France likely to work in brothels or to be sold to men seeking pleasure slaves."

"My God." Stanton sat up straight. "That is deplorable."

Mark nodded. "Cassandra is quite certain he forced young women to entertain at parties that he gave, but we know little else except that he was killed in France. The groom who tried to kill Cassandra said the Frenchman who hired him was angry because he had not received a shipment Reddington owed him. He implied that the cargo in question was young women."

"You believe this is connected to Miss Caroline's?"

"Yes, only because Reddington had a stake in it. A brothel would be a good place to train women before sending them away."

"I'll inquire about an appointment with Simone tonight."

"I plan to go to Miss Caroline's as well. You should call on me tomorrow if you learn anything."

Mark stood to leave, but Stanton called to him.

"I know you don't want my advice," his friend said. "But if I were you, I wouldn't let Cassandra go."

Mark left without saying a word.

Chapter Fifteen

When a maid showed Mark into the drawing room, Cassandra thought he looked especially impressive in a sapphire jacket and camel-colored waistcoat. The blue made his hair appear more blond than usual, and its brightness emphasized the broadness of his chest.

Amanda looked suitably impressed. Her cheeks had grown red, and Cassandra wasn't sure she'd ever seen her sister smile so broadly.

"Mr. Foxwood, this is my sister, Miss Halverston." Amanda looked at her slippers, making herself appear every inch the shy debutante Cassandra knew she'd never been. "Amanda, this is Mr. Foxwood."

Mark took her hand and bowed to kiss it. For a moment, Cassandra was actually afraid her sister was going to faint. "I am pleased to make your acquaintance, Miss Halverston. You are every bit as beautiful as your sister."

After Mark had been seated, Cassandra rang for tea, trying to suppress a laugh as she watched Mark and Amanda act their prescribed roles for each other.

Mark turned a knee-melting smile on Amanda. "Do I understand correctly that the past Season was your first?"

"Yes, sir." She had a disturbingly dreamy smile on her face. "My aunt, Lady Morgan, was kind enough to sponsor me."

"Have you enjoyed your time in London?"

The frown on her face brought back the sister Cassandra knew. "I must admit I find the constant round of balls and parties tedious."

Mark laughed. "I am pleased to see you are as forthright as your sister."

Amanda blushed. "I hope I did not give offense."

"Not in the least. It's gratifying to meet a young woman with more on her mind than dress fabric or the bobbles one can put on a hat. I take it you have not been intimidated by the dangers that await young women in London."

Amanda smiled. "Oh, no. Cassandra saw to that. She gave me excellent advice on how to avoid scandal."

Mark turned to Cassandra and smiled. "I am sure she did. I can only imagine what she must have said. I am quite sure she warned you away from men like me. If we meet at a ball, I expect my offer of a dance to be refused."

Amanda blushed again. "Perhaps, but I think you are more honest than most of the men I've met. I wouldn't have shunned you quite so thoroughly."

"Yes, but I would have spoken honestly about my desire for you as well. I fear that would have given you pause."

Amanda giggled, something Cassandra had never seen her do in front of a man. Amanda was thoroughly charmed. Cassandra imagined she would now hear nothing from Amanda but how delightful Mark was. Despite that, Cassandra enjoyed watching the banter between them.

She wondered if, after all her warnings, her sister had ever experienced this type of light, congenial flirtation. Amanda appeared to be holding her own. Perhaps she had practiced her skills while Cassandra was in the country, or perhaps Amanda had more natural talent for flirtation than Cassandra would have guessed.

Mark cleared his throat and looked at Amanda. "I would hate to spoil our delightful conversation by reminding you of the danger you sister is in, but I must ask if you have seen Reddington or either of the Linton twins during the Season."

Amanda frowned. "Reddington would not dare show his face at any of the events Aunt Claire has escorted me to, but the Lintons are occasionally invited to respectable parties. Their mother is extremely generous. She is involved with many charitable endeavors. I cannot understand how she managed to rear two such offensive sons."

Mark smiled. "Did you have the misfortune of speaking to either of the twins recently?"

"They had the gall to approach me at a ball given by the Countess of Tregar. We had not been introduced, but that did not stop them from pressing their attention on me. I gave them a set down, and they slunk off in defeat."

Neither Mark nor Cassandra could stifle their laughter "I would like to have seen that," Cassandra said. "What did Aunt Claire have to say?"

"She congratulated me and told me to give them the cut direct if they should approach me again."

Mark smiled. "Excellent advice. At the parties where you have seen them, was anyone willing to suffer their attention?"

"I can't recall seeing them talk to anyone I recognized except…" She paused and her cheeks grew rosy. "Lady Southwood."

Cassandra gave Mark a worried glance, and he put an end to his questioning.

As they discussed the lighter side of Amanda's experiences in London, Mark conducted himself like a handsome rake who knew exactly how to seduce a woman without her even knowing he was playing for her. By the time they finished the last of the scones and biscuits, Amanda, her practical, often cynical sister would have followed him anywhere.

She was seeing a side of them both that she had never seen before. Was this the relaxed, flirtatious man Mark had been before Katryn? And was the hostility that stirred in her inspired by jealousy? As much as it horrified her, she knew it was. She was jealous of the ease with which Mark interacted with her little sister. If only he could be that comfortable with her. If only they could spend even a few hours in each other's company without arguing.

As Cassandra walked her sister to the door, Amanda took her arm and whispered, "He wasn't arrogant or overbearing at all. In fact, I thought him one of the nicest men I've met since my come out."

A Carnal Agreement

"That is exactly why he can seduce women so easily. He wrapped you around his finger before you finished a cup of tea. He is subtle, and that makes his type the most dangerous of all."

"If he is all you say, you would not have stayed with him."

"I had little choice in the matter."

"You chose to fight Reddington's will, and you chose Mr. Foxwood to help you. Another man would have done as well."

Cassandra sighed. "Perhaps even I am not strong enough to resist his charms."

"Perhaps you should stop trying." Amanda hugged her sister good-bye.

Cassandra leaned against the door for a few moments, trying to ignore the temptation of her sister's words.

"Well, you certainly charmed her," she said when she rejoined Mark in the drawing room. "It was such a treat to see the Foxwood seduction method in action."

A sly smile spread across his face. "I'm glad I amused you."

"Was that a performance just now, or was that the man I might have known if I'd met you before…"

"Before Katryn?"

She nodded.

He avoided a direct answer. "I've found that it often helps to give people what they expect. Your sister expected me to be a rakish gentleman who would flirt and play with her but would not harm her because her sister was present."

"You didn't have to pretend for her. She wanted to meet you, because you sparked her curiosity. I'd already told her about you."

"I imagine you told her I was insufferable and far too willing to order you around."

There was no point in denying it. "Yes, I did."

"Then I chose wisely. I showed her what she wanted to see, not what you were hoping to show her. I could not give you the satisfaction of having your sister agree with you."

"You *are* insufferable, but I don't think the arrogant, overbearing man whom I love to thwart is the real you either. The real Mark Foxwood is the man who comes to bed with me. The man who concerns himself with my pleasure while heightening his. He's the one who…" Could she do it? Could she confess her regard for him?

"Who what?" Mark asked, his voice only a whisper.

"Who affects me most powerfully."

Heat rose in her cheeks. Her heart raced. She had almost told Mark she loved him. And only the night before she'd resolved to exert more control over her emotions.

He smiled like a large, hungry cat and pulled her into his arms, but she pushed him away and ducked from the circle of his arms, turning to gaze at the fire.

He came behind her and spun her to face him. His eyes showed confusion and pain. "Cassandra, what's wrong?"

"Nothing. I'm sorry. I did not mean to be rude. I was thinking how nice it would be to spend more than five minutes alone with you without us ripping each other's clothes off."

He drew in a breath and exhaled sharply. "I thought I was supposed to do everything in my power to make sure you have a child."

She smiled. "I think there is little more we could do without physically harming themselves."

Mark smiled. "Our appetites are rather impressive, aren't they?"

She smiled, hoping to reassure him. "I suppose so, and I am not complaining, truly. It's only that I do enjoy your company—when we aren't arguing that is—and I thought maybe we could—"

"Forget that Reddington ever existed. And spend a nice quiet afternoon talking to one another."

Cassandra smiled. "Can such a rakish gentleman spend an afternoon in conversation?"

"I'm as tired of the drama we've experienced in the last few days as you are. I know we're not safe and won't be until this is over, but I would like to pretend we are for a few hours."

"I would like that very much."

"Do you play?" he asked, gesturing toward the chess set in the corner.

"Yes. My cousin, Edward, taught me when I was ten."

"Is this the same cousin you wrote to about Reddington's crimes?"

"Yes, he's five years my elder, and he spent the summers with my family when I was little. My sisters and I all worshipped him, me especially, because he treated me like an equal rather than a silly female."

"He sounds remarkable. I might become jealous if you continue to list his merits."

Cassandra smiled. "He has faults like anyone else, but he is a crack shot and an excellent chess player."

"I will not even ask if he passed along his shooting abilities as well."

She laughed. "I'm certain you would not like the answer."

Mark moved the table containing the chess set, positioned it by the fire, and gestured for her to join him. "I do hope your cousin is as good a player as you say. It would be nice to experience some small challenge before I beat you."

"My, aren't we arrogant?"

"You may be good, but you are not as good as me."

She scowled at him. "I'd planned to go easy on you, but you are in for it now."

"As you say, my lady." Mark made a mocking bow.

Cassandra settled herself on a pillow by the table, but a knock interrupted them.

"Come in," she called.

Corwyn stood in the doorway. As soon as she saw him, Cassandra realized she had neglected to tell Mark about the incident in the park. He was going to be furious.

"Did the messenger boy return?"

"Yes, milady. He did and he was most helpful."

Mark looked both puzzled. "What's happened?"

"I went for a ride in the park this morning."

Mark jaw hardened in anger "I take it something more happened than you freezing your lovely behind."

She nodded. "Two men followed me. Brant saw me safely home and Corwyn followed them to a tavern. He left a messenger boy with instructions to spy on them and bring any information he learned here.

"And what did he learn?"

"The blond one, he's French. His name's Gaston. The frog one was real anxious to please him. They talked about getting another woman since they lost the last one, and Gaston told the other one he better not fu—I mean mess up again or he would not get another chance."

"Thank you, Corwyn. You've been most helpful."

"Glad to be of service, Mr. Foxwood. Let me know what else you need." He turned and closed the door behind him.

Cassandra spoke quickly, hoping to avoid Mark's anger. "Why would Gaston kill Reddington, but continue to work with the Lintons?"

"I wondered the same thing. Perhaps they set him up. Didn't you say they had planned to accompany him to France but changed their minds?"

"I did, but I cannot imagine them having the will or the brains to devise such a scheme. I would wager they had help."

"The Cat?"

She nodded.

"I think you are right. In the spirit of attempting to spend a pleasant afternoon, I will refrain from asking why you failed to mention this incident.

However, you will not be visiting the park anymore until this is finished. In fact, I think it best you not leave the house I am with you."

"Didn't you hire guards so I could be protected when I am not with you. And didn't they do their job today?"

"Yes, but they cannot stay as close to you as I can."

"I will not be a prisoner here."

"There is no need for that. I will accompany you anywhere you need to go."

"Yes, but I will have to wait until you are available. I don't—"

"Cassandra, I thought we weren't going to argue today."

"It's impossible. We can't talk without arguing."

He didn't respond. Instead, he continued setting up the board as if their argument had never happened. When he was done, he looked up. "Could I interest you in a wager?"

She considered refusing to accept the change of subject, but rather than be spiteful, she said, "What do you propose?"

"The loser promises to fulfill a fantasy for the winner." His smile made him look every inch the predator. "I know exactly what I will have you do when I win."

His voice was low and husky and heat surged through Cassandra. She also knew what she wanted to do to him when *she* won. She held out her hand for him to shake. "Challenge accepted."

Mark loved watching Cassandra contemplating her moves. Her brow furrowed, and she nibbled on the tip of her index finger then ran it across her lower lip. He longed to lick the same path as her finger. To chew on it in the same manner and then nibble her other fingers, her palm, her wrist, and… He had to stop the direction of his thoughts if he wanted to survive their afternoon of celibacy. His body already ached for her.

Of course he was going to a brothel that evening. Why should he deny himself what he was going to have to pay for anyway? It wasn't as if the women there wouldn't be willing to satisfy him, apparently they would do anything he asked, no matter how kinky. But he had promised Cassandra he would do nothing other than talk to them, and he would not go back on his word.

He'd had enough expensive whores in the last six months to last him a lifetime. All he wanted now was Cassandra. Unless of course one of Miss Caroline's girls could break the spell Cassandra had cast over him. They surely received all manner of odd requests, but he wondered if anyone had ever asked if they could purge a man's heart of inconvenient feeling. He imagined himself engaging the infamous Simone and begging her to do something so extraordinary that he no longer ached to make Cassandra his.

Simone might think she could fulfill this need, but she could not. No woman, no matter how talented could make him forget Cassandra. He wanted to spend every night in her bed, but worse, he wanted to spend more afternoons like this talking and enjoying her company. He wanted to know everything about her.

He watched in horror as she moved her bishop, putting his king in check. He'd been distracted by her charms, and now her success was inevitable. At least he could delay his humiliation for a little while. "I enjoyed meeting Amanda. Do I remember correctly that you also have another sister?"

Cassandra looked up surprised. "Why do you ask?"

"This is supposed to be an afternoon of congenial conversation. I thought it would be nice to know more about your family."

Her forehead wrinkled and her eyes narrowed. "You're sure? I don't want to bore you."

"Cassandra, I don't imagine you could ever bore me."

He watched the color come into her face. God, she was beautiful with her cheeks all flushed. He preferred for such color to come from desire rather than embarrassment, but it was lovely just the same.

"I am the oldest of three sisters. The youngest of us, Elise is finishing her last year in the schoolroom. She will move to London to live with Aunt Claire this summer. My aunt will sponsor her first Season the following year."

"Your aunt and not your mother?"

"Yes. Thanks to Amanda. You had a rather disastrous effect on her wits so you may not have noticed, but she is extremely determined and can be quite forceful when she needs to be."

"She wouldn't have learned this from her older sister, would she?"

Cassandra laughed. "She has taken after me in many things. I am afraid I am not very good at keeping my advice to myself, at least not where she is concerned."

"Really?" He let his eyes grow wide in false shock.

She rolled her eyes. "Oh, do hush. Amanda is only two years younger than me and should have been presented in London already, but my father hoped to make a match for her among the men near his estate in Surrey.

"She refused several offers, and father intended to force her to marry a man old enough to be our grandfather as punishment for her recalcitrance. He threatened to harm her if she refused. I don't know exactly what he said. She hasn't been willing to tell me. She had no choice but to run away."

Mark shook his head, fascinated by these strong women. "How did she get away without being harmed?"

"She sold some of her jewelry in the village, pretending father had asked her to sell it for him. A likely story since his gambling debts are legendary. That night, she climbed out of her window in a driving rainstorm and took the stage to London. When she showed up at Aunt Claire's house, she apparently looked little better than a drowned rat. My aunt's butler mistook her for one of the scullery maids.

"Our aunt was frantic but surprisingly supportive. I think she finally had all she could take of my father's ill treatment of us, and her recent marriage to Lord Morgan has given her enough money to support two girls. Amanda has lived with her since that night. I don't know what Aunt Claire said to my father, but he consented to let her sponsor both Amanda and Elise."

Mark listened with rapt attention to Cassandra's explanation. Plenty of fathers threatened their daughters and forced them into horrid marriages, but still it sickened him. If he ever met Cassandra's father, he didn't think he could restrain himself from showing the man exactly what he thought of his behavior.

Cassandra looked lost in the grip of unpleasant memories. He laid his hand over hers. "I admire your sister for what she did. She obviously learned from your strength."

Cassandra sighed. "But I gave in. I did what was asked of me."

"You married Reddington to spare your sisters. *You* chose your path. If you hadn't been concerned for their welfare, you would have found a way out like Amanda did."

"I should have tried harder to find another solution. I should have thought about going to Aunt Claire."

Mark took her hand and enfolded it in his own. "Do you think she would have overridden your father at that point? Or do you think it took what happened to you to push her over the edge?"

"I suppose it did. I guess it's selfish, but I often wish I could have saved them and myself too."

Mark came around the table and pulled her into his arms. "You've stayed sane and determined though an experience that would have drained the spirit from most women. Sometimes pain like that serves to make us stronger."

And in that moment, Mark knew he truly needed Cassandra, not as someone to warm his bed for a few months, but forever. He wanted to marry her, but he dared not ask. She would refuse. She would insist on her damned independence.

At least she wouldn't turn him down because he was a bastard. She wasn't concerned with what society thought, only with not being vulnerable to pain again. That thought gave him hope.

He would wait, see what he could do to convince her of the idea. But if she became pregnant with his child, she would marry him. He would give her no choice.

She brushed his hair from his forehead. "Are you stronger now after what you have been through?

Mark's chest tightened. Had it made him stronger? It had made him more defensive, more willing to believe the worst about people, and less willing to trust his instincts. However, it had made him study people more carefully and made him listen to his intuition.

He wanted to tell Cassandra about the hell he'd been through with Katryn. But he was afraid that if he talked about it, all the horror he had overcome would return, and he would not be able to handle seeing Katryn again. "Cassandra, I can't talk about Katryn right now. I'm sorry. I just can't."

"I understand." She caressed his cheek. The simple touch of her fingers warmed him, making the cold sickness melt away.

He looked up to see Cassandra smiling. "By the way, I hope you don't think you've distracted me so thoroughly that I forgot about the game." She turned to the board and moved her rook forward, taking his bishop. "Checkmate."

Chapter Sixteen

Mark had heard of Miss Caroline's when he and Katryn attended parties given by Langley's set. Stanton and several of his other friends had recommended it during his six months of non-stop debauchery. He had frequently considered availing himself of what the women there had to offer, and he certainly had not avoided it for any moral reason. His lack of enthusiasm stemmed from the fact that Miss Caroline catered to men of the *ton*, and he strived to avoid everyone who reminded him of Katryn.

A footman opened the door and showed him into the drawing room where Lady Caroline herself would help him make his selection from the available girls. He was startled by the lack of overstuffed furniture, garish colors, and overly painted women he'd come to associate with brothels.

Miss Caroline's drawing room could have been in a townhouse on Grosvenor Square, except that the women's attire would have scandalized society matrons. The decor was tasteful, and the women were truly beautiful. They wore simple dresses that showed off their various charms. Their hair and faces were unadorned. They did not need paint to distract from their flawless skin.

The footman directed him to a settee and told him Lady Caroline would join him shortly. He took the time to study the women who were entertaining gentlemen in the salon, wondering if any of them were unengaged for the evening and would fit his needs. One, a petite redhead, looked extremely young and rather shy. He wondered what had brought her there and hoped she had not been forced to this life.

Perhaps he would inquire about her. A young girl would be less likely to know the ins and outs of how the brothel was run. However, she would be more easily coerced into telling him what she did know.

An older woman whose ebony hair could not have been natural approached him. She looked to be nearly fifty, though her body had not an extra ounce of flesh on it.

"Mr. Foxwood?"

He nodded. "Miss Caroline?"

"I am she. How can I help you tonight, Mr. Foxwood?" She sat down beside him and allowed her hand to fall on his thigh. "I will do *anything* necessary, she paused and her hand slid up his thigh to lie tauntingly close to his cock, "to see that you are thoroughly satisfied with your experience."

A few months ago, he would have played the game with her, flirting, telling her exactly what she could do for him. He would have been aroused by it, at least his body would have. His soul would have remained as dead as ever. Tonight, he wanted only to fulfill his obligations. "Thank you. I was wondering about the redhead by the window."

"Ah yes, Caitlin. What are you are looking for this evening? All our girls have specialties. Caitlin is very popular with men who like young girls."

Mark imagined she would be. Even before Cassandra, when he was at his worst, he would not have slept with a woman who looked so young. The thought of pretending she was younger made him feel ill.

"Yes, I can see that she would be. Does she have any other talents?"

Miss Caroline grinned. "She gives the most beautiful reactions to pain. I do think she rather relishes it."

Mark forced himself to smile. She might well be one of the girls Reddington had "recruited."

Miss Caroline slid her hand further up his leg. Thankfully his body responded as it should to a woman's caress, despite his discomfort with the surroundings. "I see that appeals to you. Should you like to spend the evening with her then?"

"Only a few hours. I'm afraid I have an early engagement tomorrow."

After they agreed on a price, Miss Caroline beckoned for Caitlin to join them. She whispered something to the younger woman, probably instructions for how to handle him then ordered her to take Mark upstairs. Caitlin said nothing as they ascended. She would not look him in the eye. What did she fear he would do to her? He shuddered to think of it.

She opened the door to a room and stood aside while he entered, keeping her head bowed. Luckily there were two chairs placed by a fireplace along with the large, sumptuously decorated bed. It would be easier to convince her to talk if they sat. He pushed a chair closer to the fire, hoping to warm himself, though his coldness came from his horror of what Reddington and his accomplices had done.

Caitlin approached him, looking concerned, probably because he had chosen to recline here rather than get down to business. She knelt before him. "I am yours. You may use me as you wish." She sounded frightfully soulless as if she were a clockwork toy someone gifted with speech.

He brushed his knuckles across her cheek. "Caitlin." She flinched. She clasped her hands against her sides. He saw them shaking. "Look at me."

She looked up, her eyes filled with terror. What could he do to put her at ease? "I don't want to use you. I don't know what Lady Caroline told you about me, but I have no desire to harm you. In fact, I only want to talk to you."

He thought reassuring her would help, but tears came to her eyes. "Tell me how to please you. I will do anything."

Her hands formed fists and her eyes closed as if she fought not to cry. His anger made him want to charge downstairs and tear Lady Caroline apart. Then he would start on the men who owned this place followed by every man who condoned it by taking their pleasure with women who were obviously scared to death.

He slipped out of the chair and knelt on the floor in front of her. Taking her hands in his own, he realized how cold they were. He rubbed them vigorously as he spoke. "It would please me if you would sit here by the fire and talk to me."

Her eyes widened even more. A few tears spilled onto her cheeks. "W-why?"

"Why do I want to talk?"

She nodded.

"I need some information about the owners of this establishment."

"Please tell me what you want from me. I am very well-trained. I can—"

"Stop. I want only to talk." She pulled her hands free of his and began sliding her chemise from her shoulders, but he stopped her. "No, Caitlin. Stop." He pulled the garment back into place.

"I don't know how to play this game."

"This is no game. I need information, and you can help me. When I get the answers I need, I'm going to find a way to help you. You don't have to be scared anymore."

She looked so panicked then that he thought she would run. He reached out and cupped her face, forcing her to look him in the eye. "I promise I will not hurt you."

"*She* will."

"Who?"

"Miss Caroline will hurt me if I don't do as I'm told. She told me you wanted—"

He pressed his finger to her lips, not wanting to know what had been said about him. "I swear I will make no complaints. She will never know."

"But she will. She will see that you did not mark me."

He'd never thought of that, never thought that the level of a man's enjoyment would be measured by the harm he'd done to a woman's body. It made his stomach churn. "I will make whatever explanation is necessary to see you are not punished, but I will not harm you. I would never force any kind of attention on a woman"

Caitlin started to cry then, gentle tears at first and then wracking sobs. Mark pulled her into his arms and held her tightly.

When she quieted, he scooped her up, set her in the other chair, and covered her with a blanket. "How long have you been working here?"

"About a month."

He poured two glasses of brandy from the decanter on the bedside table and handed her a glass. She took a drink and nearly choked.

"It's strong. Sip slowly."

She made another attempt, this time managing to swallow without coughing.

Mark smiled. "Do you know who owns this place?"

She almost dropped her glass but managed to tighten her grip on it before any of the liquid spilled. "I cannot tell you that."

"You must. I want to help you and the other girls."

"Most of them want to be here. They like it."

"But you don't?"

"Please, I cannot talk about this."

"I need you to tell me who owns the place."

She took a deep breath and closed her eyes. "Everyone is afraid of those men, even Lady Caroline. I have…been with several of them, but there's one man I've never seen. He's called The Cat."

"Do you know his real name?"

Her eyes widened, and she vigorously shook her head.

"Caitlin, please. A friend of mine is in trouble. Her husband is dead and someone is trying to kill her. I believe the men who own this place are responsible."

"He will kill me. I'm not supposed to know anything."

"I'll do everything I can to protect you." He walked over, knelt by her chair, and brushed the hair from her tear-stained face. "Please."

"Southwood."

The word was said so quietly, he barely heard it. It was so shocking he had to repeat it himself to make sure he wasn't mistaken. "Southwood? Lord Southwood?"

"I overheard Lady Caroline talking to Mr. Linton, about him. That was the name they used. That's all I know. I promise."

Lord Southwood. Mark would never have guessed. No wonder he accepted Katryn's behavior. He was obviously even more depraved than she. Had she known this when she accepted his proposal? Surely she had. It must have been the real reason for her choice.

"Do you know the names of the other men?"

"Lord Reddington and a second Mr. Linton. They are brothers."

As he stood, he leaned over and kissed her on the top of the head. "Thank you so much, Caitlin. You do not know how much this information means. I need to ask you another question."

She nodded again and took a sip of her brandy.

"Did one of those men force you to come here?"

More tears flooded her eyes, and she turned her face towards the back of the chair. Mark wanted to comfort her, to tell her it would be all right. But he couldn't guarantee her safety, no matter how much he wanted to.

"Caitlin, please, I need you to tell me this."

"It was my fault. I was so foolish."

"You have been hurt, and that is not your fault. Let me help you."

She shook her head. "You can't. I've ruined my life, and no one can help me now."

"Tell me what happened." He spoke sternly, knowing he had to prevent her dissolving into hysterics.

She took a deep breath and turned to face him. "I took a job as a maid in Mr. Oscar Linton's house. I didn't like him, but I needed the work, and it was all I could find. He tried to take advantage of me, to kiss me and touch me where he shouldn't. I refused his advances, but he was unconcerned."

She paused to wipe tears from her eyes. "One night, he came to my room. He'd been drinking. He could hardly stand, but he managed to pull me from my bed and throw me against the wall. He screamed at me, told me he was tired of my refusals. He said I worked for him, and I would do what he said. I was terrified. I hit him with a pitcher and got away."

Mark wanted to reach out to her, to give her comfort, but he was afraid she would stop talking if he did.

"I...I took some money from his jacket pocket and ran. I should never have stolen from him, but I did not know what to do. I had nothing of my own, because he had not yet paid me for the work I had done.

"He must have recovered quickly. He and his brother found me not long after. I still don't know how they tracked me. They told me I could either come work for them, or they would turn me over to the authorities. I agreed to this. They took me home and both of them had me that night."

"Oh Caitlin, I'm so sorry." He reached for her, but she pushed his hands away.

"There's nothing you can do. I made a mistake. I'm stuck here now. Maybe it would have been better to let myself hang as a thief."

"Are there others who were brought here by coercion?"

"Yes."

"Do you know if any of them have been taken to another house or even out of England?"

"Two girls who came to work after I did disappeared a few nights ago. There are rumors about where they are. Some of us think they're dead, but they could have been taken away."

"Were they scared like you or did they like it here?"

"They didn't like it, but they didn't talk much. They..."

She shuddered and did not say anything else.

"They what?"

Abject fear returned to her face. She shook her head violently. "It's not important."

Mark decided not to push her further. "I want you to leave with me tonight."

"Southwood would hunt you down and kill you. I know you want to help, but it would be better if you never came back. I can't leave now, it is too late…" Sobs poured out of her again.

Mark gripped her shoulders. "Why?"

She shook her head.

"Please, Caitlin, more lives are at stake. What is it you are trying to hide from me?"

She shook her head violently. "I cannot leave with you. Accept that and go"

If he left her there, she would be abused by her next customer. He could brag about his satisfaction to Miss Caroline, but he could not protect her from other men. However, she was right, if he tried to smuggle her out, someone would come looking for them and be led straight to Cassandra. He needed time to use the knowledge he had gained if he wanted to help Caitlin and the others?

"I'm going to go downstairs and tell Lady Caroline that I changed my mind, and I want you for the whole evening. If I tell her you won't even need time off to heal, because I know how to hurt a woman without leaving any evidence, will that keep you safe from her retaliation?"

She blew her nose on the handkerchief he handed her. "It should, but you don't have to do that."

"Yes, I do."

"Please, you don't understand. These men would not mind killing you. In fact, they would probably enjoy it."

He laid his hand on her head. "I can protect myself. I'll come back upstairs to check on you. Then I'll slip out the window. I want you to get in bed and get some rest."

When he got back upstairs, he told her the address of Cassandra's house and made sure she committed it to memory. He told her that if she had a chance to escape, she would be welcomed there, but he doubted she would come.

As he was opening the window, she wrapped her fingers around his arm. "They don't give us time to heal. They use us for their own entertainment until we are pretty enough for men to pay for us again."

Rage clouded Mark's vision. "I will stop them if I have to wring their necks with my bare hands." He was damn sorry Reddington couldn't be resurrected so he could kill him again.

He had intended to return to his rooms after he left, but he needed to feel Cassandra's warm arms around him and know that she was alive and safe. Caitlin's story had shaken him to the core. How many women had Reddington and his friends treated in such a fashion? He needed the reassurance Cassandra could give him. When he was in her arms, he felt invincible.

Never would he have connected Southwood—a man who had never seemed capable of organizing anything more important than his cravat drawer—with such a sickening operation. At Eton, and later at Oxford, Southwood had come across as vapid and prideful. He'd walked around as if he had a rod stuck up his ass, but he had always struck Mark and his friends as rather prudish. He was annoying to be sure, but never did Mark get a sense of evil around him. Reddington and the Lintons wore their evil like cologne.

∝ ∝ ∝

Cassandra was still awake, sipping tea by the fire when he arrived. "Why aren't you in bed?"

"I couldn't sleep. I kept thinking about you and what you were doing."

Mark tensed with anger. "I told you I would not lie with the women there, and I didn't"

She shook her head and smiled. "No, I didn't worry about that. I feared someone would realize why you were there and try to…kill you." She held out her arms and he joined her on the settee. He pulled her into his arms, and she cradled his head against her chest. "I'm glad you're here."

He caressed her back and whispered. "I'm glad I'm here too."

She'd never seen him look so defeated or so tired. "What happened?"

He told her about Southwood's involvement first, because it was easier to talk about than the pain Caitlin had suffered. When he did tell Caitlin's story, he became so choked he could barely speak. He explained that he forced himself to leave her there and was sick that he'd done it partly to protect himself.

Cassandra held him tight against her and didn't say anything for a long time. "Katryn was a fool to leave you. You are the most compassionate man I've ever met."

His arms tightened around her waist. "I still want to strangle her every time I see her."

"She deserves far worse than that."

He pulled away and looked into her eyes. "I thought I loved her. Can you believe that? I thought I loved a woman who now makes my skin crawl."

"Even as a girl she excelled at manipulation. A man would have to be a saint to resist her physical charms."

"She deceived me so well. That's what I can't get over. At first I thought I would be miserable without her. Then I realized I had been in love with a woman who does not exist. The real Katryn is nothing but a bitch."

He stood and walked across the room. He braced himself against a table and looked at the floor. Cassandra wished she knew what to say. What could she do to heal him? If she got the chance, she would strangle Katryn herself.

"I tried everything to rid myself of her influence. But memories plagued me, the feel of her skin caressing mine, the cold look in her eyes when she refused my proposal. Nothing worked until…"

Cassandra's heart beat frantically. "Until what?"

He shook his head, still not looking at her. "Nothing. I'm sorry."

"Mark, I said I would listen whenever you were ready to talk about her. I meant it."

He pushed away from the table and walked toward one of the tall windows. "She ruined my hopes of ever marrying. I can no longer trust anyone."

Cassandra came up behind him and tugged on his arm until he turned to face her. "Do you trust me?"

The depth of emotion in his eyes made her want to back away. But she stood her ground, knowing he needed to think this through.

He held her gaze for several seconds and then turned away again. "I'm afraid to, more afraid than I've ever been of anything."

She traced the firm muscles of his shoulders, visible even through his jacket. "I won our wager yesterday. I am ready to fulfill my fantasy, but for me to do that, you will have to trust me."

That got his attention. He whirled around to face her again. "What do you want?"

"I want to see if you enjoy surrendering as much as I did."

In a matter of seconds wonder, desire, ecstasy crossed his face. He held his hand out to her. "Let's go upstairs."

Her heart pounded. Could she really do this? "Mark, I—"

"Don't you dare back out on me. You knew what you wanted last night, didn't you?"

"I did. I've thought about it since you…actually since the party. I mean, I've wondered if you would enjoy such a thing."

"Yes, I would enjoy it." The smile he gave her was enough to banish her concerns.

When they entered her room, she took a deep breath, gathering her courage. "Take off your clothes."

He complied without hesitation. She watched, giving herself permission to do nothing but enjoy the beauty of his form. His jacket hit the floor, followed by his cravat and his waistcoat. When he lifted his shirt over his head, her breath caught. Would she ever stop feeling lightheaded at the sight of his wonderful body?

He caught her eye and smiled as he stood bare-chested before her. "Wait," she said when his hands went to the waist of his breeches.

His hands dropped to his sides, and he watched her intently.

"Sit down on the bed."

He did as he was asked. She knelt before him and removed his boots. She looked up at him and felt heat rise in her cheeks. "You know how you enjoy kissing me down there?"

"Down there?"

"Between my legs."

"Yes, indeed I do."

"I was wondering if you would like that too." His eyes widened, and she held her breath.

"Cassandra, I would like that so much I think you'd better tie me up first. I won't be able to let you lead otherwise."

Her cheeks heated even more, but she smiled, glad she'd been bold enough to ask. "Take off your pants and lie down."

She opened her wardrobe and took out the ties he had made from her chemise. After he had left the night before, she had removed them from the bedposts and saved them, hoping they would be able to use them again.

She glanced at the bed and realized he was watching her, following every move she made. Pure animal lust showed in his eyes. Could she possibly hope to restrain such power, to have control over his body or his heart?

No, she would not think about his heart. This relationship would not outlast their bargain. She simply had to make the best of the time she had.

The more she watched him watching her, the hotter her body grew. She was more than ready to couple with him and part of her wanted to climb right on top of him and sink down onto his hard shaft. But she would not let her impatience spoil her fantasy. She wanted to see how he would react to being restrained even more than she wanted immediate release.

"Stretch your arms over your head." He did as she asked. She tied the arm closest to her. "Is that too tight?"

He pulled against it and shook his head. She tied the other one and let one of her hands trace the line of his side. When she reached his hips, she lingered, making circles with her nail closer and closer to the part of him that visibly throbbed for her.

He sucked in his breath, and she stopped. She let her hands continue down his leg, grasping his ankle and wrapping the silk around it. She bent to let her tongue flick across the pulse near the circular bone of his foot. He gasped and strained against his bonds.

She laughed. "It's not easy to keep still, is it?"

"Cassandra, you had better tie my other leg, now."

She took his other ankle and pulled against his leg, encouraging him to stretch it out for her.

When she had him completely restrained, she stepped back and looked down at him. "Tell me how it feels."

"Cassandra," he voice was low, threatening.

"You love it, don't you? You love knowing I can do anything to you."

Mark's hands gripped the slats in the headboard, and he pulled so hard he feared the bed would break. She was making him crazy. Seeing her revel in her sexual power was enough to bring him to the very edge of release. He did not know if he could bear the touch of her mouth.

Moving to stand by his head, Cassandra brushed something across his skin. He could not turn his head enough to see what it was, but by the feel of it, he guessed it was the remnant of her silk chemise. She covered her hand with it and stroked him, drifting across his chest and stopping to tease his nipple.

Everywhere she touched him his skin burned. All his nerve endings tingled with need for her.

Her silk-covered hand slid across his belly and paused on his hip. She bent and kissed the skin where it thinned over his hipbone. "I love this part of you. It is one of the few places you look vulnerable." Her hand moved agonizingly close to his cock. "Here on the other hand," she said, stroking him lightly, "you are all strength."

She only let the edge of the fabric graze him before she caressed his legs. His need to touch her was so strong he almost yanked himself free from his bonds. He could rip the cloth if he tried, but he wanted to fulfill her fantasy. He fought to keep still. But when her hands massaged his thighs, he couldn't. He twisted and struggled as she had done, lifting his hips upward and inviting her to take him.

She climbed onto the bed between his outstretched legs and used one hand to grip his shaft. He bit his lower lip until he tasted blood.

Her tongue replaced her hand, and his hips shot off the bed as far as they could go. "Cassandra, please!" How could she make him beg so easily, with barely a touch?

She took him into her mouth then. Her tongue flicked across the slit in the head of his cock, and he decided she had been born to pleasure him.

She moaned in pleasure as she took him deeper. He resorted to counting backwards to hold himself at the edge of the precipice, determined he would not leap over.

His mind raced, trying to think how he could enflame her enough that she would take him so he would not disgrace himself. "Turn around."

She released him and looked up. "What?"

"Turn around so I can give you pleasure too."

She turned so she faced his feet. "That's it. Now straddle my head and lower yourself to my mouth."

She did as he asked, but she kept her hips too high for him to reach her. "Damn it Cassandra. I smell your desire. Give yourself to me."

She laughed and then lowered herself. He began to feast on her. Before long she was sucking him hard as she pressed herself against his questing tongue. Her sounds of pleasure and her taste were intoxicating.

Silvia Violet

If she had waited even a second longer to release him, he would pumped his seed into her mouth. As it was, he thought he would die if he had to wait much longer to be inside her.

She turned to face him, her face flushed and her chest heaving.

"Let me fill you."

"You were right. The one who is restrained never really surrenders. How can I resist you?"

"You can't." He yanked against his bonds, but stopped himself before pulling free.

Cassandra had intended to stretch this out much longer, to take the time to touch him everywhere, to tease him with her hands and her mouth, but she could not. Her pulse throbbed and need made her dizzy.

Mark had brought her to the edge of release with his mouth. She'd pulled away, but her need did not diminish. One touch was likely all she needed to tumble into oblivion, but she wanted so much more.

"Tell me what you want," she purred, mimicking the words he had used against her. Of course, unlike her, he did not mind revealing his desires.

"I want you to sit astride me and lower yourself onto my cock. I want to feel your slick, tight passage gripping me." He lifted himself and made his cock jump. "Ride me, Cassandra."

She licked her lips and straddled his hips. He groaned when she rubbed him against her, positioning him so she could slide ever so slowly down until their hips met. She sat still for a few seconds, taking in the feel of him. His thighs were rock hard with tension.

She used her internal muscles to squeeze him. He gasped. "Cassandra, I...can't...wait anymore."

"Neither can I." She leaned over him, letting her hands rest on his chest. "Look at me." He did. She lifted and lowered herself, grinding against him at the bottom of each stroke. Within seconds, she exploded.

As if from far away, she heard a tearing sound. Then his hands were on her hips, forcing them to slide back and forth. Within seconds, he found his release and pumped himself into her.

When she had recovered enough to speak, she tried to sit up. His arms locked around her back and held her against him.

"You could have gotten free any time."

"I could have, but I didn't want to."

"But you were never truly at my mercy. When you tied me, I couldn't get loose."

"Cassandra, I have been at your mercy since the day you walked into Northamberly."

"How am I ever going to give you up?" Fear gripped Cassandra when she realized she'd said those words aloud. They were never meant to be voiced.

"Do you have to?"

Was he serious? Did he want to continue their liaison? Hope fluttered for a moment before regret sent it plummeting. Even if he did, she could not. "Yes."

"Why? I was hoping you had decided our lovemaking was more than— what was that word you used to describe it at first? An, yes, nice. You called it nice."

She shook her head. "It is far more than nice. That's the problem. The longer we let this go on, the harder it will be to say good-bye."

The sadness on his face brought tears to her eyes. What had he been thinking? He said he would never consider marriage again and so had she. "I cannot see you after our three months are over. It would be too hard on me."

"Are you always this stubborn?"

"I'm not being stubborn, I—"

"You are so determined to be independent that you would give up this pleasure so you can pretend you are in control of your life."

Pretend? Would it all be pretend? No, she would be free. She had to be. "Unless I get pregnant, I will have to find work. Governesses hardly have time for lovers."

He smirked. "I've known a few who had plenty of time for me."

She sighed, not wanting to think about all the other women he had pleasured. "Mark, I—"

He pressed a finger against her lips. "Don't say any more. I understand perfectly. Once I have done my duty, you would like me to disappear. No problem. If you want to spend your nights in a cold bed to prove you don't need anyone, I'm not going to stop you. There are plenty of women out there who would beg to spend the night with me."

He jerked his feet, ripping the ties that had held him and rolled her off him. She watched him pull his clothes back on and tried desperately to think of something to say, anything that might repair the damage she had done.

Shoving his arms into his jacket, he said, "I will call on you tomorrow after I meet with the Lintons."

"Don't go."

"I have fulfilled tonight's obligations. Thus I have no reason to stay." He slammed the door on his way out.

Chapter Seventeen

Cassandra had finally fallen asleep when the creak of her bedroom door woke her. Terror gripped her. The guards watching the house were not infallible. She reached toward her nightstand, hoping to find a makeshift weapon.

The intruder knocked something off the top of her vanity.

She screamed.

"Even when women tell me I'm not wanted, I keep coming back for more. I might as well go fuck Katryn. The funny thing is I don't want her anymore. You actually made me forget her. Now, I'm obsessed with you instead."

"You're drunk." She smelled the whiskey on Mark from across the room.

"Not drunk enough to stop me crawling back here."

"I never said I didn't want you."

"You did, but what does it matter? I'm back to give you more of what you've been promised."

"Mark, I don't think—"

He tripped over a footstool and fell against the bed. She grabbed his arm to help him right himself. He pushed her back, falling on top of her.

"Little witch, what have you done to me?"

"Nothing." She shoved at him until he rolled over, and she sat up. "I think you should go."

"No." The anger in his voice made her fear him in a way she hadn't since their first day together.

"Don't think I've forgotten."

"Forgotten what?"

"Our agreement. You must be ready whenever I want you."

"Mark, I thought—"

He pressed his finger against her lips. "You see I had forgotten too, until tonight. Other people forget things when they're drunk, but I remember. That's why I couldn't drink Katryn away. The more I drank, the more vividly I saw her in my mind, offering me more of her whore's body. Tonight, I saw you the first time I took you to bed. Then I remembered that you are mine to command."

She tried to protest, but he kissed her. Angry as she was at his arrogance, her body responded instantly to his touch. His tongue ravaged her mouth. She fought against his onslaught, trying to keep from falling back on the bed, trying to find the will to resist him.

Her head pounded with the weight of her indecision. Did she truly want to fight him? Yes…no.

She pushed at him, trying to get away, but he locked his arms tighter around her. His mouth slid down her throat. He left a trail of tingling bites all the way to her collarbone. Finally, she caught her breath enough to speak. "Stop! Now!"

The vehemence of her words got his attention. He lifted his head. "I'm in no mood to play games. Do as I say or our agreement is over."

Anger boiled inside her. "You're not going to leave. You need me as much as I need you."

He made a sound of disgust. "I do, and I hate myself for it."

"Then get out."

Ignoring her, he brushed her nipples with his thumbs. "No. You're right. I don't have the strength to leave."

She bit her lip to hold in a moan. He continued to torment her. Alternately flicking his thumb or fingers across her nipples and squeezing them. The tightness between her legs grew unbearable.

He shoved her nightgown up and lowered his mouth to her breast. She let her head drop back and supported herself on her elbows. His hot breath warmed her as he spoke. "You'll spend the rest of your life missing this, longing for just one—" he stroked one nipple with his tongue, "caress."

"No." Tears filled her eyes as he bent to pull the tight bud into his mouth. "Let me go."

"I tried to warn you when you first came to me. I told you I was dangerous. You chose not to listen. Now you will suffer for it."

"No, please." Tears fell down her cheeks, but she pressed his head against her. Her denial was a lie. She would die if he left, but she could not let him touch her soul as he touched her body. If she did, she would give in to his demands to extend their liaison.

Focus on the pleasure, she told herself. *Don't look at him. Don't think about how much you care. Let your body do as it will.*

"You want this as much as I do." He slipped a finger inside her and used his other hand to wrestle her nightgown over her head. She helped him, wanting to see the fire in his eyes when he looked at her naked body.

He thrust his fingers in and out of her pussy. "You're always ready for me, aren't you?"

She arched against him.

"Tell me damn it. Tell me you want this. Tell me to stay."

"I—"

"Tell me."

She squeezed her eyes closed, but she saw him none-the-less. In her mind she saw how his gaze penetrated right to her heart. "I need you." She whispered the words slowly as if each one were being pulled from her.

She opened her eyes, realizing how futile it was to try hold back from him. She couldn't hide the desperate need that consumed her every time she saw him. When he touched her, she was his.

She wasn't sure how he got his pants open. His hands never left her for more than a second. But suddenly he was bearing her back. She was happy to fall this time. She sank into the mattress and accepted his hard shaft inside her.

He immediately set a rough, pounding rhythm, making no effort to hold back the tide of his furious passion. She was thankful for it, because it kept her from thinking. Only the deep pleasure of him filling her to the core registered in her mind

"Tell me again. Tell me you need this."

But she never had to say a thing. Her orgasm wracked her body. She screamed. She expected him to follow immediately, but he didn't. He pushed at her thighs until they were doubled against her chest.

The position gave him even greater access to her. When she thought surely he could not take her any faster or harder, he did. The look on his face should have frightened her. She was not sure he would hear her if she spoke to him, not that she could catch her breath enough to speak.

He looked as if he were torn between killing her and pleasuring her, as if he wanted to punish her for denying him and surrender his soul at the same time. When he finally let himself go, pain and pleasure swirled together in his eyes. It tore at her heart.

Mark rolled to his back and pulled Cassandra into his arms. Within moments, she was asleep. Despite his exhaustion, he lay staring at the ceiling, suddenly achingly sober.

He prayed he had not misinterpreted her desire. He would never have taken her if she had not wanted it as he did.

Had he become a monster in the last few months? She had told him he was like a wild beast, and he feared she was right. Yet the wilder he became, the more it excited her.

He also feared his eyes had revealed all the things he could not say. He hated nothing more than the ease with which women stirred his emotions. When he'd reached his climax, he'd been unable to disguise his need for Cassandra. He couldn't keep the pain from his eyes anymore than he could hold back the storm of pleasure that surged through his body.

Mark stayed the night with her, unable to leave the security of her arms. Neither of them spoke after their emotional coupling. But they had remained in each others' arms until well after dawn.

During breakfast, he intended to once again broach the subject of continuing their liaison. He feared he might have even begged, but he did not have the chance.

She had grown cold again. He watched as she cut her food with deliberate movements, taking only small bites. For several long minutes, the only sounds in the room were the clanking of their silverware and the ticking of the mantel clock.

"I have been thinking." She looked down at her plate, at the floral centerpiece, at the empty chair beside her, anywhere but at him. "Perhaps I should start inquiring for positions now. There's only a small chance that I'm with child. I need to be realistic. I—"

"Cassandra!" He refused to listen to anymore nonsense. "You will do nothing of the kind, not until you are safe. We have no idea who else may have been involved with Reddington. Neither of us would have suspected Southwood. But apparently he is even more dangerous than your husband."

"I would not take a position until the killer is found. But...I've been a fool. I should never have come to you, never have tried—"

Mark resisted the urge to shake her. "If you had not come to me, you would probably be dead by now. Would that be better?"

"No, I—"

"We will continue as we have and pretend this conversation never happened."

"I must find a way to support myself. My aunt does not have the funds to take care of me and my sisters. I will not go back to my parents' house."

193

He sighed. "Cassandra, I can arrange for you to you have everything you need."

She slammed her teacup onto its saucer. He expected it to shatter. It only teetered there, it's rattling echoing across the room. "I will not be your whore."

"Why not? You don't mind making me yours."

"I am not paying you for this."

"More's the pity. I should have struck a better bargain."

"Having a sex slave at your beck and call isn't good enough?"

Mark threw his napkin onto the table and stood so fast his chair turned over. He stared at her for a few seconds, then forced himself to walk away.

He'd been too angry to stay. In such a wild state, he might have thrown more cruel words or worse, a confession of love. He couldn't decide what he wanted to do more, throttle her or fall down on his knees and beg her to stay with him.

When she'd dismissed the idea that she might be with child, a knot formed in his stomach. He'd been too angry to understand his reaction. As he walked in the chill morning air, he realized he wanted nothing more than to see her body swollen with his child.

Every time he spent himself inside her, he hoped his seed would take root. It must be some primitive desire for procreation, some elemental need. Whatever it was, the knowledge that a baby might grow in her womb increased the ecstasy of their joining.

This feeling was entirely new. Even when he was mired in his obsession for Katryn, he'd never fantasized about seeing her with child. But when he imagined Cassandra's breasts full with milk, and her belly increasing with his child, a strange warmness grew deep inside his chest, thawing the cold Katryn had put there.

Perhaps she was with child already. Then he would be justified in convincing her, hell, in ordering her to marry him. He would not allow her to refuse him no matter what their agreement had been. She would not raise his child elsewhere. He knew what it was like to grow up without a father. He'd be damned if he would bestow the same fate on his own child.

With great effort, he managed to push his thoughts to the back of his mind as he neared the address Linton had given him. More important than convincing Cassandra not to leave him was keeping her safe.

He rang the bell and presented his card to the butler. The man returned quickly and showed him into a small study. He was contemplating examining the papers that lay scattered on the desktop when Walter Linton entered. "Foxwood, how nice to see you."

Once again he was stuck with the less desirable brother. He'd expected Oscar to be the one to handle the actual negotiation. Walter extended his hand. Mark took it, managing somehow to shake it without shuddering.

Walter poured Mark a drink. "I trust you are still interested in finding a girl for your party."

Mark nodded.

"There is a young woman we are hoping to…acquire shortly that might fit your needs. I assume you do not mind if she requires a bit of coercion before she complies with your wishes."

Mark fought his revulsion. "I assume you could advise me on the best methods to deal with…reluctance."

"Of course. For an additional fee, we can give you a special concoction we like to give the girls we acquire. It makes them far more biddable. The more they take, the more they need. They are not anxious to leave us."

Bile rose in his throat. He had to force himself to relax his hold on his glass lest he break it. Was this what Caitlin had refused to tell him? "Price is not an issue as long as I get what I have requested. Tell me about this girl."

"She's well bred. She came out this year. Quite the little ice queen. Breaking her in would sure give me a thrill."

A girl from society? Never would he have thought they took girls from anywhere but the servant class or the streets. "Do all your girls come with such a pedigree?"

195

"No, most of them come from less fortunate situations. This one is special. She rebuked my brother and me. We feel she needs some attitude adjustment."

His smile made Mark's stomach churn. "Where is your brother by the way? I rather expected to see him today."

Walter stopped smiling. Mark thought his color faded a bit, though his sickly skin made it hard to tell. "He's…not in town at the moment."

Mark did not believe that for a minute. Walter was far too flustered. Something was wrong. He would have to look into the matter later that day. "Tell me about this girl. What does she look like?"

"Oh I am certain you would enjoy her. She is small but lush. Her breasts simply beg for a man's hands…or his lash." Linton laughed.

Mark squeezed his fist to keep from hitting him.

"Her hair is thick with big loose curls. But her eyes. They are most unusual. So deeply gray they are almost lavender."

Mark's heart skipped beat. He ceased to breathe. A young woman who'd given them a set down. A woman with lavender eyes.

Amanda. Mark was almost certain of it. Did Linton know he'd been with Cassandra at Langley's party? Was Linton baiting him or were they unaware he was involved?

Mark had to force himself to continue listening to Linton.

"Those eyes will reflect pain beautifully. I am certain you will be pleased."

Thank God Linton hadn't noticed his discomfort. Mark had to pretend to reach an agreement and get out before he killed Linton. Yet, he didn't want to let the man live even another minute.

"She sounds like exactly what I am looking for. But as for breaking her in. I want that pleasure."

"That will—"

"Yes, yes. It will cost more. Money is not the issue here. When could you deliver her to me?"

"Give us a few days, we will contact you when we have her in our possession."

"Excellent. We can negotiate the price after I have seen her and assure myself that she is all you have promised."

"Where can we contact you?"

"I've got rooms at the Clarendon."

"Excellent. You will not be displeased. This girl is of the highest quality."

"I would expect nothing less. I must go now. I have some less pleasurable business to attend to."

As soon as he left, Mark looked around for a hack, wishing he'd ridden instead of walking. He had to get to Amanda as fast as he could.

Finally he saw a driver waiting on the next block. Hopping in, he handed the man a handful of coins. "If you get me to Grosvenor Square in record time, I'll give you twice that."

They hurried along at a reckless pace, but soon got stuck behind a delivery cart. "Come on, man. I could walk faster than this."

The driver forced his way onto the sidewalk, nearly running down an elderly woman and her dog. The hack tipped as they rounded the next corner, but all Mark could think about was arriving too late and finding Amanda already gone. His heart beat so hard he thought his ribs might break.

Finally, they pulled up in front of Lady Morgan's townhouse. He tossed more coins at the driver as he leapt from his seat and ran to the door.

A footman answered. Mark pushed past, asking for Amanda as he went.

"Stop. Sir. You must come back." The man tried to halt Mark's progress, but Mark shook him off and searched each room until he found Amanda working a sampler in the conservatory.

"Mr. Foxwood, whatever is the matter?"

He was overcome with relief. He tore the embroidery hoop from her hands and pulled her to her feet. "Come with me."

"What? Why?"

He was dragging her toward the door when her aunt appeared. "What is going on? Release her at once, or I will call my men to throw you into the street."

"It's all right, Aunt Claire. This is Mr. Foxwood. Cassandra introduced us yesterday."

Lady Morgan took her niece's arm. "I don't care who he is. He has no right to barge in here and take such liberties."

"I am not sure what he is so upset about, Auntie." Amanda paused, giving Mark the same look Cassandra always did before telling him he was insufferable. "I am sure he meant no harm."

"What do you have to say for yourself?" Lady Morgan gave Mark a piercing glare.

"Forgive me Lady Morgan, Amanda is in great danger. It is imperative that I take her to her sister immediately."

"In danger? Whatever for?"

"Lord Reddington's most unsavory acquaintances have made threats against Amanda."

Amanda sucked in her breath. "Threats?"

"Yes, but I will see you are not harmed."

Lady Morgan gave Amanda a quelling look. "I knew there was more of a story to Cassandra's sudden appearance in London." She turned to face Mark, her face no less imposing. "How are you involved?"

"I am a friend of Cassandra's, and I have sworn to protect her. She and her house are under guard. Amanda will be safe there."

"A friend?"

"Aunt Claire, please. Cassandra trusts him. We should do as he says." Amanda tugged on Mark's arm, trying to pull him from the room.

Lady Morgan raised her brow. "Are you Cassandra's lover?"

Mark was rarely shocked, but this woman's personality was even more forceful than Cassandra's. And she rattled him to the core. At least Lady Morgan had not asked the question indignantly as one might expect. Instead, her tone was hopeful as if she approved of the idea. He decided to honor her forthrightness. "Yes, I am. I will do all I can to protect her and her sister."

Lady Morgan smiled. "It's about time she took a lover. It's the most sensible thing she's done since she married that goat's ass of a husband. She needs a man like you, one who knows how to take charge."

Mark started to speak, but she held up her hand. "I don't need to hear anymore. Take Amanda and keep her safe." She turned back to her niece. "I will expect a message from you once you are settled."

"Might we make use of your carriage?"

"Of course." Lady Morgan rang for a servant as she shooed them towards the door.

Mark's mind whirled as he helped Amanda into the carriage and took the seat across from her. Had he really told Lady Morgan that he and Cassandra were lovers? Were the Lintons and God knows who else after Amanda?

"Mr. Foxwood? Mr. Foxwood!"

He realized Amanda was trying to get his attention. "I'm sorry. What were you saying?" He forced himself to focus on her words.

"What is all this about? Why have I been threatened and why in the world did you tell my aunt about you and Cassandra?"

"In answer to your second question, I gambled on the notion the news would be well-received. As to the other matter, some of Reddington's men intended to kidnap you and...well, what they would do to you once you were in their custody does not bear repeating. Once we are safely within Cassandra's townhouse, you are not to leave until this is settled."

"How long will I be there? You did not even allow me to pack anything."

"Cassandra will provide you with clothes or a servant will deliver some. You are not to go out for any purpose. Ultimately, Reddington's associates would kill you, but not until they made you wish you were already dead. Do not convince yourself you can handle this on your own. The last thing I need is another woman as stubborn as your sister."

Amanda laughed. "I don't think I could be as stubborn as Cassandra if I tried. Thank you for taking care of her."

"I could do no less."

"You love her, don't you?"

Mark's gut twisted as if she'd punched him. He studied her intently, wishing he knew how she read him so clearly.

She smiled. "You don't have to answer. I know you do."

"How is it you can be so certain of my feelings when you have only spent a few hours with me?"

"I read people easily."

"And what does your insight tell you about Cassandra? Do you fancy her in love with me as well?" Did he really want to know her answer?

"I would never betray my sister's trust in such a fashion." But then she twirled her hair and pursed her lips, seeming to reconsider. "Don't let her get away. My aunt was right. You are the best thing that could have happened to her."

Mark scowled. "I wish you'd tell her that.."

Chapter Eighteen

Having attempted to distract herself from the aching knot in her chest, Cassandra wrote her sister, Elise, outlining a modified version of the week's events. She was sealing the letter when her maid, Rebecca, entered the library. "A gentleman is here to see you." The young woman handed her a calling card.

She looked down at the name. Mr. Rhys Stanton. She closed her eyes and took a deep breath. He would not have come unless he had news about the killer. "Show him to the study."

"Yes, my lady." Rebecca left to comply with her wishes.

Cassandra hoped Mr. Stanton would be gentlemanly enough to ignore her disheveled appearance. When she had mentioned Mark in her letter, stubborn tears had begun to fall.

Stanton stood near the fire, holding his hands out to the flames. He was immaculately turned out in a perfectly tailored heliotrope jacket and a gray waistcoat embroidered with silver thread all set off by an intricately tied cravat, sleeves that were trimmed in lace, and Hessians polished to perfection. He turned and bowed when Cassandra entered. "Lady Reddington."

"Please call me Cassandra." She wished she could drop her title altogether so people would no longer link her with her husband.

"Then I must insist you call me Rhys. I apologize for bothering you, but I've learned something I think you should know. I called at Mark's townhouse, but he was not there. I was hoping he was with you."

"Please sit down." Cassandra gestured toward the chairs near the fire and sat down herself. "Mark is meeting with the Lintons. I am unsure when he will return."

Stanton shook his head. "Oscar Linton won't be meeting with anyone. He's dead."

Dizziness forced her to lean back in her chair. "How did you find this out?"

"I went to Amelia's. It's another establishment like Miss Caroline's." He paused and ran his hand through his hair.

His sheepish grin made Cassandra smile. "You can hardly expect me to be shocked by how you spend your evenings. I rather expect such from men."

"If your expectations are based on your husband's behavior, then I must correct you. All men do not behave in that fashion. I would never—"

"You would never beat a woman who did not please you or kidnap a young girl and force her to do your bidding. No, I do not think that of you. My husband rather excelled at depravity. While I imagine your conquests are legion, you strike me as more the run-of-the-mill rake, harmless to all but young debutantes or women who give their hearts too easily."

Stanton smiled. "I am not sure I like being described as harmless, but I suppose you are right. Though debutantes are safe from me. I'd rather be with a woman who knows the measure of her desire."

"I suppose you fancy yourself able to fulfill all those desires."

"I assure you, it's not fancy." He grinned, but his face reddened as if he'd just realized who he was speaking to.

Cassandra laughed. "I must say it amazes me that a man who professes to be a danger to women blushes when attempting to discuss topics of a scandalous nature."

"You are under Mark's protection."

She raised her brow. "Are you afraid of Mark?"

"I wouldn't say afraid, but certainly wary. Any man would be a fool not to be. He is a force to be reckoned with though you seem to be faring rather well."

"I think my ability to hold my own is driving him crazy." *And driving him away.* She remembered the look on his face as he'd turned to leave her that morning and wondered if he'd ever look at her with tender concern again.

"Perhaps you are, but…"

She studied his face. His lips were pressed together. He looked as if he was working hard to put the right words together. "You are free to speak your mind to me. I prefer forthrightness."

"No. It's nothing. I should finish telling you what I heard at Amelia's."

She wanted to press him, but instead, she nodded in agreement.

"I was leaving one of the rooms, ready to go home, when I overheard Walter Linton talking to Amelia, the proprietress. The door to the room they were using stood ajar. I stopped to see what I could learn.

"Amelia was crying. It took me a few moments to piece together what had happened. But I figured out Oscar Linton had been murdered by a man named Gaston. I think he's the same man who ordered Reddington's death."

Cassandra's heart beat so rapidly she feared it might explode. Fear, anger, hope all raced through her. "Why? What did they say?"

"Amelia was certain they would be killed as well, but Walter assured her he'd made a deal with Gaston. He said he wasn't going to be stubborn like Reddington or his brother. He said if Gaston wanted more girls, he would give him what he wanted, and Amelia would have to help him."

"So Reddington and Oscar Linton crossed Gaston by failing to deliver what he wanted," Cassandra said, more to herself that to Rhys. "Why would Reddington have risked angering him?"

"I don't know. Walter and Amelia began arguing about money, but I had to leave when two men exited a room down the hall. Maybe Gaston wasn't paying enough."

"Maybe not. Mark went to Miss Caroline's last night. The woman he talked to said several women have disappeared from there recently. She said the other girls feared they were dead. This woman was forced to work there after taking a job as a servant in Oscar Linton's household."

Stanton looked stricken. "Damn! I do hope you realize I would never condone such behavior. The women I've been with showed no sign of reluctance." He leaned over, spearing his hands into his hair. "I pray they had not been forced. They gave no impression—"

She reached out and placed her hand on top of his. "You meant no harm. I know that."

He smiled. "I hope Mark appreciates you."

Cassandra sensed the heat in her cheeks. Stanton was as great a charmer as Mark, more dangerous in a way, because he was more subtle. Even when dressed in formal attire, Mark presented a rough exterior. His animal power was never successfully concealed.

Stanton on the other hand did a smashing imitation of an *effete*, hiding his strength beneath the clothes of a dandy.

"Why do you hide who you really are?"

"What an impertinent question." His smile showed he wasn't offended.

"Perhaps so, but I'm curious. You are more like Mark than one would ever guess from your appearance."

"Who in society ever shows their true self? I find this façade amusing and convenient. It gets me into places a man like Mark could never go."

She smiled. "I'm sure that is true. Although I imagine Mark opens plenty of doors with his…rougher methods."

Stanton grinned and nodded his agreement. Cassandra told him the other things Mark had discovered at Miss Caroline's. Stanton was stating his disbelief at Southwood's involvement when Mark burst into the drawing room with Amanda in tow.

"Amanda? What are you doing here?"

Mark and her sister both began to speak at once, and Cassandra understood nothing from either of them. Finally, Mark gave Amanda a quelling look. She sighed and gestured for him to continue.

He told them what he had learned from Walter Linton. When he mentioned that Oscar was not there, Cassandra caught Rhys's eye but said nothing. By the time he finished, Cassandra's stomach had tightened into a knot. She gripped her sister's hand, but she wasn't sure who needed the comfort more, Amanda or herself.

She took a deep breath, trying to still her nerves. "Come let's sit down. Mr. Stanton has some important news as well."

Mark looked around when she said "Mr. Stanton" as if registering Stanton's presence for the first time. Rhys stood from his chair and bowed toward Amanda. "We have not been properly introduced, but I can only assume you are Cassandra's sister. You are a perfect replica of her except for your most exotic eyes."

He walked behind Amanda and reached his arms around her as if to undo the clasp of her cloak. "May I?"

Amanda nodded and he took the cloak from her shoulders. Rather than putting it down, he held it over his arm, letting his fingers run absently over the fabric. Cassandra should have scolded him for flirting with her sister in such a ludicrous manner, but she found it rather amusing, so she simply introduced them.

"Rhys, as you guessed, this is my sister, Miss Amanda Halverston. Amanda, this is Mr. Rhys Stanton. He is a friend of Mark's."

Amanda gave Stanton a withering look. "I would prefer if you did not maul my cloak. It was given to me by my aunt, and I am rather attached to it."

Stanton looked down at his hands as if he had not realized what he was doing. "Of course. I meant no harm. It is a beautiful garment, almost as beautiful as you."

Mark scowled at him. "What's wrong with you, Stanton? This is no time for your ridiculous games."

Stanton shook his head. "Do forgive me. I was quite overcome by the young lady."

Mark gave him a withering look. "Take a seat."

"I'll take the cloak." Cassandra pulled it from Stanton's hands. "Rebecca can hang it when she brings in tea."

The four of them sat, Mark and Rhys in the two Windsor chairs and Cassandra and her sister on the sofa.

Rhys told Mark that Oscar Linton was dead and explained the rest of what he'd overheard. When he finished, Mark leaned back against the chair and let out a long breath. He looked exhausted. Cassandra wanted to kiss the worry lines from his face, but he had not looked her in the eye since he entered the house.

She'd hurt him in her attempt to keep them from crossing a line that would only bring them worse pain. As long as the end was established, she could prepare herself. Anything else taunted her in a way she could not bear.

"I'm going to see her." Mark's voice was low and dark.

"What?" Cassandra and Stanton asked at the same time.

"Katryn. It's possible she knows what her husband is up to and…I think I can convince her to tell me."

"You don't have to do this." The pain she saw on his face made her cringe.

"Yes, I do." The intensity of his gaze compelled her to lean back against her seat. "I must do everything in my power to keep the two of you safe."

"What about *your* safety?"

"I hardly think Katryn intends to harm me. She's much more likely to use seduction rather than violence with me."

Cassandra decided not to bring up the emotional harm the encounter would cause. "Her husband will kill you if he finds you there."

"It is a risk I must take."

She twirled an errant curl, trying to think of some other way to get the information they needed. Cold fingers of fear played over her when she thought of him approaching Katryn alone. "At least take Stanton with you."

"No. The only way I will get anything out of her is by pretending to accept her offer to renew our acquaintance. Stanton will stay here with you and Amanda until I return." He glanced at Rhys who nodded in assent.

A knot formed in Cassandra's stomach. Would Mark bed Katryn to get this information? The thought sickened her. She could not bear the idea of that woman putting her hands on Mark. Cassandra had balked whenever Mark insisted that she belonged to him. But sometime in the last few days she'd come to think of him as belonging to her, and she'd be damned if she'd let Katryn hurt him again.

Mark rose. "I'll be back as soon as I can."

Cassandra followed him, but he did not turn around or stop until he was forced to wait for his coat at the door.

She took hold of his arm and turned him to face her. "I don't want you to do this."

"Why not? You made your feelings clear. You prefer taking a position where you will be treated like a servant to extending our liaison."

"Mark, I never said that."

He glared at her but said nothing.

"Whether or not I think it is best for us to continue our relationship, I do not want to see you hurt."

"I don't see why. You've used me as surely as she did."

Cassandra gasped. His words cut like knives. Tears sprang to her eyes. She ran toward the stairs past a bewildered Rebecca who carried Mark's coat and hat.

She rushed toward her room. As soon as she shut the door, she crumpled to the floor and let the tears flow. She cried harder than ever in her life, pounding her fists into the floor as the sobs bent her double.

Mark's cruel words had prompted this release. But once the tidal wave of tears began, she cried for everything cruel that had ever been done to her. In that moment, she hated herself for falling prey to Mark's charms, and she hated Mark for making her feel something she never intended to feel. He'd shown her she would not be as happy on her own as she had thought.

She had fended for herself her whole life. Her mother had never been strong enough to stand up to her father so her sisters depended on her to protect them from her father's cruelty. She'd had no one but herself to lean on.

Once she'd married Reddington, she spent most of the year in isolation at Reddington Abbey. Of course she had been able to write to her sisters and share some of her grief, but for the most part, she'd been forced to endure the hell of being Reddington's wife on her own.

If only she'd had a strong ally whom she could rely on. Someone who made her safe. Someone she could trust. Someone like Mark.

Why hadn't they met years before? She could have saved him from heartbreak, and he could have saved her from fear and guilt and loneliness. Now it was too late. Neither of them had the strength to open their hearts.

She was kneeling on the floor, tears streaming down her face when Amanda opened her door.

Her sister sank to the floor and pulled Cassandra into her arms. Several minutes passed before they pulled apart. Amanda wiped at her eyes, and Cassandra realized her shoulder was damp where her sister had joined in her tears. "I didn't mean to upset you, I—"

Amanda shook her head. "This is the first time you've let all this out isn't it?"

Cassandra said nothing.

"You didn't even cry when you married that son of a bitch."

"Amanda!"

"Cassandra, I'm twenty years old. You do not have to censure my language. Now answer my question." She handed her sister the handkerchief she'd extracted from her sleeve.

Cassandra blew her nose and attempted to dry up all her tears. "Reddington wasn't worth crying over."

"But Mark is?"

"No…yes…I don't know."

Amanda smiled. "What happened?"

"We argued this morning, and I hurt him."

"What did you say?"

"I don't want to discuss it. Mark and I won't be seeing each other after Reddington's killer is found. Right now, I'd rather concentrate on keeping you safe."

"So that's it? You're going to walk away from him?"

Cassandra nodded.

Amanda shook her head. "You love him, Cassandra. I know you do."

"I will not discuss this further. Where's Stanton?"

Amanda sighed. "He is quite well occupied with a scandalous novel I found for him. I was glad to have an excuse to abandon him. He looks at me as if he is thinking of doing things one could not mention in polite company."

Cassandra sighed. Perhaps she had overdone the warnings she gave her sister. "Stanton's a good man. You like Mark well enough, and he is the epitome of a rake."

"Yes, but he's harmless. He's meant for you."

"No, he's not," Cassandra said, as a few last tears wet her face. "He is definitely not for me."

Cassandra stood and pulled Amanda with her. "Let's rejoin Stanton. I promise to protect you from any unwanted advances."

Chapter Nineteen

Mark raised his hand to knock on Katryn's door. Before he made contact, it opened suddenly. Katryn stood before him, looking him up and down, lust plain on her face. She wore nothing but a crimson wrapper so thin she might as well have been naked.

"I was glancing out my bedroom window when I saw a hack slow and then stop. Imagine my surprise when you descended. I had to race down here to see if my eyes had deceived me."

"No deceit. I'm truly here." He swallowed his pride and gave her an appreciative glance. "Do you always wear so little where the servants can see you?"

"Oh, they're quite used to my eccentricities." She smiled lasciviously. "Do tell me you've reconsidered my offer."

He willed his lips to curve upwards. "Indeed I have. You were right. Why should you be denied my skills because you are married?"

"Mmmm. Why indeed? Come. Have a seat. We should talk."

They entered a dark, richly appointed sitting room. Katryn pulled on the bell. Two footmen appeared almost instantaneously. "Take Mr. Foxwood's coat and see that refreshments are brought to us."

He watched as both men let their gaze roam over her body. Was she bedding them too? She certainly made no effort to cover herself in their presence.

"Brandy?"

"Thank you." He forced another smile.

When she had filled two snifters, she handed him one and joined him on the settee. She sat suffocatingly close and rested her free hand on his thigh. He had to fight the urge to scoot away from her. "What prompted this change of heart? Did Lady Reddington prove too boring?"

Mark nearly choked on a sip of brandy. Katryn *had* recognized her at Langley's. He tried to recover though he feared he'd given himself away. "Whatever makes you think I've been with Lady Reddington?"

Katryn sat her glass on the marble-topped table in front of them and brought her hand up to caress his cheek. "I would recognize that ridiculous hair of hers anywhere. No mask could hide her identity."

"Katryn, you are quite mistaken. I told you my companion at the party was someone you did not know."

She smiled, far too knowingly. "Have it your way."

He took a few more sips of brandy. "I found I enjoyed Langley's party more than I expected. I've been missing too much by staying away from such events. I thought by resuming contact with you I could insinuate myself into a world I wish to learn much more about."

"Ahhh. What is it you wish to know?"

The look of rabid anticipation on her face unnerved him. What was she hoping he would say? "I've heard that your husband is involved with men who procure young women and train them to...entertain at parties. I thought perhaps I would give such a party myself and—"

He stopped when Katryn began to laugh. "What do you find so amusing?"

"My *husband?*" She laughed so hard she barely choked the words out.

He downed the rest of the brandy, needing fortification for what was to come. "Yes...I assumed you knew."

"Southwood is the biggest prude I've ever met. I think he might have been a virgin on our wedding night. Oh Mark, you don't get it, do you?"

"Get what?" His head pounded, and the room spun. Surely her presence couldn't actually make him physically ill.

"Southwood is the perfect stooge. All I have to do is smile, and he gives me all the money I ask while staying quietly hidden away in the country."

It hit him then. Katryn. Kat. The Cat. How could he have been so stupid? "It's you, isn't it? You're The Cat."

"Of course I am. Oh Mark, I'm so disappointed in you. I thought surely you would have figured that out by now."

Mark's vision began to blur. He couldn't think clearly. She had deceived him once again, and this time, it wasn't only his heart that was in danger. It was his life and the life of the woman he loved.

"Walter came to see me earlier this morning. Apparently, he found you most entertaining when he described what he wanted to do to little Amanda Halverston. The look on your face must have been priceless."

Mark's stomach roiled. "You disgust me."

"And you used to find me so delightful."

Her maniacal laugh beat against his head.

"I've wanted you at my mercy for a long time. It will be so good to have you inside me again."

"You won't get away with this."

She stood. He reached for her, but his hands wouldn't work properly. The brandy. She'd put something in it.

She pulled the bell rope and turned to face him. "Cassandra has to die and, eventually, so do you. It's a pity. The two of us could have been so good together."

He lunged for her again, but her image divided into two and then three. He collapsed at her feet. "Tie him tightly and take him to the carriage." Those words echoed in his head as he lost consciousness.

CR CR CR

Mark had been gone for hours, and Cassandra could not help but worry. She paced the length of the drawing room, wishing Stanton and Amanda made better company. Both were reading at opposite ends of the room. Amanda studiously ignored Rhys while he spent far more time staring at her décolletage than at the pages of his book.

Cassandra supposed she should be concerned by his interest in her sister. But he was Mark's friend, and she did not think he would harm Amanda. Perhaps her sister could use an invigorating flirtation.

"Cassandra, do sit down before you wear a hole in the carpet." Amanda laid her book on the sofa table. "Would you like a game of chess?"

Cassandra glanced at the chess set and thought of the wonderful afternoon she had spent with Mark. He'd shown her such tenderness that day. An invisible hand squeezed her heart. He'd hurt her that morning, but the thought of him being injured made her tremble.

"Mark should have been back by now."

Stanton looked up. "We don't know what he had to do to get the information he needed."

"All she needs is to be reminded of that," Amanda snapped. "Do you have any sense at all?"

"Amanda, there is no need to be rude. Rhys is right. But, even if Mark…had to be especially persuasive, he should be back now."

Amanda went to her sister and embraced her. "I'm sure he will be here soon. Don't worry."

"I feel uneasy. I can't explain it, but I know something is wrong."

A loud, insistent knock interrupted their conversation. Cassandra raced from the room. When she threw open the door, she saw a young woman. A threadbare gray cloak was pulled tight about her head, but strands of fiery red hair escaped to frame her face. Cassandra looked closer and gasped. Even in the shadows of the cloak it was obvious the woman had been beaten.

"I'm so sorry to come here like this ma'am, but Mr. Foxwood said I was to find him if something happened and I—"

"You're Caitlin, aren't you?"

"Y-yes."

"Please come in." Cassandra took the woman's arm to pull her inside. Caitln winced.

"I'm sorry." Cassandra let go. "I should have realized. How badly are you hurt?"

"No worse than I've been many times before."

Cassandra didn't know what to say. She beckoned for Caitlin to follow her to the drawing room. Amanda looked up and froze when she saw the woman's battered face.

Rhys's book clattered to the floor. He rose and took Caitlin's arm, helping her to the sofa.

"Caitlin, this is my sister, Amanda Halverston, and Mr. Stanton, a friend of Mark's. You may speak freely in front of them. They know about Mark, and they know I've been helping him."

The young woman swayed. Cassandra sat next to her, helping her steady herself. "I'll get you a brandy."

"Should we summon a doctor?" Amanda asked.

"No, please." Caitlin's eyes widened in fear. "I must tell you everything. They came and got me from my room this morning and started questioning me. They tried to force me to tell them what I knew about Mark and about you. When I wouldn't tell them, they did this." She indicated her face.

"Who were they, Caitlin?" Cassandra asked. "Do you mean the men who own the brothel?"

"Yes and another man, a Frenchman. He told them they were all idiots, and he would be running things from now on. She didn't like that. They were fighting before they came to get me."

Rhys handed Caitlin a snifter. She extended her arm to accept it, and her breath caught. She pulled her arm back, cradling it against her body. He sat the glass on the small table beside her. "You said she, Caitlin. Did you mean Miss Caroline?"

She shook her head. "That's why I risked coming here. I had to tell Mr. Foxwood. I was wrong. It's not her husband. It's Lady Southwood. She's The Cat."

A wave of acute pain snaked through Cassandra's body. She had to lay her head back against the sofa. "Dear God, what has he done?"

What little color had been in Caitlin's cheeks drained away. She looked around the room frantically. "What's wrong? Where is Mr. Foxwood?"

Cassandra couldn't make herself speak. Rhys joined the women on the sofa and took hold of Cassandra's hand. "He went to see Lady Southwood. He wanted to convince her to help us."

"Then, I'm too late. He…he was so kind to me. No one has ever…" Her voice trailed off as tears poured down her cheeks.

"It is not too late." Everyone turned toward Amanda. "We're going to find him."

Rhys nodded. "Of course we are."

Fear paralyzed Cassandra. What if Mark was already dead? What if she never got to tell him she loved him? She could only manage shallow breaths.

Stabbing pain sliced at her heart. But she had to pull herself together. She had to believe they could save him. And to do that, she needed all her wits about her.

"Caitlin, tell us what else you learned. We need to gather all the knowledge we can before we plan a rescue."

Rhys gave Caitlin a handkerchief. She blew her nose and took a few more painful breaths. "Lady Southwood's the one who's been keeping the women after the men capture them. She's hiding them at one of her estates, Southwood Grange it's called. They hardly need to keep the women locked up though. They have this drug. They give it to all the girls, and then we can't escape. I…I need more right now. I'll have to go back."

Cassandra gapsed. "You cannot go back. They will kill you."

"It's my only choice. I can't go long without their potion, and I can't get it elsewhere. I don't even know what they put in it." Caitlin began to cry, and Cassandra pulled the young woman into her arms.

"We will not sentence you to death after the service you've done us." Looking up at her sister, Cassandra said. "Find Rebecca and have her summon a doctor." Amanda left, and she focused her attention on Rhys. "We have to go after him."

"*I* have to go after him," he corrected. "But not until tonight."

"He may not be alive tonight."

"We will have to take that chance. I can hardly waltz over there in broad daylight and ask them to hand him over."

"We can't let him die."

"Mark is capable of taking care of himself. If they killed him on sight then we can do nothing for him. If he's alive, we have a better chance of him staying that way if we are patient."

Caitlin took a tiny sip of brandy and coughed. Cassandra reached out and touched her cheek. One of her eyes was swollen shut, and the other had a cut beneath it. Seeing her like that made Cassandra want to track down Katryn and rip the woman apart with her hands. "Thank you. You can't know how much your bravery means to me."

Caitlin smiled. "I don't think they'll kill him, my lady. At least not right away. They want you. I think they hoped to use him as bait."

"Do you think she'll drug him, like she does the women?" Rhys asked.

Caitlin nodded. "I think so. I heard her say she would enjoy making him helpless."

"No!" Cassandra stomach churned. She would do anything to prevent Mark being used like that, even if it meant giving herself over to them. "Rhys, we have to go now."

"You heard what Caitlin said. They intend to kill you or feed you this drug and sell you."

"Mark can't handle this. Think what Katryn has already done to him."

"He is both strong and stubborn, Cassandra. He will make it."

Stanton stood and reached for the bell pull. "Let's call the guards in. They can help us make the best plan to get Mark out."

"They'll be others there too," Caitlin said. Her voice was shaky, but she took a breath and continued. "Women whom they've captured. They were hoping for some deliveries today." She looked at Cassandra with tears in her eyes. "They'd planned to take your sister, my lady."

Rhys leaned down and patted Caitlin's shoulder. "Linton gave their plan away and Mark got to her in time. We won't let them hurt her, and we'll get the others out."

"I'm going with you." Cassandra gave Stanton a look that dared him to contradict her.

"So am I," Amanda said from the doorway.

Both Cassandra and Rhys looked at her and spoke simultaneously. "No, you're not."

"I am. They intended to drug me and sell me to men for entertainment. I have as much right as Cassandra to see they are not allowed to do this to me or anyone else."

Stanton scowled. "Cassandra will not be going either."

"I will."

"I cannot help Mark and protect you at the same time."

Cassandra tried to keep a handle on her anger. "You don't have to protect me. Thanks to my cousin, I'm a crack shot and I'm not bad with a knife either."

"I see." Stanton raised his brows. "Still, I cannot let you go. Mark would have my head."

"Mark may not have his own head if we sit around arguing all day." Amanda scowled at them both. "Cassandra and I are both going."

Stanton shook his head. "Absolutely not—"

Amanda exhaled sharply. "I do not wish to hear any further argument from you."

Stanton stood. "I'm going to round up Brant and Corwyn. I'm also going to order the other guards not to allow impetuous young women to leave the house."

Amanda turned to face Caitlin, ignoring his last comment. "Rebecca is off to find a doctor. Caitlin, what can we do to make you comfortable?"

The young woman's hands shook, and she labored for breath. "I have to go back." Her voice so low it was nearly imperceptible. Then she fainted.

"We're not going to let you die," Cassandra whispered, overcome with emotion for this woman who had risked so much for Mark.

∞ ∞ ∞

Mark nearly choked as one of his captor's forced wine down his throat. This was the second time he had awakened to such treatment. The first time, he lay on the floor of a moving carriage, a rather poorly sprung one at that, before he passed out again.

This time his mind cleared rapidly, perhaps they had misjudged how much wine he had swallowed. He tested his bonds, but his wrists and ankles had been tied too tightly for him to slip free. A rope connected the two sets of bonds, forcing him to keep his legs bent and his back arched. Katryn's footmen had made quite a neat package of him, but he would get his revenge.

He was no longer in the carriage. Now he lay on a cold, hard floor. This wine had no bitter aftertaste, and he did not feel the overwhelming tiredness that had come on him instantly when he had been drugged. Perhaps he was being given a reprieve.

As his mind cleared, he focused on his surroundings. He had a vague memory of being carried down stairs, and the floor beneath him was made of nothing but packed earth. His cell contained only a tin cup and a ragged blanket. The cup appeared to be full of water, but thirsty as he was, he had no intention of drinking it.

He rolled over on his stomach and worked at freeing his hands. The coarse ropes tore at his wrists, but he ignored the pain. After a few minutes of trying, he realized he had no hope of tearing the ropes. But perhaps, by rubbing them against the stone wall, he could make them fray.

As he scooted toward the wall, he realized he was sweating. The thick, oppressive air of his cell rested heavy on his skin. Was it getting hotter? That didn't make sense. There was a small window near the top of the cell, and he saw that night had fallen. The underground cell ought to be freezing. Instead, he was as warm as if he lay in front of a blazing fire.

Within minutes, he realized he'd been drugged again, but this potion had different effects. His skin grew more sensitive. His clothes irritated and aroused him everywhere they touched his skin. All over his body, sharp points pulsed beneath his skin. Apparently, they'd given him some type of aphrodisiac. It took all his concentration to work his way to the wall where he could rub the ropes against the rough rock.

To keep from going crazy from the riot of sensations, he focused on the need to get free. But his mind kept clouding. He was slowly losing control of himself. He wanted to scream in frustration. If he couldn't fight this incredible urge for satiation, he would never get free.

He twisted his head over his shoulder and saw that the ropes beginning to fray. He increased the vigor with which he chafed them against the rock. Unfortunately he could not avoid catching his hands on the rock as well. The skin at the base of his palms and his wrists was torn and bleeding, but he did not stop. The pain helped him ignore the fire raging in his body and alleviate the confusion in his head.

He had to be under control when Katryn came. He assumed he'd been given the drug so she could torture him with his need. She would revel in his humiliation.

He clung to that thought and to the sensation of blood trickling through his fingers as the pulsing sensations changed. They were no longer localized. Now imaginary hands stroked up and down his limbs. He had to be touched, had to gain relief. Sweat ran from his forehead in streams.

Chapter Twenty

Cassandra, Amanda, Rhys and several of the guards had been discussing possible scenarios for what Cassandra thought was far too long. Time was critical and she would rather act on a plan than continue to sit in her drawing room while Mark's life was in danger.

Suddenly Amanda looked up from the map she had been studying. "I've got it. The perfect solution."

Rhys eyed her suspiciously. "What is your plan?"

She ignored him, turning instead to Caitlin. "Do you have any idea who delivers the captive women to Southwood Grange or who is there to receive them?"

The young woman had regained consciousness after the doctor arrived. The doctor said she would have a rough time of it until the first round of cravings wore off. If he'd guessed right as to what the drug contained, there would be no lasting harm. He'd bandaged her injuries and put her broken arm in a sling. But she'd refused to take the laudanum he offered, saying she must remain awake to help them save Mark.

She continued to shake with chills despite the feverish feel of her skin. To relieve some of her discomfort, Amanda covered her with blankets, and Rebecca brought her hot tea laced with brandy. Cassandra sat by her, holding her hand and wiping the perspiration from her brow.

Caitlin opened her mouth to answer Amanda's question but then bent double. The pain on her face made Cassandra cringe. She squeezed

Cassandra's hand so hard Cassandra feared her fingers might break, but she would not let herself pull away.

The spasms passed and Caitlin sat up, leaning her head against the back of the sofa. She took a few deep breaths. "They try to use different men, thieves they hire off the street. They..." She paused as another, smaller spasm shook her. "They don't want any one man to know how many woman they've taken."

"So some of our men could pretend to deliver a woman, and Lady Southwood might never know the difference?"

"No," Caitlin gasped. "They watch Lady Reddington." She paused again. "You must use someone else."

Corwyn spoke up. "I've some friends, three brothers. Their sister was in service to Walter Linton. She's lucky to have escaped him with her life. I'm sure they'd be more than willing to help us."

Amanda smiled at him. "Excellent."

"Whom do you propose they deliver to Lady Southwood?" Rhys asked, his voice too low and cold for Cassandra's comfort.

"Me, of course," Amanda responded.

Rhys closed his eyes for a moment and took a deep breath. "Under no circumstance. If you think for one moment-"

"Do you have another way to get to Mark?"

"There is no logic in this whatsoever, only madness."

"It is unlikely Walter Linton has given up searching for me. I am certain there are men on the streets with instructions to bring me to Southwood once they find me. Our men can get inside to find Mark and the women they have already taken."

Stanton made a low sound like a growl. "You can't seriously think we would allow this?"

"I would hope that as Mark's friend you would do anything to rescue him and keep other women from being treated like this." Amanda gestured toward Caitlin.

Rhys scowled. "As Mark's friend, I am willing to do anything. However, I am not willing to let you risk your life."

"Why would you do this, Amanda?" Cassandra asked, trying to intervene before Rhys and Amanda's anger escalated further.

Color crept into Amanda's cheeks, and her eyes glowed with indignation. "Because Southwood, Linton, and their allies deserve to die for what they've done to you, to Mark, to all the other women and for what they wanted to do for me."

Cassandra had never seen her sister look so impassioned or so determined. As surely as Cassandra knew Stanton could not keep her from putting her life on the line to save Mark, she knew nothing would deter Amanda. "Tell us the rest of your plan."

"Am I the only sane person here?" Stanton ran his hand through his hair roughly, destroying its perfect shape. "Will no one else protest this madness?"

"Rhys, one or more of us is going to have to risk our lives to save Mark's."

"Mark would never want you or your sister to endanger yourselves. He would never let you serve as bait."

Ignoring him, Amanda began to outline her plan. In the end, all of them, even Stanton, agreed that it was the best chance they had.

ଔ ଔ ଔ

Stanton, Cassandra, her sister, and four of Mark's hired guardsmen approached Southwood Grange on horseback. They used an overgrown path that would bring them to the house from the back of the property. The trees concealed them, but the going was slow and Cassandra's impatience grew with every step. *What if we are too late?* She asked herself this question over and over until she wanted to push her horse to a gallop, risking the animal's life and hers.

Brant led them, using a small lantern he would have to extinguish when they neared the house. She just made out the shadowy form of Amanda's rigid back as it swayed up and down with her mount's movements. In the brief intervals when she wasn't agonizing over whether Mark was alive, she berated herself for agreeing to Amanda's reckless plan.

Caitlin had finally taken the laudanum she desperately needed. But first, Caitlin had described the layout of Southwood Grange. She knew it well, since the Lintons had taken her there before forcing her to work at Miss Caroline's.

Cassandra and Brant would position themselves near a door leading directly to the cellar while Stanton and Corwyn stayed near either side of the main entrance. Corwyn's friends, John and Ryan, would knock on the door and enter, pretending to deliver Amanda. Once inside, they would eliminate anyone who was in the foyer and let Stanton and Corwyn in. Amanda would leave and circle around to find her sister.

When the four men had fought their way to the basement and gotten the prisoners free, they would exit through the basement door with those they had rescued, and the whole party would ride to safety. At least that's how it would work in theory. Cassandra feared they would meet with more resistance than they could handle, and some or all of them would not survive the night.

When the trees began to clear, the back gardens of the estate appeared. The party halted, dismounted and tied their horses. After urging everyone to circle up, Rhys gave a few last instructions.

Cassandra's heart thundered in her chest. She listened intently to all the sounds around her as Rhys went over the details of getting Amanda and the men inside. Leaves rustled in the woods, and the screech of a nearby owl made her jump. She expected to be discovered any second, but no sounds came from the house. The horses stood still and calm. They were likely to sense any strangers before she would.

Finally Rhys waved her and Brant on. They began to move with painstaking slowness toward the spot where they would wait. The boxy hedges of the classical garden failed to hide them. The illumination from the moon was welcome as a light for their path, but it increased their exposure. She held her breath until they were on the far side, within the shadow of the house.

They crept along, pressing themselves against the wall and pausing every step to listen for any sign of movement within. When they rounded the corner of the house, the land began to slope downwards. They found the cellar door exactly where Caitlin had said it would be. Also as she had promised, a wilderness garden stood several yards from it.

As they left the protection of the wall to make their way towards the garden, a cat appeared out of nowhere. It streaked across the lawn in front of Brant and nearly tripping him. Cassandra fell against him, and they both went down in the grass.

They lay there for the space of one heartbeat, then two, then three. Brant rolled her off of him and whispered against her ear. "Are you all right?" She nodded, and he pulled her up.

She was certain she would be bruised. She had bitten her tongue painfully to withhold a cry of surprise, but that was inconsequential. They were still alive, and they had only a few yards to go before they could conceal themselves in the trees.

CR CR CR

Mark's mind was in overdrive. His body pulsed. He clenched his teeth against need that had the potential to drive him mad.

The scrape of a key against the lock of his cell made him tense. He deliberately rubbed his ragged palms against the wall to help him control his racing thoughts.

The door swung open. It was Katryn. For a moment, he lost his grip on sanity. His entire world narrowed to the juncture of her legs, deliciously outlined in riding breeches so tight they must have been made for a small boy. In that brief second, he would have traded anything for the relief she could bring him. A squeeze of his fists brought back the pain and his grip on reality.

"I can see that my little preparation has taken effect. It is most potent, isn't it?"

He glared at her and said nothing. He pressed himself against the wall so she would not see the frayed ropes at his wrists, but try as he might, he could not keep his body still.

"Hmmm, I can't decide what I desire more? Watching you suffer while I deny you release or fucking you while you beg me for more."

"Bitch."

Her smile widened. "I wonder how long our potion will hold you in its throes. Perhaps even too long for me. Some of my guards prefer men. I wonder what would it be like to see them toy with you?"

Mark knew she would do it. He had no intention of being raped by her or any of her foul, perverted guards. He fought against the surge of anger that only served to heighten the effects of the drug.

He needed to distract her, but it was so hard to think, to construct the words he needed. "Why, Katryn? Why...are you...doing this?"

"You refused to comply with my wishes and instead sought to humiliate me. Now you will be the one who will grovel. You will beg for death before I kill you."

"No. Why are you selling the women?"

She smiled. For a moment, her lips captivated his senses. "It's my inheritance."

Had he heard her right? "Your inheritance?"

She paced back and forth before him, more agitated than he'd ever seen her. "My father introduced me to this world when I was but fifteen. He—" she stumbled over her words. Mark thought for a moment he saw tears in her eyes. "He would have sold *me* if I had not done his bidding, but I learned to enjoy it. He was right. Pleasure is worth any price, and men will pay dearly for it."

Her confession made Mark sick. Her father? He swallowed the bile that rose in his throat.

He gathered his wits again, wishing to speak. But even after such a vile story, he was losing the battle to keep his body still. As he watched her move in her tight breeches, his hips rocked forward of their own accord.

He would have to make his move soon. Despite his hatred of her, he gave her one last chance to admit she was wrong. "Katryn, you-you don't have to do this. No matter what your father did to you."

She bent down and traced the line of his jaw with a long, sharp fingernail. "I don't have to, but I want to." She stood again, laughing. "God, it's good to see you like this. You won't be able to hold onto your arrogance for long. Soon I'll break your body like I broke your heart."

He pulled his feet under him and kneeled up. "Don't do this, Katryn."

"Beg me, Mark." She took a step closer to him. "Beg me to stop."

He swung his arms, snapping the last thread of the rope that connected them to his feet. His clasped hands connected with her head and she crumpled to the floor. He ripped the frayed ropes at his wrists and wrestled with those holding his ankles.

Fortunately, Katryn had been so sure of the drug's power she'd dismissed his guards. Groans echoed from one of the women imprisoned near him. He had no intention of leaving them to the fate Katryn had devised, but first he had to escape and find help.

CR CR CR

Amanda slumped against John's shoulder, letting her eyes stare straight ahead as if she were in a stupor. John's younger brother Ryan lifted his hand to knock. Once she heard the firm tap, there was no turning back.

A young but severe looking footman opened the door. "What'd'ye want?" He asked, making no attempt to be proper or pleasant.

"As ya can see, we've come to make a delivery to yer mistress," John said, pushing at Amanda. "Stand up there, ya haughty miss. Let 'em get a

226

look at ya. Is this the woman they've been waiting for, Reddington's sister-in-law?"

"Aye."

"I'll take her." The man reached for Amanda's arm.

"Not so fast." John put an arm around her waist and pulled her roughly to his side. She tried her best to let her body go limp as if she didn't have the will to resist. "We was instructed to deliver her straight to Lady Southwood. How's we to know you won't sport with her yerself before turning her over? She won't be worth near so much if yer grubby hands've been on her."

The man snarled. "Give the girl to me and leave. Your continued presence is dangerous to your health."

"I'm not moving 'til I see Lady Southwood." John nodded to his brother who pushed past the sputtering footman and entered. John dragged Amanda inside.

"Stop, right there."

John released Amanda and punched the footman.

He staggered back but managed to grab hold of the bell rope. John punched him again, harder this time. The footman slumped to the floor. Footsteps and shouts echoed through the foyer.

Ryan grabbed Amanda, intending to send her back outside. Two men appeared in the doorway. Both carried pistols. The three of them had no choice but to run.

Chapter Twenty-One

Mark crept along the passage between cells until he came to a set of stairs leading to a door. Anyone or anything could be on the other side, and he had no weapon. Fire burned through his body. He stopped and leaned against the wall, seriously wondering if he could go any further without relieving his raging need.

The sound of voices reached him from the far end of the corridor. Trying the door was his only option.

He turned the handle, exhaling only when the latch gave. The door opened into a side yard. Trees stood a few yards away. After closing the door silently, he ran toward the small wilderness across the lawn.

He saw nothing but the shape of small trees, but he pushed ahead. He froze when he heard a gasp and the crunch of leaves. Looking all around and digging his nails into his palms to keep his tortured body still, he studied the darkness. He willed his eyes to make sense of the shadowy forms of trees and shrubs.

Then he saw something. A face peeked out at him from behind a small tree. It disappeared after a second. Mark dashed in that direction and caught the lurker.

He knocked the man to the ground, tumbling and rolling. He managed to pin his opponent beneath him. Except it wasn't a man. Soft curves and the scent of roses told him a woman lay beneath him. A woman his raging body responded to instantly.

Why hadn't she screamed? Her rapid pulse beat against his hands where they pinned her wrists to the ground. He could not keep from grinding himself against her behind. Yet she remained silent and motionless.

The cold barrel of a pistol pressed against Mark's temple. "Get up slowly. Make a sound and you'll regret it," a male voice whispered.

"Brant?"

The woman shifted beneath him. "It's Mark."

Dear God. "Cassandra?"

"Please, you're crushing me."

Brant lowered the pistol. Mark rolled off Cassandra, pushing her away and trying to get his body under control. What must she think of him rutting against her without even knowing who she was.

"What are you—"

"Where are—"

They both paused. Then Mark spoke again. "Katryn...I knocked her out and...ran." He couldn't get enough air. Cassandra's scent assailed his nostrils. All he thought about was pulling her beneath him and plunging into her. Without relief he feared he would disintegrate.

"Mark, what's wrong?" She looked down at the dark stains on her dress. "You're bleeding, aren't you?" She reached for him.

He scooted away from her. "Don't touch me."

"Mark, what is it?"

"She gave me the drug. The one she gives the women."

"Oh, my God. But the blood—?"

"My hands. The ropes. It's nothing. I'll be fine."

"Stay here. Both of you. I'm going in." Before Mark could protest, Brant disappeared into the darkness.

"Did you see any of the others inside?" Cassandra asked.

He shook his head to clear it. Her words made no sense. The only thing he understood was the demands of his body. "What do you mean?"

"Some of the guards are here and Amanda and—"

"Amanda!"

Cassandra realized how foolish it sounded, how crazy and desperate she'd been to let her sister risk her life like this. "Two of Corwyn's friends pretended to deliver Amanda. They were supposed to get to you and the captive women."

"I'm going to find them." Mark tried to stand but he stumbled and grabbed a tree for support.

"You're in no shape to go anywhere. Sit down."

"I'll be all right. It has to wear off soon." He tried to stand again and pitched forward onto his hands and knees.

"Mark! Stop it!" She grabbed his arm to pull him back to the ground.

He flinched. "Don't touch me!"

Cassandra barely contained her panic. Mark was half delirious and he wouldn't let her help him. And something had gone terribly wrong inside. She didn't know if her sister were alive or dead. Her gaze flicked to the house then back at Mark. She couldn't leave him like this.

She knelt in front of him and put her hand under his chin, forcing him to look at her. Even in the moonlight, she could see that his pupils were fully dilated. His skin burned hot where she touched him.

"Tell me how I can help you."

"No!" He pushed her away and sat back on his heels.

"Mark, what the hell is wrong with you? What has she done?"

She moved forward. He scooted back on his hands and feet like a crab until he made contact with the trunk of a tree. "You can't touch me." His voice was wild, frantic. "My skin is alive. I feel—"

She studied him. He seemed unable to keep himself still. Then realization hit. "Oh, God. The drug. It's an aphrodisiac."

"Y-yes."

"Caitlin told us about it, but I thought it made the women groggy, unwilling to fight."

"Caitlin?"

"She came to the house to warn us. They had beaten her to make her talk, but she's going to be all right, if she can survive without their potion."

"Where is she?"

"At my house, with Rebecca. A doctor is seeing to her."

Mark pushed away from the tree and got to his feet. "I have to go help them."

Cassandra watched him teeter and lean against the tree. She knew what she had to do. It was the only way to bring him back to sanity. Amanda needed her desperately, but she wasn't foolish enough to think she could save her sister on her own. She needed Mark's help.

She closed the gap between them and brought her hands to the waist of his pants.

"No!" He tried to pull away, but he was trapped by the tree.

"Shhh!" She placed a finger against his lips. "It's the only way I can help you."

"No." This time his voice held less force. His hips bucked against her hands as she pulled his breeches open and found his cock.

She'd intended to bring him relief with her hands or her mouth, but once she touched him, she lost control of the situation. He growled, a low tortured sound. Then his arms locked around her waist, and he pushed her to the ground.

Twigs and stones dug into her back, and the weight of him took her breath. His hands tore at the breeches she'd worn for ease of movement. She feared he would rip them. He pushed them down and freed one of her legs, giving him the access he needed.

Mark's flesh burned her, and his thighs were slick with sweat when he pushed them between hers. She realized he had no control over his need, and a shiver of fear ran over her.

He thrust to the hilt in one brutal stroke. She gasped, biting down on the sleeve of her shirt to keep from screaming. His hands were everywhere. They grabbed roughly at her breasts, pinching her nipples and pulling at them. They slid over her belly and drew her legs up, trapping them against her body. Hoarse cries came from his throat as though they were being ripped out by an unseen hand.

Mark gripped her calves and pushed her legs up until he could hook her ankles over his shoulders. He plunged so deep he penetrated straight to her heart, breaking the wall she'd built there. She lay trapped beneath him, a willing sacrifice.

The familiar fire raged in her body. Her hips came up against Mark's, meeting him stroke for stroke. She should have been embarrassed to be so easily aroused, ready for him to take her on the ground with no preliminaries. Instead she abandoned herself to pure sensation. The rush of fear and anger that had thrummed through her transformed into a desire so fierce it rivaled what the drug had done to Mark.

There was no finesse to his actions, no attempt to be gentle. Mark was mad with need. Yet her crisis built until suddenly the night lit up, and she saw an expression of pure bliss on his face. He sent his seed into her, choking out her name.

He lay atop her, resting his full weight on her body. She feared she would suffocate before she got him off of her. But the sound of creaking wood echoed across the lawn, bringing him rapidly back to consciousness.

They scrambled to straighten their clothes, and Cassandra gave Mark her second pistol. They crept to the edge of the wilderness and saw Corwyn slowly making his way toward them. Cassandra rushed out to meet him, Mark close on her heels.

Corwyn fell to his knees. His hands gripped his abdomen where blood soaked his shirt.

Mark put his hand on Corwyn's shoulder. "Where are they?"

"Cellar."

Mark looked back at Cassandra. "Stay with him. Try to get him to cover. I'm going in."

"No," Corwyn whispered, but his voice was too low for Mark to hear.

Cassandra's heart constricted as she watched Mark go. If lives hadn't been at stake, she would have run after him. Despite the fact that he'd been under the spell of Katryn's drug, their coupling re-opened barriers they'd both erected with their cruel words. She had much to say, and yet she wouldn't have been able to find the right words even if they'd had the luxury of hours.

"Can you make it to the trees? We'll be less exposed there." Cassandra took hold of Corwyn's arm.

"They took Amanda." Corwyn looked up at her with tears in his eyes. "I'm so sorry."

His words sliced her like knives. "What happened?"

"The footman at the door. He alerted others. Amanda couldn't get away. There were too many of them."

Cassandra pulled a knife from her boot and used it to cut a strip of cloth from the long man's shirt she wore. After folding it over, she tugged Corwyn's hands away from his wound and placed it under them.

"Can you move, now?"

He nodded.

"When we get to the trees, I'll examine your wound." She tried to speak calmly, not wanting to agitate him more when he was obviously in great pain.

She wondered if any of them would survive this night, but she tried to block out her fear and focus on helping Corwyn. She wanted to ask if anyone else was injured or…worse, but she couldn't bear to.

She got him into the wilderness area and helped him sit down at the base of a tree. She lit the lantern Brant had left with her, deciding the risk of detection was less important than saving Corwyn. When she raised his shirt, she saw a nasty slash. It was still bleeding, but it wasn't deep. He would survive if they bound it tight enough to staunch the bleeding.

She ripped more fabric from her shirt and wrapped the strip of cloth all the way around him, tying the cloth pad to him and putting pressure on the wound. "You're going to be all right. I'm going to see what I can do for those who are still inside. I promise we'll come back for you as soon as we can."

"Don't. It's too dangerous." His eyes pleaded with her. She knew he blamed himself for the plan going awry.

"I have to," she said and patted his arm.

ঙ ঙ ঙ

Mark gripped his pistol tightly as he descended the stairs to the cellar. He heard muffled voices but could not make out what was being said or who was speaking. One of the voices was female. Probably Katryn. He didn't think his blow had been strong enough to kill her.

As he reached the end of the passage where he had been held, the voices grew louder.

"You stupid whore, couldn't you manage one man's capture? I do not make a habit of working with bitches who cannot deliver." Mark easily identified the speaker as the man who had attacked Cassandra.

"Gaston, you cannot blame me. Those idiots you hired as footmen did not give him enough of our potion. If they had the brains of a rat, they would have done as I said, and he would even now be tied to my bed, begging for more."

"That is all you think of, isn't it? Your own pleasure. This is a business. You can't think with your cunt all the time."

"He deserves to be humiliated. It is his fault we are behind with our shipment."

"Then he should be dead. Instead, your lust has caused us to lose him. Now we have more prisoners who must be dealt with."

Mark crept closer. Finally, he reached a doorway through which he saw Katryn and the Frenchman. Guards held Amanda and John at gunpoint. Ryan lay on the floor either dead or unconscious. Where were the others?

Suddenly an arm came around him, and a hand covered his mouth. "Don't move, it's us."

Mark nodded. The hand fell away, and Mark turned slowly to face Stanton and Brant. They motioned for him to move back down the passage. When they were far enough away to whisper without detection, they made a plan. If Katryn and Gaston's argument continued to escalate, they would rush the room in the ensuing chaos.

Brant and Stanton would aim for the guards who held Ryan and Amanda. Mark would train his weapon on Gaston. There were two other men around the perimeter of the room, but their weapons were holstered. Their best chance was to eliminate the others quickly then deal with the secondary threat.

They inched back to the doorway, standing two on one side and one on the other.

"I am not your slave," Katryn screeched at Gaston.

He slapped her. "You will do as I say. That is part of our agreement."

She pulled a knife from a sheath at her waist and pointed it at him. "Don't ever hit me again."

He shot her. Point blank in the chest.

Shock rattled Mark, but he forced himself to ignore it. Stanton gave the signal, and they launched into action.

Brant's and Stanton's shots connected, but one of the unoccupied guards tackled Mark. His shot went wild.

Gaston pulled a second pistol from his waistband and aimed it at Amanda. Stanton dove toward him as Mark watched the scene from the ground.

Gaston squeezed the trigger. Stanton hit his arm, throwing the Frenchman off balance.

Amanda fell back. She knocked her head on the wall and slumped to the floor.

Mark elbowed the man on top of him and looked for his gun. But it had skidded just out of his reach.

Gaston wrestled free of Stanton's hold and unsheathed his knife.

ભ ભ ભ

Cassandra eased the cellar door open. She kept her hand clenched around the pistol Stanton had given her before they left her townhouse. And she heeded his caution to keep her finger off the trigger lest her shaky nerves make her shoot before she was ready.

When s gunfire echoed down the long hall, she sped up. She was running by the time she came to the doorway of the room where her friends were fighting for their lives.

The first thing she saw was the Frenchman who'd attacked her raising a knife to throw at Mark. She lifted her pistol and fired.

Gaston slumped to the floor, a bullet in his head. Mark spun to see where the shot had come from. His face paled when he saw her.

With Gaston out of the picture, the two guards who were left held up their hands, declaring their surrender.

Cassandra saw Amanda lying on the ground and raced over to her. Stanton was already there, bent over Amanda, inspecting her wound. "I don't think the bullet hit anything vital," he said. "The bleeding's mostly stopped."

"What happened?"

"Gaston shot her. Then she fell and hit her head against the wall."

"She would be dead if it weren't for Stanton," Mark informed her as he leaned over to look at Amanda. "He knocked Gaston off balance and kept the bullet from meeting its real target."

Cassandra looked down at her sister. The bullet had hit her shoulder, but it was only inches above her heart. "Thank you." She placed her hand over Rhys's.

"Don't thank me yet. She hit her head hard and…"

Mark held Amanda's wrist. "Her pulse is strong. Her skin is warm but not feverish. She's got a good chance, but we need to get her upstairs."

Cassandra turned to face Mark. "Are you all right?" He reached out to caress her cheek.

"Y-yes." Suddenly the impact of what she'd done hit her. She'd actually killed a man. "I had to do it, didn't I? He was going to kill you."

"Yes, he was. I owe you my life."

John interrupted them. "I'm sorry, but I need some help. One of us should go check on Corwyn while the other sees to the prisoners. Brant's gone to the village to find the local magistrate and a doctor."

Mark reached out to cup Cassandra's cheek before he stood. The look on his face made her ache. She'd never seen him look so sad.

Before he left the room, he looked down at Katryn's body. Cassandra turned her head from the gruesome sight, and her gaze met Rhys's. He must have read the question there. "Gaston killed her, not Mark. I think it was easier that way."

She nodded. If Mark had killed her, he would always wonder if he had no other choice or if he had done it for revenge.

She surveyed the rest of the room. Ryan was still seated. His head rested in his hands. "He got knocked in the head with the butt of a pistol," Stanton explained, "but he looks as if he'll recover."

Amanda moaned and stirred.

"Mandy? Mandy? Can you hear me?" Cassandra squeezed her sister's hand.

Stanton caressed Amanda's cheek. "Wake up, Amanda. Come back to us." She moaned again but didn't wake.

John returned with the few servants who hadn't fled. They swore they'd worked for Katryn only because their lives had been threatened. They were willing to do anything necessary to aid those who had been injured.

John explained that there were three women locked in the cells, but they were all unconscious. The men would get them upstairs as soon as Amanda and Ryan were settled.

Cassandra gave orders to the servants while Stanton carried Amanda upstairs. John helped his brother. Ryan protested that he could walk on his own and then fell to his knees as soon as he stood.

When everyone was settled, Cassandra sought out her sister. She tucked blankets around her when someone knocked on the door. "Come in."

Mark entered and gave a report on the injured. "Brant and John are bringing the women upstairs. I helped Corwyn to a bed, but he says he's feeling better already. I doubt that, but with a few stitches I believe he'll be all right. He's lucky. We all are."

Cassandra nodded. "What will happen to these women when they leave here?"

Mark ran his hand through his hair. "I don't know. It's unlikely they have anywhere to go."

"Do you think we could find them positions, possibly as servants in respectable homes? I imagine my Aunt Claire would hire one of them at least."

Stanton looked up from his seat by Amanda's bed. "My sister might be willing to help out."

Mark nodded. "If you are willing to vouch for them, I think it might work."

"I will do whatever I have to, but I can't let them go back to selling themselves. I know some women choose such a profession but to be forced like that…" She let her words trail off, not wanting to think of the horror anymore.

Mark tensed. Cassandra knew he must be thinking of how Katryn had hoped to find her revenge. She moved toward him, but he backed away, a wary look on his face.

"Brant should be here soon with the magistrate. I need to be available when they arrive."

Cassandra watched the door close behind him. She was tempted to go after him and tell him she had changed her mind about their relationship. But she let him go. There would be time to talk when they got back to London.

C๏ C๏ C๏

After a grueling few hours explaining the events of the day to the magistrate, Mark was ready to collapse on the nearest bed. He was gathering his energy to help Stanton make arrangements for everyone's return to London, when the doctor Brant had summoned from town knocked on the door of the study. Mark bade him enter.

"Miss Halverston is awake now. I expect her to make a complete recovery."

"Thank God." Mark patted Stanton on the back. "You did save her after all. How are the others?" he asked, looking back at the doctor.

"I have stitched up Mr. Adams, and I gave Mr. Claxton some laudanum so he could rest. The latter has a wretched headache, but he should be fine. I'm happy to say all of them should pull through."

Mark shook hands with the doctor and offered to show him out. But the man told Mark he could find his own way and exited, leaving Mark and Stanton alone. Mark picked up the torn jacket he'd lain across a chair and pulled it on over his soiled shirt. "Can you spare a horse for me?"

Stanton looked confused. "We brought an extra for you to make your escape. And I'm certain we can have the use of Southwood's considering our circumstances, but you can't mean you are leaving now."

Mark nodded. "I am."

"What about Cassandra?"

"She does not wish to continue our relationship."

Stanton shook his head. "She's in love with you, Foxwood. Anyone can see it."

Mark gave his friend a bitter laugh. "If only that were true."

"I saw the look on her face when she shot Gaston. She would have done anything to save you."

"You risked your life for Amanda. Are you going to profess yourself in love with her?"

"No, but—"

"Tell Cassandra I wish her all the best. I will not bother her further."

"You're a fool."

"I may be, but I'm a fool who wishes to keep his sanity." He walked out and closed the door behind him.

Chapter Twenty-two

"You look worse than the last time I saw you, and I would not have thought that possible."

Mark glanced up to see Stanton leaning against the doorframe with feigned casualness

"I told you not to call on me unless you could be civil."

"And I told you I have no intention of leaving you alone until you see sense and go after Cassandra."

"If you mention her name once more, I will end our acquaintance all together."

Stanton pushed himself away from the door and took the liberty of pouring himself a drink. "What are you going to do? Call me out for daring to care enough to want to see you happy?"

Mark snorted. "You're one to talk. You've done nothing to pursue Amanda despite your obvious regard for her."

"Amanda is an innocent. While I appreciate her charms, she is better off without me. I've no taste for virgins anyway."

"I've seen how you look at her, Stanton."

"Do you want me to seduce Cassandra's sister?"

"God, no." Mark shook his head. "I don't know what I want."

Stanton took a seat and sipped his brandy. Mark longed for his friend to leave him in peace. How dare he keep pestering Mark about Cassandra, reminding him of what he had lost? It wasn't as if Mark ever stopped thinking about her. Even at night, he lay awake longing for her to be by his side or dreaming of her. Every morning he woke to emptiness.

He wanted nothing more than to see her again, and Stanton wasn't the only one encouraging him to go after her. Amanda had written him a scathing letter, and her aunt had visited and given him a set down so harsh his ears still burned. They all said Cassandra was languishing without him, but he knew that wasn't true.

He remembered their last days together with painful clarity. They'd done their best to hurt each other. Cassandra would not want to see him after that. He'd let himself believe differently for a few moments while Katryn's drug wracked his body, and Cassandra offered him salvation. In the midst of that haze of need he'd thought, they could make it work. But once his mind cleared, he could not bring himself to risk another rejection.

Cassandra had made no attempt to contact him after she left London, not even to let him know what had happened to the women they had found at Southwood Grange. Of course, Stanton had been there to tell him everything she hadn't. His friend had visited Amanda once, though despite the service he'd done her, he hadn't been allowed to see her again since her aunt feared he would ruin her reputation. But in that single visit, he had learned the details of Cassandra's departure for Devon.

As soon as Amanda was transported to her aunt's and the family was assured she would make a complete recovery, Cassandra had set about securing positions for the women they'd rescued. She took one woman, Mary, to Reddington Abbey with her. Caitlin had stayed in the service of Lady Morgan, and the other two women had been employed by Stanton's sister.

With those arrangements made, Cassandra quit London, intending to claim her belongings from Reddington Abbey and prepare her former home for the distant cousin who succeeded Reddington's heir. Once the authorities had become involved, Mark and Cassandra had been unable to keep Reddington's death a secret. Mark assumed Cassandra would reside with her aunt while she looked for a position, but no one had mentioned her returning to London.

The French authorities had been given the names of Gaston's accomplices, and several of the kidnapped women had been located and returned to England. The only missing link in the whole business was Walter Linton. He had yet to be found. Mark assumed he had fled the country. Hopefully, he would never have the nerve to return.

The Earl of Southwood suffered a nervous breakdown when the details were revealed to him. He was currently sequestered at his mother's estate. It wasn't known if he would ever recover.

"Reddington's heir offered Cassandra the Abbey." Stanton's words startled Mark out of his reverie.

"She won't take it, but it makes no difference to me. I've put Northamberly on the market."

"What? You love that old heap."

"I thought you'd be thrilled. You hate the place."

"But you don't." Stanton set his glass down with a thump. "Giving you that estate is the only fatherly thing Gillinvray's ever done. You can't sell it."

Mark scowled at him. "Why ever not? I can't go back there. Whether or not Cassandra stays in Devon, I'll never enjoy it again."

"You would enjoy Northamberly if she were there with you."

Mark growled. "Don't make me throw you out."

Stanton shook his head "Fine. I won't mention her again, but I can't sit around and watch your continued decline. You haven't left this house in days.

"It's snowing, and there is no one in town."

Stanton snorted. "That's never kept you in before. In fact, you once recounted the story of a marvelous evening during which you watched the snow fall from the carriage window while a woman I won't name performed certain services on you with amazing skill."

Mark clenched his fist. "I'm not as young and foolish as I once was."

"You're hardly elderly, nor has your penchant for trouble left you. I refuse to see you sit here, drinking yourself into oblivion every night. I'm going to a supper at Langley's tomorrow night."

Silvia Violet

Mark raised his brow.

Stanton smiled. "It's not like the affair you attended, but there will be plenty of women there. Several of whom would not be averse to spending the night with you."

Mark studied his friend intently. "What are you up to?"

"Nothing." But he wore a grin like a cat. "If you aren't going to pursue Cassandra, you need to work on forgetting her. Say you'll come."

"Will you promise not to mention her name?"

"I promise," Stanton said, but the unnerving smile didn't leave his face.

"Fine." Why did he already know he'd regret his acquiescence?

ભ ભ ભ

"Have ye heard Northamberly's up for sale?"

"You don't say. I wonder what will become of the servants. Hope the new master keeps them on. My Letty needs that job somethin' awful what with her husband's leg busted."

Cassandra couldn't help but overhear the conversation as she looked at ribbons in the milliner's shop. She gripped the counter to steady herself as the weight of the statement hit her.

How could Mark let that beautiful old castle go? But she knew the answer. He had no wish to see her, no wish to think about what might have been.

She'd thought of nothing but him since leaving London. Her heart ached so much she couldn't gather her wits enough to start the search for employment. The new Lord Reddington had told her to stay on as long as she liked, but she could not live on his charity indefinitely. She had to get herself together and make plans for her future.

If she were honest with herself, she'd admit she was stalling, hoping Mark would change his mind and seek her out. Why she allowed herself to think there was the remotest possibility that would happen, she did not know.

244

She had told Mark in no uncertain terms that their liaison could not continue after they found Reddington's killer.

But what if he didn't just want a liaison? What if, as she'd begun to suspect, he wanted more? She would not have accepted his proposal a few weeks ago, no matter how much she might have wanted to. She would have stubbornly clung to her desire for independence. But now she would accept without reservation. If only it wasn't too late.

She suspected she had pushed him away when he had been trying to say his feelings for her went beyond the physical. She'd been so cold, letting him think he *had* been nothing but a stud to her. She'd been so angry then and so foolish.

By the time she returned home from her errands, she had a splitting headache and cramps in her lower abdomen and back. All she wanted to do was curl up in bed, pull the covers over her head and refuse to speak to anyone for-how long? The night? A week? The rest of her life?

Loring opened the door and took her cloak. "Lady Reddington, are you feeling unwell?" he asked, studying her face.

Her headache was making her sick to her stomach, but she did not want Loring fussing over her. "I have a touch of headache, that's all. I'd like some tea sent up to my room. I'll be resting there."

"Would you like a hot bath? The steam might ease you?"

"Yes, that would be lovely." Perhaps a bath would also ease the cramping. "After the bath, I'd like a tray sent to my room. I plan to retire early."

"Yes, my lady. I will see to your hot water and tea."

She knew Loring wished she'd confide in him, tell him what had been bothering her since her return. He was worried that all she did was sit and stare out the window, unable to even concentrate on a book. But what could he do? No one could make her feelings for Mark go away.

And she certainly couldn't tell him why she was more depressed than usual today. The cramping in her belly was surely a sign of her impending menses. She was always crabby and uncomfortable at this time of the month, but these particular cramps were worse than any others. They meant that her last hope for a link with Mark was gone.

She had told herself it would be best for her not to be with child. Such an eventuality would only complicate her situation further. Mark would feel he had to marry her. She did not want him trapped like that.

Still, part of her wanted desperately for there to be a child. The idea of creating a life with Mark, of sharing such a gift warmed her inside. When she'd begun their affair, pregnancy had been a means to an end. How foolish she had been. She would never have been able to pretend the baby was Reddington's and ignore what she and Mark had shared.

She was able to relax for a time in her bath. Both her headache and her cramps diminished. By the time she stood and began to dry herself, her mood had improved. At least she would have enough appetite to eat her dinner.

But as she was drying off, it became evident that her menses had begun. She had known it would come soon, had told herself again and again that there was not a baby. But until that moment she'd let herself believe the cramps could be a symptom of pregnancy instead. When she saw the stained towel, the full impact of her separation from Mark hit her.

Tears poured from her eyes as she dressed herself. She could hardly see as she made her way to the sofa where she allowed herself to curl up and let the sobs come. Her tears had soaked the pillow by the time Mary, her new lady's maid, opened her door to deliver her tray.

"Lady Reddington, whatever is the matter?"

Cassandra sniffled and tried to draw in enough air to speak. "I'm fine...I—"

"You're not fine, my lady. Pardon me for saying so, but you haven't been fine since we left London. I know it's not my place to scold. I shouldn't think to after all you've done to help me, but you've got to stop sitting around feeling sorry for yourself."

Cassandra wiped her eyes. Mary was right. She couldn't keep on like this. "I'm not with child," she blurted out, as if that could possibly explain what had upset her so.

"You're *not* with child?"

"No, I…my menses started tonight."

"I see. It seems to me most women in your position would be upset if they *were* with child, not the other way round."

Cassandra had to smile at the look of bewilderment on the young woman's face. "You're right, Mary, they would be. Sit down. I'll explain." Cassandra patted the sofa cushion.

Mary looked a bit startled. She sank down onto the sofa but sat so close to the edge Cassandra feared she might fall off. "I can't talk to you if you are going to hover like that. I need a friend right now, not a servant."

"Yes, Lady Reddington, it's only—"

"Make yourself comfortable," Cassandra admonished and Mary obeyed.

She told Mary everything, starting from the day she decided to approach Mark with her plan which now seemed foolish in the extreme. The young woman listened intently, nodding occasionally but remaining completely silent.

When Cassandra finished, she took a deep breath and leaned back against the sofa. Mary covered Cassandra's hand with her own. "There's only one thing you can do," she said.

Cassandra opened her eyes and studied the young woman's face. "What do you mean?"

"Well, I suppose you have two choices, although there's only one I approve of."

"Well, what are they?"

"You can sit here and let your heart break until you die of despair. Or you can let me pack your most alluring dresses and ask that the carriage to be prepared for a journey to London."

Cassandra knew right then what she would do. Talking to Mary, hearing her own voice tell someone else how much she loved Mark had shown her he was worth any risk she had to take. She hugged the young woman. "Thank you so much, Mary. Inform Loring that I will leave for London at first light. Then return so we can pack."

CR CR CR

"I'm sorry. I can't do this." Mark tried to turn his back. But Seline, the lovely young widow Stanton had introduced him to, slid her hand down Mark's chest and wrapped it around his cock.

"This feels more than adequate to me."

"My body is responding quite properly. That, thank God, is not one of the plagues I suffer from." He pushed her hands away and turned to face the fire. Seline was beautiful, intelligent enough to carry on a lively conversation, and known to be an excellent lover. A few months ago, he would have pounced at the chance to take her to bed and explore the many ways they could pleasure one another.

But not now. He'd known from the moment he'd entered Langley's house that he didn't want any of the women there. He wanted Cassandra.

But Cassandra didn't want him. He had to move on. That's what he'd told himself when Seline gave him several not-so-subtle hints that she would be more than happy to spend the night with him.

He had let her accompany him to his rooms, and as soon as they reached his bedroom, she'd attacked him with a ferocious passion he should have appreciated. She was obviously well-versed in removing men's clothes, and she had him stripped to the waist before he had a chance to tell her he couldn't go through with this.

She slid her arms around him and rested her head against his back. "What's wrong? Your thoughts have been far away all night. If I weren't so vain, I might think you were less than impressed with my charms."

He turned back to face her, bringing both her hands to his lips and kissing them each in turn. "I assure you, your charms are more than enough to bring a man to his knees."

"Some men, but not you." She studied his face carefully. "Who is she?"

He sighed. "Seline, I—"

"You don't have to tell me if you don't wish to. I will go, but whoever she is, she's a fool to leave you like this."

"I left her. Well, I guess you could say I left her before she could leave me." He exhaled slowly and ran a hand through his hair.

"Come and sit." Seline gestured toward the winged chairs by the fire. Mark slipped his shirt back on while she filled two snifters from the decanter by his bed.

"This might help." She handed him some brandy.

"Thanks." He took a large swallow and settled into a chair.

"Now, what made you think this woman was going to leave a charming, handsome man like you?"

"We agreed to end our affair after a certain time. I asked her to stay longer, but she refused."

"Was she hoping you would marry her?"

"No, it wasn't that. She is a widow. Her first husband treated her cruelly. She has no wish to marry again."

"How much longer did you hope to keep the affair going? Would it not have been better to end it before you tired of each other?"

"I could never tire of her. That's the problem."

"So you *would* marry her if she agreed?"

Mark couldn't believe he was having this conversation with a woman he'd known for a few hours. A woman who by all rights should be insulted at his refusal of the pleasure she offered. But somehow it was easier to talk to someone who didn't know his circumstances. He needed an unbiased opinion.

Taking a deep breath, he answered her question. "Yes, I would."

She smiled. "Then you have to change her mind."

"I tried, but—"

"If you've already tried and failed, then it is time to forget her and move on."

"I'm not ready to let her go."

"As I see it, you have two choices. You can let her go, or you can fight for her. Which is it going to be?"

Mark's heart pounded against his chest, He no longer saw what was in front of him. Instead, scenes of his time with Cassandra flashed before his eyes. Their first meeting when she strode into his study and asked him to bed her. The first night they were together. The wonderful afternoon they'd spent playing chess. The pleasure she took from riding him while he was tied down. The hurt look on her face as he'd backed out of the room where Amanda lay unconscious.

"I hope you are going to decide before too long. If I stay here much longer, I'm won't be able to keep my hands off you. You are more tempting than any man has a right to be."

Mark smiled. "I'm going after her."

"Excellent. I think you've made the right choice, though I must say I envy her."

He stood, helped Seline to her feet, and gave her a light kiss. "Thank you."

She smiled and let her hand trail across his cheek. "You're welcome."

She picked up her cloak and reticule and retied the ribbon that circled the neck of her dress. "If things don't work out, I do hope you will call on me. I'd be happy to help you recover your spirits."

He smiled. "I'll keep your generous offer in mind."

When Seline left, Mark considered calling for his horse and starting the journey to Devon immediately. Now that he'd decided on a course of action, he hated to delay for even a few hours. But as tired as he was, riding alone at night would not be wise. He decided he'd get a few hours sleep and leave for Reddington Abbey at first light.

As he readied himself for bed, he thought about the smirk Stanton had given him when he'd introduced Seline. He'd known. Damn it. He'd known Mark wouldn't be able to spend the night with her. That was why he'd been so insistent that Mark go to Langley's. When he saw his friend again, Mark wasn't sure whether he'd thank him or punch him. Perhaps it would depend on Cassandra's reaction to seeing him again.

Chapter Twenty-three

Cassandra arrived in London late in the evening. She had intended to go straight to see Mark, but her hair was a fright, and her skirts were damp from the stops they'd made on the snowy roads. If she arrived on her aunt's doorstep, she would be questioned relentlessly and admonished for not informing Aunt Claire of her journey. Reddington's townhouse had been closed and the servant's dismissed after his death was announced.

Knowing it was highly improper, she decided Stanton's rooms were her best option. He would certainly provide her with a place to freshen up and leave her things, and she'd have a place to return to if Mark turned her away. The thought made her throat constrict, but she had to remind herself that it was a distinct possibility.

Stanton's valet opened his door. For a brief moment a look of unease flashed across his face. Then, he quickly replaced his bland expression.

Cassandra clasped her hands to stop their shaking. "I'm sorry to disturb you at this hour, but I was hoping to speak to Mr. Stanton. It is a matter of some urgency."

"I'm afraid Mr. Stanton is not at home."

The sound of female laughter floated from one of the rooms. Cassandra felt herself blush. Why hadn't she thought Stanton might have a woman here? "I'm sorry. I'll return tomorrow." But before she could leave, Stanton stepped out from a room wearing a dressing gown.

"Who is it, Meadows?"

"Lady Reddington, sir."

Stanton strode quickly toward the door. "Cassandra, do come in."

"I'm so sorry. I wasn't sure where to go."

"Is something wrong?"

"No, I've come to see Mark. I wanted to freshen up before I sought him out. I didn't want to go to my aunt's. I knew you would understand and—" She stopped speaking when she realized Stanton had grown quite pale. "What's wrong?"

"You intended to go to Foxwood's tonight?"

"Yes, I know it's late, but I'm afraid I'll lose my nerve if I don't."

"He might be out, and if he's not, then he's likely asleep. You would be welcome to stay here until morning."

She detected a frantic note in Stanton's voice. "What aren't you telling me?"

"Nothing. I think you might rather go in the morning, after you've rested."

Then the realization hit. "He's not alone, is he?"

Stanton took a deep breath. "I don't think so. I encouraged him to come to a dinner party with me, but I…"

"You what?"

"I thought it would help him see how much he missed you. I hoped that by forcing him to be around other women, I could make him realize that he only wanted you."

Cassandra's heart pounded. "But it didn't work."

"I don't know. He disappeared while I was otherwise occupied."

"I see. Well, I'll just have to find out." She turned and rushed through the door. Stanton called for her to wait, but she ignored him.

Why should it bother her? She was the one who'd said their affair should end. Yet the thought of Maek touching another woman the way he'd touched her filled her with rage. He was hers.

As the carriage rolled to a stop in front of the house Mark had rented, she hesitated. What *would* she do if he wasn't alone? Throw the woman out of his bed and inform him he was never to touch another woman again?

The butler looked none-too-pleased when he opened the door for her. He tried to tell her she should return in the morning, but she pushed right past him.

"I'm not leaving until I've seen Mr. Foxwood. It would save us both time if you show me the way to his chamber."

"Mr. Foxwood must not be disturbed. He is embarking on a journey in the morning. He needs his rest."

A journey? Thank God she had not waited to see him.

"What I have to say cannot wait." The man remained rooted to his post. "Are you going to help me, or do I have to open every door until I hit upon the right one?"

"Madam, this is most irregular. I cannot allow—"

"You have no choice." She started up the stairs.

The butler started after her, and she picked up her pace.

"Madam, please, if you would but give me your name, I inquire whether Mr. Foxwood will see you."

She wanted to ignore him but forced herself to be reasonable. She stopped and turned to face him. "I am Lady Reddington."

Suddenly, he smiled. "I'm sorry, my lady. I did not realize it was you. His chamber is the third one on the right."

Cassandra frowned at his retreating back. What one earth had Mark been telling him about her?

She pushed open Mark's door and tiptoed across the room, hoping to see if he was alone before she woke him. The room was too dark for her to see clearly, but it appeared he was the only one there. He lay on his stomach, his limbs sprawled out. If he was sharing a bed, the other occupant was certainly left with little room for herself.

Cassandra pushed the door closed and tip-toed across the room. Ever so gently, she lowered herself to the bed. She could not resist reaching out to stroke his back. He purred and inched closer, but he did not wake.

She longed to stay like that, suspended in time, able to believe he might take her back, might even agree to spend the rest of his life with her. But she had to face reality even if it brought disappointment.

She laid her hand on his shoulder and shook him. "Mark. Mark, wake up."

He turned on his side and opened his eyes to slits.

"Mark, it's me, Cassandra."

He mumbled something that sounded like "dreaming, stop dreaming" and closed his eyes.

"I'm not a dream." She shook him again.

He reached out and touched her leg. His hand patted her thigh and then slid up her abdomen to cup her breast. She slapped it away, but he opened his eyes fully. "You *are* real." His voice was still clouded from sleep.

He sat up and slid out of bed. She could not help but admire his body as he began lighting candles. Apparently he slept without the hindrance of clothing whether or not a woman shared his bed.

When the room was light enough for him to see her clearly, he pointed to two wing chairs. "Have a seat."

When she had done as he asked, he pulled on a dressing gown and joined her, a wary expression on his face. "Why are you here?"

Not an auspicious beginning, but she could hardly expect him to fall at her feet the moment he saw her.

"I'm not with child." She realized immediately those were not the words she had meant to begin with.

"You came all this way and disturbed me in the middle of the night to tell me that you are *not* with child."

"No." She paused and took a deep breath, wishing she read him more easily. But he was working hard to mask his emotions. "Having a child was my last hope for a link with you. When that hope died, I realized I had to take action. I decided to do what I'd been longing to do ever since you disappeared from Southwood Grange."

A touch of eagerness began to show on Mark's face. "And what would that be?"

"Track you down, tell you how wrong I was, and try to make you understand that the only reason I refused to continue our affair was because I'd never want it to end. Every day I spent with you would make it harder to leave. Mark, I love you."

By the time she finished speaking, he was kneeling at her feet. He brought both of her hands to his lips. "I have loved you since the first time I touched you. I knew I would never find another woman like you."

"Did you take home a woman tonight?"

"What?" His look of confusion amused her.

"I saw Stanton before I came here. He said he'd tried to force you to see that you were in love with me, but he was afraid I would come here and find another woman in your bed."

"He said that?"

"Not exactly. He tried to discourage me from seeing you tonight. I guessed why."

Mark exhaled sharply. "I did bring a woman home, but I sent her away. She wasn't you, and you were all I wanted. I had planned to leave for Devon in the morning. It appears you saved me the trip."

The constriction in her lungs eased. "Please don't sell Northamberly. It's so beautiful and—"

"Would you like to live there?"

"Well, I…"

"I will only consent to keep it if you will make it your home as well."

Cassandra's heart pounded in her chest. Could she throw caution to the wind in such a fashion? Did she truly have the nerve to take up residence with her lover?

"If I do, I will never find a position anywhere."

He looked puzzled. "Why would you need to do that?"

"I cannot ask you to support me forever."

"Isn't it is a husband's duty to support his wife?"

"Husband?"

"How else—oh, you thought I meant that we would simply remain lovers?"

She nodded.

"No, Cassandra. The only way you can get me back is to consent to be my wife." He reached out and cupped her face, tilting her head so she looked straight into his emotion-filled eyes. "Cassandra, will you marry me?"

She was delirious with happiness. "Yes, I will marry you. I was so foolish to ever think I could be happy any other way." •

He stood and pulled her to her feet. "I will call my solicitor first thing in the morning and take Northamberly off the market. But for now," he brought her body against his, "I have much more important matters to attend to."

He mouth crushed hers, and she opened at the insistence of his tongue. Fire spread through her body as he picked her up and carried her to the bed. Finally, he lifted his mouth so he could sit her down, giving her a chance to speak.

"Mark, do you want children of your own?"

His eyes widened. He opened his mouth as if to speak but then stopped. He sat down beside her and pulled her onto his lap. He held her gaze with a look more serious than any she'd seen on his face. "Until I met you, I didn't. I tried very hard to avoid such complications. When you asked me to get you with child, I thought I could do so and walk away. But for some time I've known that if you became pregnant, I would make you marry me even if I had to drag you to the church."

"You wouldn't."

"I dashed well would." He toyed with one of her curls. "I desperately want to see you increasing with our child. I never thought I would say that, but I want it more than I can express."

She smiled. "Then can we keep trying as hard as we were?"

He laughed and gave her a kiss. "My darling Cassandra, we will try twice as hard."

About the Author

To learn more about Silvia Violet, please visit http://violet.chaosnet.org. Send an email to Silvia at silviaviolet@gmail.com or join her Yahoo! group to join in the fun with other readers as well as Silvia!

http://groups.yahoo.com/group/silviaviolet

Sometimes even the strongest magic can't protect you from the heat of passion.

Magic In The Blood
© *2006 Silvia Violet*

Liz Carlson lives a quiet life in a small mountain town, but she carries a dangerous secret. She is a practitioner of Deep Magic. When a rogue Deep Magician comes to town, bent on increasing his own power, Liz's only hope to stop him lies in a partnership with a devastatingly sexy vampire.

When Avran Niccolayic meets Liz and she intrigues him more than any woman has for six hundred years. He wants to show her pleasure greater than she's ever imagined. He's willing to do anything to get what he wants, even if it means risking his life in a dangerous game between Deep Magicians, and risking his heart every time he touches her.

Available now in ebook and print from Samhain Publishing.

Enjoy the following excerpt from Magic In The Blood...

Reaching up, she cupped his face and stroked his cheek with her thumb. His skin was smooth and cold. She wanted it pressed against her, but even more, she wanted him to taste her. She who had kept herself aloof, who had always prided herself on controlling her life, wanted to surrender to him, to fall into his eyes and feel his teeth piercing her.

She traced the line of his jaw and ran her fingers along his neck and down across his chest, feeling the hardness of the muscles there. He caught her wrist before she could move lower and placed her hand back on the floor.

He bent over her and used his tongue to trace the path his fingers had followed. Starting at her palm, he ran his tongue up and over her wrist, stopping ever so briefly on the pulse point there. Then he drew a wet line up her arm to the pulse that beat in the curve of her elbow. Back and forth he stroked her.

How could something so simple be so arousing? Each time he licked her pulse points, her heartbeat accelerated. The throbbing of her heart echoed between her legs. Lines of searing heat ran from her arm to her center. She felt ripe and heavy, ready to be taken. Never had a man made her feel like this. She thought she should be afraid, but she wasn't. Everything was exactly as it should be, as if she'd been waiting for this her whole life, waiting to surrender.

When his tongue reached her wrist again, he stopped. He laced his fingers with hers and placed his other hand on her forearm, all the while stroking her wrist with his tongue. His fangs brushed her. Once. Twice. Then a sharp pain jolted her as his teeth sank into her flesh. It was immediately overshadowed by the most intense pleasure imaginable.

As his mouth sucked at her wrist, waves of heated bliss swam over her. She felt the pull of his lips all the way to her core. If she hadn't seen him bent over her arm, she would have sworn he was licking her swollen clit.

She writhed and twisted, praying he wouldn't stop. Reality rushed in for a moment. She wondered how much blood he could take without killing her. Would he stop in time? Then she was lost again to her passion. Her free arm fisted in his hair, locking him to her. She cried out, begging him not to stop. Then, she went over the edge and darkness consumed her.

He is a desperate prisoner escaped from the dungeons and she is his beautiful and daring captive.

A Knight of Passion
© 2006 Ingela F. Hyatt

It was only three months ago when I, Lord Reynard Devin de Fauconer, learned of my father's death, making me Baron Rothwell. When I returned to the family castle after a five year absence, I certainly did not expect to find my cousin, Sir Garron, sitting in my stead, having stolen my identity. Then to imprison me in the darkest hole of my own dungeon, accused of the most vile treachery. And yet I cannot blame him for his perfidy, for truly it was I who killed Maggie of Maidwell - his woman. I fear my actions, my desires brought about her death. After this tragic incident I vowed never to touch another woman - gentle or baseborn.

However all is not lost - with the aid of a loyal servant I escaped the dungeon. I must tell you that during my flight I stumbled upon the most exquisite creature. Even half dead as I was, I could not resist the desire to kiss those lush lips. But what happened next was most unexpected - the lovely girl took it upon herself to sneak me from the castle, away from Garron's grasp. It was then I realized the spirited beauty was none other than Lady Rianna de Termonde, my own betroth, come to marry the imposter Baron Rothwell! The thought of him touching her, kissing her, makes my blood boil. And so I have done the unthinkable - I have kidnapped her.

We've been racing across England for several weeks now, eluding Sir Garron's men and battling brigands intent upon killing me and stealing her. But I wonder if I am deluding myself. Rianna believes me to be Baron Rothwell's cousin, and I have not dissuaded her from this belief, using it as a shield to protect her. But I tell you honestly, I do not know how much longer I can resist the passions brewing between us. There is something about her which touches me in a way I have never felt before. Should I reveal my true identity to her? Confess my darkest secret? Or will my love bring about the death of yet another woman? I seek your wise counsel in this matter.

Desperately Yours,

(the true) Baron Rothwell

Enjoy the following excerpt from A Knight of Passion…

Reynard watched, captivated, as Rianna slowly opened her eyes. A deep crimson flush stealing into her cheeks as the whirlwind of passion receded from her gaze. He saw a hint of the emotions she must be feeling flash through her delicate features—shock, dismay, and finally anger. Without warning, she pulled back and slapped him full across the face. The blow so hard his head twisted to one side.

And then she was jerking out of his loose embrace as if to escape.

Growling, he grabbed her arm in a steel grip, yanking her back to him.

"I may have deserved that, *demoiselle,* for taking such liberties as kissing you, but do not even *think* that you are going to get away from me so easily," he hissed.

And then all was calm.

Reynard rose, attempting to mask the lust and anger boiling in his veins with indifference. He tightened his grip in warning, mashing flesh and bone, causing her delicate knuckles to turn white. She gasped in pain, her eyes widening in shock and fear as she began to tremble.

He instantly loosened his hold, but refused to let go. Turning away from her, he dragged Rianna behind him to where Strum stood stock motionless, waiting for his master's further command. Reynard was appalled at himself for harming her. But her slapping him in the face, the rejection of the passion they had just shared, cut through him like a knife, and sent fury careening out of control to clash with the lust already pounding through his veins. That she could so easily disregard the fact she had helped him escape the castle and the baron's wrath, though he'd not asked her. Or the amorous kisses they had shared when she'd merely thought him an escaped prisoner. But what stabbed deeper than he would ever admit, was her forgetfulness—she did not recognise him. Nor did she recall the oath which had bound them together for the last seven years. It only served to remind him why he had not dallied with such women in recent times, not since Maggie's death.

Taking hold of the horse's reins, he guided his captive and mount into the now empty clearing. Without giving her a chance to run, he swung Rianna up into the saddle, mounting behind her. His arm around her waist, he pulled her hard against his chest, leaving the maiden no choice but to lean against him. Taking the reins in his free hand, he clucked at Sturm, digging his spurs in the charger's flanks. The warhorse sprang forward, directed toward the left path and Tove River.

A long moment of silence passed as they made their way through the heavy brush dotting the winding path. Rianna sat still as stone in his hard embrace, seemingly trying to keep her back from touching his chest.

"Where are we going?" she suddenly asked, so softly he might have imagined it.

"To the river," he responded sharply, coldly.

He felt a shiver run down her spine as her back became more rigid.

Reynard stared down at her golden head, aware he was playing the fool for even caring he'd frightened her again. Anger still rolled through his veins from her rejection of his kiss, his touch. But then he should have stayed the hell away from her.

Had not the death of one woman been enough to teach him?

Reynard thought he'd learned his lesson well. But apparently he had not learned well enough, for he'd wanted her, and she had rejected him. Gritting his teeth against the fury rising within, he swallowed down the anger. One thing was certain, he would keep the madness from controlling him, no matter how alluring this maiden might be. Nor would he *ever* touch or kiss her again.

The Book of the Damned reads "Know ye this—a Merciful God hath provided release from the damning curse of vampirism. If the creature be righteous, loving truly and truly loved in return, God may grant he become human once more."

Blood Atonement
© 2006 Sara Saint John

But at what price…?

Szeretni's days are spent translating occultic texts and her nights dreaming of romance. Shunned by Society because of family madness, she despairs of finding a man with whom to share her life. Then she meets the enigmatic Baron Corvinus, and she dares to hope love has found her at last.

A once great king, Matthias Corvinus, has lost his faith in love. Three hundred years before, aided by a woman's betrayal, Vlad Dracula changed him into a vampire. When Matthias finds himself drawn to the innocent Szeretni, he wonders if she too will betray him, or if he will gain peace for a brief moment in his never-ending lifetime.

When Dracula again makes his presence known, Matthias must face his past. Should he save the woman he's come to love before Vlad makes her his prey…or let her go before she can "feed" on him. Sucking out his heart, his mind, his very soul…

Available now in ebook from Samhain Publishing.

Enjoy the following excerpt from Blood Atonement…

A swan moved toward her and Szeretni paused to scrutinize the strange apparition. The woman's costume consisted almost entirely of feathers. A white feathered bodice, a white-feathered cap and a black-feathered mask—how it must have tickled. Pretty, yet somehow comic. Who did she know that fit that description? Recognition came with a smile. "Anne! You clever girl. It's a beautiful costume."

Knees bent, wobbling, yet somehow graceful, Anne gave her an exaggerated curtsey. "Your servant, Majesty."

The butler's voice rang out again, his tone one of grudging respect. "His Majesty Matthias Corvinus, King of Hungary."

The servant's announcement took her completely by surprise— this was something she hadn't anticipated. Curious to see what kind of man dared portray such a legendary figure, Szeretni turned to see her king. The crowd parted to reveal him and she gasped—it was as if the man had stepped right out of the gallery portrait. Clothed in royal splendor, his costume fit him to perfection. She couldn't help noticing how his black velvet tunic gaped slightly at the neck to reveal dark, curling wisps of hair. Silk hose, also black, covered his legs, accentuating their form. A scarlet mantle, embroidered with golden ravens, flowed majestically from very broad shoulders, to end in a swirl around short kidskin boots. A golden crown rested in his thick, ebony hair.

She thought him a magnificent sight. In truth, she could only find one flaw, and this flaw was an old mystery. As with the portrait, his face remained secret, the upper half completely concealed by a silver mask. But this enigma would answer at the time of unmasking. Finally she would see the face of her king.

Szeretni wondered if his face might be anything near the perfection of his body, then blushed at her crassness. What was she thinking? Never before had she scrutinized a man in quite this way.

Certainly hers were not the actions of a theologian's daughter, even one whose father's main interest was the occult. But then this was a night for alternate identity. If Beatrice's king had been anything like this man, she was a fool to leave him.

Open-mouthed, Anne stared as her feathers shook with her trembling. Szeretni nodded. Anne wasn't the only woman in the ballroom bewitched by the king. She surely was and this enchantment was pleasant sensation indeed. Awestruck, she watched the royal mystery walk grandly forward, to stop in the center of the dance floor.

Come to me.

"What did you say?"

Anne seemed puzzled. "I didn't say anything. Are you all right? You look pale."

"It's my porcelain skin."

Come to me.

An eerie sensation—the voice seemed to come from inside her head. Her gaze caught that of the king's. His eyes held her.

Come to me, my queen.

The statuesque monarch held out his hand, strong fingers outstretched in a gesture of command. The crowd stared, clearly eager to see if this Beatrice had the courage to take up the gauntlet thrown so obviously in her face.

She felt a tingling of anticipation. This challenge she could not resist.

Outside the manor, trees swayed with the might of the gusting wind at the arrival of an unexpected storm. The gale's force drowned out the whispered speculations of the merry-makers, their attention riveted to the drama unfolding before their curious eyes.

Szeretni cloaked herself in dignity as she walked toward him. Whatever Beatrice's motives, she meant to do better by this man than her cruel ancestress. She knelt before him, suddenly shy in the vital power of his presence.

Taking her hand in his, he drew her to her feet.

Lightning ripped the sky outside the large picture window, a visual display of the electricity that coursed through her body at his touch. She stood trembling, head bowed, no longer eager to meet his gaze. His fingers were warm when he placed them under her chin and lifted her face. The king looked into her eyes and she felt her secrets revealed, vulnerable to her very soul. Realization choked her. His eyes were a beautiful golden brown, the same as her wolf-prince.

The king turned toward the waiting orchestra. "Why do you stare? Play for me—I wish to dance with my queen."

The room burst to life as musicians scurried to do his bidding, striking up an elegant waltz. Celebrants caught up in the masquerade stood respectfully by, waiting for the royal couple to begin the first dance. The powerful monarch swept her into his arms and whisked her away. Bewitched by his touch, she felt they were floating as they moved gracefully to the music's spell. She cherished the feel of his hand around hers—flesh to flesh, it took her breath away.

Szeretni could not tear her gaze away from the tall, dark stranger's. Nothing else existed but those arresting eyes. This ruler yielded a haunting familiarity, something beyond the costume. Unlike other men she had met, he bestrew a masculinity that drew her like a thirsting woman to cool water. She felt powerless to resist.

He moved his face closer to hers. His warm breath caressed her cheek. "It seems an eternity since I've held you in my arms."

Samhain Publishing, Ltd.

It's all about the story…

Interested in writing for us?

Samhain Publishing is open to all submissions and seeks well-written works that engage the reader. We encourage the author to let their muse have its way and to create tales that don't always adhere to trends. One never knows what the next trend will be or when it will start, so write what's in your soul. These are the books that, whether the story is based on "formula" or an "original", are written from the heart, and can keep you up reading all night!

For details, go to http:

http:// www.samhainpublishing.com/submissions.shtml

Samhain Publishing, Ltd.

It's all about the story…

Action/Adventure
Fantasy
Historical
Horror
Mainstream
Mystery/Suspense
Non-Fiction
Paranormal
Red Hots!
Romance
Science Fiction
Western
Young Adult

http://www.samhainpublishing.com

Breinigsville, PA USA
10 November 2010
249114BV00001B/44/A